The Doll
in McCallaway's Store

To Jean

I hope you enjoy
reading this as much as
I enjoyed writing it.

Bedside Books
An imprint of American Book Publishing
P.O. Box 65624
Salt Lake City, UT 84165
www.american-book.com
Printed in the United States of America on acid-free paper.

The Doll in McCallaway's Store

Designed by Jana Rade, design@american-book.com

Publisher's Note: This is a work of fiction. Names, characters, places, and incidents either are the product of the author's imagination or, are used fictitiously, and any resemblance to actual persons, living or dead, events, or locales is entirely coincidental.

Library of Congress Cataloging-in-Publication Data is available upon request.

ISBN 1-58982-149-1

Krogh, Kevin, The Doll in McCallaway's Store

Special Sales

These books are available at special discounts for bulk purchases. Special editions, including personalized covers, excerpts of existing books, and corporate imprints, can be created in large quantities for special needs. For more information e-mail orders@american-book.com or call 801-486-8639.

The Doll
in McCallaway's Store

Kevin Krogh

A Christmas gift to my family

December 2001
-Kevin Krogh-

Part One

Since his the sway of circumstance,
I would not wince nor cry aloud.
Under the law that men call chance,
my head with joy is humbly bowed.
-Dorthea Day-

"And it shall come to pass, before they call, I will
answer...."
-Isaiah 65:24-

All my life when I'd ever been lonely
and I prayed to Him, He always came.
And tonight when I need Him I've only
to call out His name.
He comes with the cure for my sadness:
if I would receive, I must give,
share the grace I've been given with gladness,
so that others may live.
For it's only by helping another,

The Doll in McCallaway's Store

it's only when I fill the needs
of a Heavenly sister or brother
that He intercedes
and lightens my cross, shares my burden,
gives me strength, whispers peace to my soul.
With the oil He gives me, my lantern
continues to glow.
If I now would be raised from my sorrow
and partake of His Heavenly gift,
I must temper my tears and tomorrow
find a soul I can lift.
-Annabelle McNeely-

Chapter One

Molly Kikkert was enjoying her evening bath. The six-year-old had more than her usual number of toys in the tub, so it would be at least ten minutes before Ann could wash her daughter's hair. Ann left the bathroom door open so she could hear her playing from the kitchen, where Jacob had almost finished cleaning up after supper. Ann knew something was wrong. He had been unusually quiet since coming home from work, and she was curious to find out why.

"Okay, Jacob, what's bothering you?" she asked.

"And what makes you think something is bothering me?" he countered, acknowledging his wife's perceptiveness with a smile.

"Come on," she coaxed, gently brushing his hair away from his forehead. "I know you too well...I'm listening."

Ann expected something small, something work-related, something requiring a quick expression of confidence in her husband's abilities, a listening ear and a few words of encouragement. She did not expect him to turn her world upside down.

Jacob motioned for her to sit. She moved the chair closer to the doorway, so that she could still hear Molly singing softly in the tub. Jacob placed his chair in front of hers; their legs interlocked.

"You okay, Molly?" Ann called out over her shoulder.

"Yes, Mommy," came the answer. Molly continued her song, something in Spanish about a mother duck and her gaggle of ducklings.

Ann looked at her husband. His uncharacteristic seriousness worried her.

"Are *you* okay?" she asked, almost in a whisper.

Jacob sighed hard.

"I want to quit my job and write again."

His words took her entirely by surprise. She was stunned.

"Quit your job? But why?" she asked. "It's a good job, and you're good at it. And you *are* writing."

Ann did not know that Jacob expected just such a reaction, nor that he had his argument all planned, even rehearsed.

"Yes, it is a good job and I am good at it, but it's not what I'm meant to do. It's a technical-writing job, Ann, an extremely dull technical-writing job; it's tedious and unchallenging, a waste of my talent. I am not a technical writer. I'm a poet; I write verse. I write—"

"But Jacob," Ann interrupted, "your poetry is not our livelihood. No one will buy it. No one will publish it. I thought you had accepted that." She was fighting back the urge to cry. "You said yourself that nobody makes money writing poetry, no matter how good it is. Remember, Jacob? You said that only novels sell."

"Exactly!" Jacob agreed in a broken whisper, reminding her by that whisper and by leaning closer to her to keep her voice low.

Ann realized by the enthusiastic promptness of his answer and by the spark in his eyes that she was saying precisely what he knew she would say, and precisely what he wanted her to say. That they both spoke quietly to not disturb or alarm Molly also gave him an advantage.

Ann was right, of course. Few poets made a living writing poetry. Oh, he had tried—Ann knew he had tried. They had tried together. Every publisher had given them the same story: "Everybody wants to write poetry," they explained, "but no one wants to read it. I'm sorry," they would almost invariably add, "but our current policy is to not consider the work of unpublished poets. If you have a novel," some continued, "have your agent contact us."

Jacob had not believed them—not at first—and had persisted, sending his poems to countless presses and agents, hoping that some enlightened agent or editor would see the uniqueness and market potential of his work.

"It will be profitable, if you'll only give it a chance," he promised.

None would, and he had finally resigned himself to the reality that he was just another frustrated poet without a public. Self-publishing was out of the question. The risk was too high. School loans and other bills had to be paid; and Ann, who trusted her husband implicitly and whose encouragement and support had been stellar, was growing increasingly impatient. She abhorred their increasing debt. For a year, they had lived without health insurance, a constant worry to both of them but especially to Ann. The young family desperately needed an income. Poetry would have to be, for the time being anyway, Jacob's hobby—his distraction.

Jacob was a gifted writer, so he easily landed a good job as a technical writer. Although his starting salary had been modest and although it had taken him time to make the adjustment—writing poetry and writing technical manuals were worlds apart—he had proven his value to the company and had begun his second year with a generous pay increase.

"We're pleased," Mr. Hendricks had told him. "Your worth will continue to rise as you gain experience."

Ann should have realized that Jacob's character required he at least pretend to like his job. Ann wanted him to like it and had convinced herself that he did. He often put in late hours at the office or brought his work home, leaving little time for her and Molly. But Ann reasoned that it was because he was used to writing at a slower pace. In time he would learn to be less of a perfectionist; he would adapt and become more comfortable and efficient.

Ann's perception of Jacob's attitude toward his job was further clouded by her own dreams for their future. After more than four years working her part-time cashier's job at Cardona's Market, she was thrilled with the security of a decent, steady paycheck. For the first time in her life she felt safe; and for a year and a half now, she had reveled in being a full-time housewife and mother. School loans were slowly but surely being repaid, and they were even saving a little. Although Jacob's dream had been shattered, part of that dream, her part, the dream of having her own home, would soon—in a few years, perhaps—become a reality. It all depended on Jacob's steady and growing salary. The prospect now of him quitting his job to again write poetry was terrifying to her.

Ann's love for Jacob had not allowed her the luxury of entirely disregarding the subtle evidence that he was not as happy at work as she wanted him to be. She well understood, or a least she thought she understood, his passion for creative writing. She didn't question his talent; his poetry thrilled her; it always had. It had sweetened their courtship, lightened their load in hard times, and sustained and nourished their shared dream of the future.

Some day, they had together imagined, Jacob would be "discovered." His work would be found on thousands upon thousands of bookshelves, nightstands, and coffee tables, and his name would be known and respected in literary circles everywhere. Ann would have a home, a house in the country with a garden—a garden was the crucial ingredient—a cherished place where her own talents and maternal instincts could find fertile ground. It would be a place where Molly and, perhaps, other children, like the flowers in Ann's dream garden, could blossom and grow. Little Molly would have things that Ann had longed for as a child but had been denied: piano and dancing lessons, a new dress now and then, a playhouse, a swing in an oak tree in a backyard, and maybe even a collection of porcelain dolls—Molly loved dolls.

Jacob had been a tireless and disciplined poet. He had written more than a hundred poems during their courtship and the first five years of their marriage, an average of almost two per month. Molly was born one year to the day after their April wedding. For four long years, they had lived a life of subsistence in the married-student apartments at the university where Jacob took classes in creative writing and Ann studied both interior design and landscape gardening. Both worked part time, Ann at first as a waitress and then, after she became pregnant with Molly, as a cashier at Cardona's Market. Jacob had tutored in the university writing lab and worked on Saturdays and full time during the summer break in a locally owned furniture factory.

Money was tight; scholarships and student loans were their salvation. Free time was scarce, but somehow Jacob found ample time for the three loves of his life: Ann, Molly, and his poetry—in that order, of course. Jacob was a loyal husband and father. His poetry sometimes distracted him from his studies but seldom from his family responsibilities. Ann knew that his time with her and Molly was sacred to him. He called them "my two best sources of inspiration," and he almost always gave them his full attention when he was with them. When he didn't, Ann was quick to remind him.

She completely understood when, as ideas occurred to him, he stopped to write in the little black notebook, his constant companion, which he kept clipped inside his shirt pocket—inspiration was fleeting and must be recorded in the moment; but on those rare occasions when he became preoccupied with his thoughts to the neglect of his family, she did not hesitate to gently scold him. She had trained him well.

Often late at night, long after Molly had been tucked into bed and after she too had drifted off to sleep, Ann would wake to find herself alone. Sometimes she would slide quietly out of bed, tiptoe down the hall, and peek around the frame of the kitchen door, where she always found Jacob sitting at the computer, his notebook open on the desk on his left, and giving full rein to his imagination, absorbed by his world of words, rhyme, and meter.

Ann called her husband "the people's poet." His verses explored the feelings, passions, dreams, triumphs, and disappointments of the common man about whom and for whom he wrote. Selected poems had placed well in several competitions at the university, fueling his cautious confidence. He had also done well in several regional competitions and had published three poems in three separate literary journals. He once won a five-hundred-dollar prize, and many of his poems had been published in multiauthored collections. More important to Jacob was the response his poems received from those for whom they were written—his family, of course, but also those he perceived to represent who he hoped would become his public: the men on his father's construction crew, Luis and his brother Tony and the others in the furniture shop, and Ann's coworkers at Cardona's Market.

Most of his poems were narrative and fairly long. They were fictional stories in metered verse, based on the lives of people he knew and admired or others he had observed or imagined. His collection was impressive, but he had not understood the market or that the few publishers who accepted collections of poetry had an inflexible bias for free verse. Jacob remained loyal to traditional metrical forms in his poetry. For him, poetry without rhythm, rhyme, and meter wasn't poetry at all.

So on he wrote, unaware that his themes too were out of favor, not spicy, erudite, provoking, or esoteric enough for the in-vogue tastes of those few circles of society who do buy poetry. He knew his intended audience but did not yet understand what the publishers and agents well understood: that those for whom he wrote—common everyday people with everyday challenges—were not the type of souls you would find browsing the poetry sections of the fashionable bookstores that catered to the literary tastes of the upper-middle class.

Jacob and Ann had been optimistic in charting a course for their future. As they approached graduation, they formulated what they felt was a conservative, short-range, yearlong plan. Ann would continue working her part-time job at the market. Jacob would do some tutoring at the university and work as needed at the furniture shop but would spend most of his time polishing and adding to his poetry, the best of which he would then submit for publication as a book-size collection. After that first year, once the royalties started coming in, Ann would quit her job and become a full-time mother. They would pay their debts and buy their house in the country. Jacob would give occasional workshops, lectures, and recitations, and every couple of years publish another volume of poetry. He might even teach at a university. They would, in essence, live happily ever after.

This was their dream; a pie-in-the-sky dream to be sure, but they were not entirely naive. Ann allowed herself to give more rein to her hopes than her personality permitted only because she knew Jacob would always keep their collective feet on the ground. He had inherited his passion for poetry—along with his dark eyes and hair—from his mother, but the reserved and calculating attributes of his personality were entirely paternal. He trusted no one and was even suspicious of his own instincts. Ann knew he felt guilty that she had to work so hard and that Molly had been deprived of a full-time mother. She knew also that his greatest fear was that she might be disappointed. He had cautioned her that this first book might not be as successful as they hoped.

"And if it fails," he had assured her, "I promise I will make it up to you."

And his book had failed, not because he wrote poor poetry but because he wrote very good poetry that he could not sell. He knew he had a readership, the masses of hard-working, decent people who now had a poetic voice, his voice, but there was no way they could hear it, no way he could get his poems into their hands.

So, Jacob had resigned himself stoically to his lot—or so Ann thought—and for the past year and a half, he was making good on his promise. He had never complained. He had never said anything. Ann was confused now by his new resolve to try again.

"Exactly, Ann!" he repeated even more softly. "Only novels sell, and that is why I am going to write a novel."

Chapter Two

It was 8:15. There was a hint of fall in the morning air. Annabelle McNeely looked up from her embroidering and out the large picture window she had insisted Tom install when they built the home. Any moment now, the children would begin walking by across the street on their way to their first day back at school after summer vacation. She knew they would stop for a few minutes to look at the display in the window of McCallaway's store. They always did, and she loved watching them on their way to and from school. The children who knew her would always wave, and she would answer. She knew most of them by name.

They came every fall just before Halloween to pick pumpkins from the famous McNeely pumpkin patch. The scarecrow was in place for the children's benefit—crows were no threat to pumpkins. The patch promised to be especially productive this year. Some of the small pumpkins had already started turning orange. The children in the neighborhood, of course, had first choice. The ones she taught in Primary were especially dear to her.

She and Tom—especially Tom—had strongly objected when the zoning mysteriously changed, extending the business district ever so slightly and allowing Jed McCallaway to build his store on the large wooded lot they had enjoyed for years from their chairs in the parlor, the same parlor from which Annabelle now waved to the children. The Norway maples Tom had planted and so carefully pruned in their own yard had framed the lot perfectly, giving them the illusion that they lived deep in the woods instead of just blocks from the commercial center of town.

The view was one of the reasons they had purchased the land more than forty-five years ago. They had stretched their finances considerably to buy their half-acre lot, and several years passed before they could afford to place a home on it. But fortune had at last smiled on them. Tom's printing business, after a few years of initial struggle, had done very well, and life here had been good to them. Here they had raised their children, a girl and a boy, here they had made their truest friends, and here they had become acquainted with God.

It was the perfect place to raise their family, a college town, not too large and not too small. Their neighborhood was safe—they cherished their neighbors—their home was spacious and comfortable, and they had, they were often told, the most beautiful yard and most productive garden and orchard in town. The elementary school was close enough that they heard every school bell. Susan and Paul, if they ran, could leave the house when the first bell rang and be at their desks before it rang again.

The church where they worshiped was also within easy walking distance. Annabelle could still see the white steeple from the back porch through the two catalpa trees that Tom had planted to shade the gazebo he had built in the southeast corner of the yard. The picture that Paul had taken late one July afternoon framed the steeple in the trees' white summer bloom. It had won him first prize in the high-school photography contest and still hung on the parlor wall above the piano.

The steeple was a constant reminder of the faith they had made the center of their lives, and their greatest desire was to instill that faith in the hearts of their children and grandchildren. They had had their disappointments and challenges but in the long run had been successful. They were very active in their ward congregation and also in the community. Their church had helped them raise their children; the youth programs were wonderful—Tom worked mostly with the Aaronic priesthood quorums and the Boy Scouts, and Annabelle taught in the Primary and Sunday schools. The whole family joined in the service projects organized by the priesthood quorums and ward auxiliaries. They tithed their increase faithfully and contributed generously to the fast, humanitarian, and missionary funds; they visited the widows and widowers—like Jed McCallaway—and gratefully shared the abundant harvests from their garden and orchard. Yes, they were very happy here and would never think of leaving the place that had given them such a busy and full life.

Although Paul was still single and was now living in Europe, Susan had married. She had met Andrew Harrison at the university in the capital. They had gone away to graduate school for several years but had returned and settled nearby. They wanted to raise their family where Annabelle and Tom could be a constant influence on their children's lives. Their home was close enough that their daughter Camille could easily walk the distance to and from Grandma's house. She called it "over the river and through the woods" precisely because a footbridge crossing the river in the park was the safest and most direct route.

Andrew taught ornamental horticulture and landscape design at the local college and got along splendidly with his in-laws. He enjoyed working side by side with them on their property. His expertise was a large part of the reason for the famed beauty of their gardens and yard. Yes, life had been good to Tom and Annabelle McNeely. Both had enjoyed excellent health and looked forward to Tom's retirement and a Church mission, and to many years of delighting in their family and reaping the fruits of their many labors.

However, Annabelle was alone now. Life had not gone as they had planned. Tom had died suddenly and unexpectedly—a heart attack—just days before his fifty-eighth birthday, the very morning crews began to clear the lot across the street to begin construction on Jed McCallaway's store. Tom had become very upset as he watched the maples across the street being felled one by one.

"You needn't cut them all down," he protested.

He was in the parlor on the phone with Jed, venting his Irish anger, when the heart attack came.

That was more than twelve years ago. Annabelle had long since forgiven Jed McCallaway. After all, it wasn't really his fault that Tom had died, and if not for his store, the children would now have no reason to stop and wave. Over the years, she and Jed had become good friends. They sometimes sat together in sacrament meeting, and both sang in the choir. They often read the same books simultaneously and discussed them over lunch. Annabelle supplied Jed with fresh vegetables from her garden and fruit from her orchard—he was too busy with the store to grow his own—and Jed paid Annabelle to design and put up the holiday and seasonal displays in the store window, one of which the neighborhood children had now stopped to admire. This year's back-to-school display featured some of the early apples from her orchard that had ripened just in time. The children appeared to like it very much.

The sound of the second bell meant that no more children would pass by, and Annabelle turned again to her embroidering. Even though Christmas was months away, she was putting the final touches on her Christmas gift to Camille, a dress for her porcelain doll. This would be the twelfth Christmas since Annabelle found the doll in a shop at the end of a narrow alley in Milan, Italy.

She and Tom had planned to travel to Europe together to visit Paul and see the sights. She and Susan had made the trip instead. Susan had insisted, hoping it would lift her mother's spirits. Annabelle knew from the moment she saw the doll that it was the perfect gift for Camille's sixth birthday. The doll's eyes had caught her attention, blue as the Italian sky, not like the eyes of other dolls. Most doll eyes stared blankly into space at nothing in particular, but these eyes looked into Annabelle's own eyes, smiling their assurance that life was still beautiful and good.

No, this was no ordinary doll; Camille loved her so much that Annabelle began their tradition the following Christmas. Every year she made a new dress so Camille could outfit her favorite doll—actually, her only doll, because no other could compete for Camille's affection. This year Annabelle had made a high-collared, red satin dress trimmed in white, gold, and silver lace. Only the embroidering remained, the personal touch that so delighted Camille. As she had done so many times before, Annabelle carefully stitched, in gold and silver thread, the doll's name, "Molly Ann," on the back of the dress just above the hem.

Camille had at first wanted to name the doll Annabelle, in honor of her grandmother, but at Annabelle's suggestion she changed her mind and named her Molly Ann.

"Annabelle is a fine name for a grandma," Annabelle had reasoned, "but not for the world's most beautiful doll. Annabelle sounds so old. Why don't we think of another name?"

"I'll call her Molly Ann," Camille resolved decidedly. "Molly after my friend who moved away, and Ann, short for Annabelle, after you, Grandma. She'll be like us, Grandma," she added excitedly. "We all have two L's in our names: Annabelle, Camille, and Molly Ann."

Camille was like that, very bright, even witty, but not one to waste time mulling over decisions, surprisingly opinionated for a little girl, a little too impetuous sometimes for her own good, yet always sincere and willing to accept the consequences of her impulsive nature.

Camille was right about one thing: In many ways, grandmother and granddaughter were much alike. After Tom's death, Camille became Annabelle's new best friend. They enjoyed many of the same things in life, and they enjoyed them together: long walks in the canyon, listening to Susan play the piano, early Saturday morning garage sales, gardening, and most of all, poetry, and especially Annabelle's poetry.

Annabelle had never ventured to write until after Tom died. It was her loneliness that finally reawakened the long-dormant talent. She was no stranger to poetry. As a small child, she memorized every nursery rhyme her mother read to her; she loved to hear herself say them. She spent many hours as a youth in the county library, and by the time she finished college, she had surely read almost every poem ever written. Whenever she found one she really liked, she committed it to memory. Her knack for memorization was truly remarkable. She easily knew two, maybe three hundred poems. When she wasn't with Tom, with her children, or with her friends and neighbors, these poems were her constant companions, her defense against loneliness and discouraging thoughts. She often repeated them aloud and without error while walking, gardening, or in the evening quiet of the parlor as she embroidered or sewed.

It was on one such quiet August evening in the parlor that Annabelle discovered her hidden gift for writing poetry, precisely, the first night after Tom's death that she found herself entirely alone. Circumstances had combined so that she would have to be alone—later she would credit it to divine will and providence. Annabelle had been caught unprepared by Tom's sudden passing. Though she was a woman of unwavering faith, she was having great difficulty pulling herself out of her grief. She had no doubt whatsoever that she would be with Tom again—her hope in the resurrection and in the covenants they had made in the temple was unshakable—but she missed him deeply.

Because of her mother's emotional condition, for several weeks after her father's funeral, a perhaps over-protective Susan saw to it that her mother was never really by herself, at least not for long, and never at night. Someone—Camille mostly, but sometimes the whole family—was always there. Camille loved spending the night with her grandmother, and because Annabelle did all she could to hide her grief and melancholy in Camille's presence, Susan thought it good therapy.

But that night, Annabelle would have to be alone. It couldn't be helped. Camille had just come down with the measles and had a fever. Susan was a talented pianist and once every year was the guest soloist with the symphony orchestra in the capital. The concert that night would keep her away until very late, even should she try to drive back. Andrew insisted that she stay and return in the morning. Annabelle had a slight cold herself and was also sure she had never had the measles. All agreed it unwise that she stay with her granddaughter.

"Why don't you come with me," Susan suggested, but Annabelle knew she would only be in the way. If Andrew were also going, it would be different. The concert wouldn't end until well after 10:00 P.M., followed by a reception. No, she just wasn't feeling up to it.

There was no other solution. Andrew stayed with Camille, Susan drove alone, and Annabelle spent the night by herself.

"Well," Andrew had reasoned, "it's as good a time as any to wean your mother from Camille's company. After all, she'll soon be in school. It's been over three weeks since your dad's funeral, and we can't have her staying the night forever."

Susan had reluctantly agreed, provided that Andrew call often to check on her. Annabelle also agreed. She was embarrassed to be such a burden on her daughter's family. Andrew was right; it was time.

"I'll be fine," she said.

Despite her slight cold, Annabelle spent most of that day in the garden. The pumpkins had to be rotated, or they wouldn't be the perfect shape that the children had come to expect. Tom had always turned them religiously every couple of weeks. Likewise religiously, Susan stopped by early in the afternoon on her way to the concert. She had several hours of driving ahead of her, but it was still early, and it was their tradition. Susan always played her pieces for Annabelle, for good luck, on the parlor piano she had played as a child. That night it was a concerto by Debussy.

Debussy was Annabelle's favorite, and Susan played him beautifully.

Later that night, Annabelle sat in the darkness of the parlor, unable to sleep, unable to conquer her loneliness. She had prayed desperately, pouring out her soul to God, pleading that He would take away her sorrow, her loneliness, and most of all, that she might be rid of the enmity she felt toward Jed McCallaway, but her despair persisted. She sat in a half daze, staring out the window, reciting poem after poem, accompanied only by the measured chirp of the crickets in the yard, slower now because of the slightly cooler night air. Only her voice and their song tempered the otherwise absolute silence. Across the street a solitary lamp cast its tenuous light on the pile of maple trees that had been felled the day of Tom's death and that now lay subdued and lifeless, waiting to be cut up and hauled away, to Annabelle, a haunting reminder of the reason for her solitude and pain.

She returned again to her poetry.

"Whose woods these are, I think I know," she muttered, staring out the window. "His house is in the village though."

Robert Frost was not very comforting.

She started another: "Two roads diverged in a yellow wood," she whispered, "and sorry I could not travel both and be one traveler, long I stood and looked down one as far as I could," she proceeded, her eyes filling with tears. But as she reached the poem's last few verses, the reason for her tears had changed. She smiled softly.

"And I," she continued slowly and thoughtfully, "I took the one less traveled by; and that has made all the difference."

The warmth and peace she had prayed for had finally come to her, and as she finished the poem, something new, a voice, still and small, within her mind, within her whole being, more felt than heard, but more real than if she had heard it with her own ears, a voice that spoke clearly and firmly.

"Take that road, Annabelle," it said.

She looked around, startled but unafraid.

It was not the first time she had had the feeling, though it was the first time she had heard a voice. The feeling was the familiar product of her prayers. It had been her comfort in the shyness of her childhood and youth, and her assurance as a young woman facing important life decisions. It had come to strengthen her often throughout her life. When Tom's business was struggling, it had given her hope. It had filled the emptiness in her heart after the stillbirth of her second child. It had spoken peace to her often during Paul's rebellious teenage years. When three-year-old Susan had been very ill and near death, it had promised her that all would be well. Whenever she had prayed in earnest, it had come. But after Tom's death, until that night, that moment, it had delayed its coming. For some reason God, she thought, had left her alone and comfortless in her bereavement, but she now understood why. The road she must take was the road of forgiveness. Jed McCallaway was not to blame. Tom had died because it was his time. It was now her time to cast off her self-pity, to forgive, and to get on with life.

She at last felt relieved of the burden she had carried. But what to do now? After her prayer of gratitude, she retired to her bed but lay awake, still full of the warmth and energy of the Spirit, when the voice inside her came again a second time.

"Write," it said.

"Write?" she questioned aloud.

"Write a poem, Annabelle," was the immediate response.

She had attempted to write a poem once, long ago, in college, and had failed miserably. It had been a frustrating experience she had never again repeated. But now, urged on by the voice and the feelings inside her, it seemed entirely possible, even necessary. She got out of bed, put on her robe, and walked down the hall and into the parlor. She sat at the desk, turned on the lamp, removed several clean sheets of paper from the drawer, and sharpened a pencil.

"And what should I write about?" she wondered.

She thought of Tom, of the day they had met, of the night he had proposed, of their walks in the woods, their trials and triumphs. She thought of her children, their birthdays, their camping trips, their smiles, and their tears. She thought of Camille. She reflected for a good hour on her life's experience, but she wrote nothing. It was very late. She was suddenly very tired and decided to go back to bed.

Annabelle put the paper back into the drawer and turned off the lamp. In the dark she sat for a moment and tried to clear her mind. On the other side of the room, the light from across the road spilled through the window and reflected in the piano's black lacquer finish on the right side of the keyboard. Annabelle thought of Susan and wondered how the concert had gone. Of course it had gone well; Susan did everything well. Even as a child, she had demanded so much of herself. Annabelle recalled her daughter's first attempts to play. Susan had been so determined. She nodded excitedly and smiled. She knew now what she would write.

In a moment the lamp was on again, the drawer open, and the paper on the desk. Three hours later, Annabelle copied the poem's final draft carefully onto a clean sheet of paper.

Each Time She Plays
(for Susan)

Two feet too small to reach the floor,
a glance in search of needed praise
from eyes that leaped from keys to score,
I well recall those yesterdays,
when little hands so awkwardly
tried hard to play notes gracefully.
These memories return to me
each time my daughter plays.

And now, years hence, her grace and poise
no longer need her mother's praise;
the music bears its own sweet joys

as sacrifice and practice pay.
Rachmaninoff or Debussy,
the common thread I clearly see
in piano, prayer, and poetry
each time my daughter plays.

My spirit soars to hear the sound;
   its purity of tone betrays
a birthright from celestial ground,
a dowry chance could never raise.
In her I see God's grand design;
she is His child, as well as mine.
I glimpse that heritage divine
each time my daughter plays.

Annabelle read it over again and again, amazed that she could have written such a thing. Her wonder was still there in the morning when she awoke with a start, questioning for a few moments if it had all been a dream. Where had the words come from? She repeated them from memory and tearfully thanked God again in her morning prayer.

Her mother's improved spirits pleasantly surprised Susan when she stopped by on her way back from the capital. She had left early, anxious to get home to see how both Annabelle and Camille were doing. She found her mother in the garden, cheerfully weeding the pumpkin patch.

"I'm fine," she insisted, "never better. You get home to Camille, and call me and tell me how she's feeling."

Part One
Chapter Two

Annabelle was equally insistent that no one stay that night either, although she didn't tell Susan why. She said nothing about her poem, nor that she now wanted to be alone in order to see if her experience could be repeated, if she could write another. And she did write another, and another, and another. None came as easily as had the first. She labored over most for weeks, sometimes months; but with each poem she completed, her gratitude grew. Each was a gift from God.

Although Annabelle considered herself to be an amateur poet, those few she allowed to read her work knew better, Susan more than anyone. One day, while looking for a piece of paper, she opened the bottom drawer of the parlor desk where her mother kept her finished drafts. There, she discovered twenty-six separate poems, each written neatly by hand on pale gray cotton parchment, each dated and ordered chronologically, twenty-six poems written in a little less than two years. When she saw the date of the first, August 21, Susan immediately understood.

"Why didn't you tell me you were writing poetry?" she asked a few days later.

"You never asked," was Annabelle's evasive reply. "Besides, I don't write them to be read. How many have you read?"

"All of them, Mother. They're beautiful. They made me cry."

Mother and daughter embraced.

"I'm very proud of you, Mother. I had no idea. You should share them, at least with your family. It's a sin to hide your talent, you know," she playfully chided. "There are a lot of magazines that print poems. You could at least put them in the church newsletter from time to time, or read them whenever you give a talk in sacrament meeting. They might help someone."

"Well, maybe someday, but not now." She paused, and then added, "I'm glad you like them."

She was relieved that Susan had at last read her poems. She had often wanted to show them to her, but she was uncomfortable with the idea of publishing or reading them to others. Annabelle was extremely compassionate and eager to do all the good that she could. She filled her life with service to others, but she was shy by nature. She had struggled throughout her life to overcome her timidity, and she had mostly succeeded, but she would never force her affection, or now, her poetry on anyone.

Annabelle was glad Susan had discovered her secret, and she was happy to make her poems available to the members of her family. It was, after all, she realized, as much for them as for her that God had let her write them. But share them with others? Perhaps someday, but not just yet.

After she had entered them into her computer and printed a hard copy (just in case), Susan placed the originals—each in its own plastic cover—in a three-ring binder that she displayed openly on the shelf in the parlor. As time passed, one binder became two, then three, and finally four of them graced the parlor shelf. It pleased Annabelle when those she loved took them down to read, but she always remembered to hide them before receiving other visitors.

Camille especially, and to her grandmother's delight, from about age twelve, was drawn to Annabelle's poetry. Almost every Sunday afternoon after dinner—the family often had dinner at Annabelle's after church and on holidays—she could be found at the parlor desk or on the parlor couch pouring over an open binder, and she was invariably the first to read Annabelle's newest offering. She had her favorite poems, of course, and she never tired of hearing her grandmother recite them during their leisurely walks in the canyon.

Camille tried to follow her grandmother's example with her own attempts at writing, but she had little aptitude for verbal organization; she lacked the patience. It also quickly became clear that she would not follow in her mother's footsteps; music too was too structured and rigorous for her impetuous nature. Camille wasn't sure what she wanted to be in life; she only knew she wanted to try everything. For her, life was an adventure. In high school she tried almost everything available: sports, drama, debate, dance, and more. If you named it, she probably tried it at one time or another. Annabelle delighted in her granddaughter's zest for life, and Camille adored her grandmother. She was Camille's confidant and counselor, and the doll Molly Ann was the symbol of their relationship.

Shortly after Annabelle had given her the doll, Camille started talking to her Molly Ann. At first, it was "cute" but had soon gone beyond what one might judge to be normal for a little girl's imagination. Camille also insisted that Molly Ann talked back.

"Molly Ann says I don't have to eat my cabbage," or "Molly Ann says you're being mean to me."

Camille's behavior soon became worrisome to Susan and Andrew. They contemplated taking the doll away and even discussed arranging for some kind of professional counseling. Annabelle scoffed at the idea.

"A six-year-old doesn't need counseling," she argued. "She'll grow out of it. What she needs is a little brother or sister."

"Mother!" Susan protested. "That's really a matter for Andrew and me to decide, don't you think?"

Annabelle knew she had overstepped her license—it was a touchy subject between Susan and Andrew—but she didn't hesitate for a moment to take at least part of the credit a little more than nine months later, when Camille's little brother Mark was born.

Annabelle was right. Camille chatted with Molly Ann for about a year but eventually grew out of it. It was only a phase, as Annabelle suspected, but it had its vestiges. Even now, whenever Annabelle wanted Camille to tell her how she really felt about something, she sometimes asked, "And what does Molly Ann say?" Their tradition of a new dress for the doll each Christmas renewed and strengthened their relationship.

Annabelle usually waited until early November before even thinking about the dress she would make for Camille's Molly Ann, and because of this, she often rushed to complete it in time for Christmas. But here it was, late August, and the red satin dress with the white, gold, and silver lace was finished. Even the embroidering was almost done. She had begun the task on Camille's eighteenth birthday and had completed it quickly because she had extra time on her hands.

Camille and her family were far away. Andrew, on sabbatical from the college, had arranged to work a year for the urban forestry department of a large city on the East Coast. His college encouraged its faculty to take a break from academia and touch base with the "real world" every six or seven years. Andrew had taught for thirteen years without a sabbatical and was long overdue. The timing was right; Camille had graduated from high school, and Mark was entering the sixth grade and would be changing schools too when they returned—from elementary to junior high school. Susan likewise had a good reason for going. She would be teaching piano to advanced students at a nearby state university and studying with one of the best concert pianists in the country. She was also to be a guest performer with the university and the city symphony orchestras. Only Camille had hesitated, reluctant to leave her grandmother. Susan and Andrew left the decision entirely up to her but urged her to stay with Annabelle and begin her first year of college at home. The allure of new places and people, however, proved too strong for Camille's adventurous disposition.

"I can't decide, Grandma. I'll stay here if you want me to."

"And what does Molly Ann say?" Annabelle inquired.

Camille hugged her grandma. "Molly Ann says she wants to go, but she'll miss you so much."

So Camille had gone too, planning to live with her family and attend her first year of college at the university where Susan would teach. The following year, she would either find roommates and an apartment near campus or come back in May after Andrew's sabbatical and study at the college in town. That, of course, was what everyone hoped for. It would be the less expensive option—her tuition would be free because she was a professor's daughter. Annabelle had been sure she would return, but Camille's recent letters hinted that she had already decided to stay east another year.

Camille had been gone for less than four months, but Annabelle missed her immensely. The summer hadn't been the same without her. Her morning walks in the park and in the canyon were solitary now, great for reflection and for her poetry—some of her best ideas occurred to her in the canyon—but she would willingly sacrifice all of that creativity to have Camille with her again. She worried about her granddaughter's impulsiveness. She hoped the values and the legacy of faith that she and her parents had worked so hard to give her would see her through her college years away from home, without the immediate support of family. Annabelle wrote to her faithfully every week, encouraging her to be strong. Two poems had already been inspired by her love and concern. She had been working on another for the past several weeks. This poem would be special; she planned to give it to Camille, along with the dress for Molly Ann, when she visited for Christmas.

Part One
Chapter Two

The embroidery on the dress was complete. Annabelle tried to imagine how Molly Ann would look in her new dress. Perhaps Camille was too old for dolls now. Perhaps this would be the last time she would lovingly stitch the name Molly Ann. Perhaps a special poem each Christmas would become their new tradition.

Annabelle rose from her chair and carefully placed the dress on the piano. In less than a year she would be seventy, but she didn't feel old. Today she needed to turn the pumpkins. Andrew had arranged for Larry, one of his students, to help in the yard. He had done an excellent job, even by Annabelle's exacting standards, but she insisted he leave the pumpkin patch to her.

Chapter Three

Molly continued her song in the bathtub, while in the kitchen Ann glared wide-eyed at Jacob in disbelief. It was clear to him that he had caught her completely unawares and that she did not know what to say.

"Not just any novel," he continued enthusiastically. "A new kind of novel, a novel only I can write."

Jacob's voice betrayed his emotion. He paused briefly to regain control.

"The publishers are right. People read novels, not poetry, but only because—"

He paused again. He was getting ahead of himself.

"Ann, you read my poetry. Why do you read it?" he asked as he took her hand. "You don't read anyone else's poetry. Why do you read mine?"

The question, of course, was rhetorical; Jacob answered it.

"You read my poems because you know the poet. Am I right?" Jacob knew she had read very little poetry before they met, and only his poetry since then.

"Yes, you're right, but—" Ann inserted, trying to get in at least a word or two, but Jacob was eager to make his point and interrupted her with his next question.

"What do you read when you're not reading my poetry?"

Ann smiled a weak, forced smile and then bit her lower lip before looking away and letting go of Jacob's hand. Jacob sighed but continued to watch her eyes. He knew instantly what Ann's reaction meant, but this was no time for a discussion about religion or, better said, about his lack of it.

"Besides the Bible," he clarified, trying to keep the slight annoyance he felt out of the inflection of his voice.

Jacob had always admired his wife's faith and spiritual nature. She was profoundly religious, and he loved her for it. Why she had so much faith was a mystery, but he could not imagine her without it. Her devotion to God and her hope in Christ were essential to who she was. Ann referred often in their conversations to her past, and he knew her story well.

She had grown up as an orphan. She was three years old when she survived the car accident that killed both her parents. Her maternal grandmother had raised her. Grandma Molly, as Ann affectionately called her, had only one child and only one grandchild. Grandmother and granddaughter had lived alone together for fifteen years in their small inner-city apartment, a fixed, minimum-wage, hand-to-mouth existence, supplemented only by the money from Ann's parents' small insurance policy, food stamps, and later, her grandmother's Social Security benefits and

Ann's part-time job. But they were happy. Their shared love and faith more than compensated for their lack of material possessions.

For as long as Ann could remember, she and Grandma Molly had read from the Bible and prayed together every night before going to bed. Theirs was a simple form of religion. They belonged to no congregation or church, although they often attended meetings with friends. They were content with their own interpretations of what they read. They prayed to a Heavenly Father who loved and watched over His children. They believed in a Savior who had atoned for their mistakes and weaknesses, and whose New Testament example showed them the way they should live. They did not expect an easy life—it had never been so, and there was much to be learned from adversity—but they had great confidence that if they knocked, God would open the door. Prayer was their strength, their solace, and Ann's only dowry.

Then, just a few weeks before Ann graduated from high school, Grandma Molly suffered a debilitating stroke. Because there were no other relatives, and because Ann was not yet eighteen, the state assumed the responsibility for her and her grandmother's care. State social-service agencies moved Grandma Molly into a nursing home and Ann into a center for homeless youth to await either foster care or her eighteenth birthday. Ann protested the separation. Less than two months separated her from the freedom of adulthood. She did not understand why she was not allowed to care for her grandmother. Ann, too, had once been helpless and alone. She now longed to repay that debt but was powerless to do so.

Although they lived apart during the two months between Grandma Molly's stroke and her death, Ann made sure they were still a family. Her daily visits to the nursing home kept them close, and their evening devotional—earlier now because of the distance between them and the dangers inherent in the night—continued uninterrupted. The two remained together as much as possible until Grandma Molly's death. Then, Ann had been alone for almost two years, until she found someone with whom she could again share her love and faith.

Love and faith. In Ann the two principles were inseparable, and that harmony in her character immediately impressed her young poet. Jacob's own capacity to love was no less than Ann's, but Godly faith was something he had never explored, not for want of respect or reverence for things sacred but for lack of habit and interest.

Jacob's story was much different than Ann's, and that difference explained, in his mind, the disparity in their spiritual temperament. He was the second youngest of four children, and the only son of honest, unpretentious, working-class parents—ordinary people, if there be such a thing. His father was a construction foreman who worked long hours but who was entirely devoted to his wife and children. Reserved and cautious as he was, it was a wonder he had ever met Jacob's mother, a shy though energetic woman as guileless and trusting as her husband was wary and vigilant. They had met and married while he was stationed in Spain with the Air Force. Jacob's mother was proud of her Spanish Republican heritage—both her father and mother had fought with the Marxist militia against fascism and Carlist conservatism during the Spanish Civil War—and she had insisted on raising her children in a bilingual environment. She spoke only Spanish whenever they were alone, and she taught them to read and write her native language. College and his life since had verified for Jacob the wisdom in his mother's determination to give him this advantage.

His mother's passion for literature in general and poetry in particular assured that all her children would have the opportunity to embrace that same passion. She had read to Jacob almost daily from the works of Spain's greatest authors, including its most beloved poets: Machado especially, but also Bécquer, Espronceda, Lorca, and others.

Religion, on the other hand, was simply not an ingredient in the family character, not for any lack of civility or charity toward their neighbors and acquaintances—the family undeniably possessed many of what are often called the "Christian" virtues—but for lack of devotion. Jacob's parents were good, kind, decent people who kept mostly to themselves and their small circle of friends. They treated others with respect and compassion but felt neither the need to commune with Deity nor the desire to affiliate with any religious group or organization; there had never been extraordinary events in their lives, no major trial or crisis that might have led them to spiritual self-searching.

Although from the beginning Jacob had embraced Ann's spiritual temperament as an essential part of her identity, Ann had at first been apprehensive about Jacob's lack of religious background and sentiment, and fearful of its potential for conflict in their relationship. While there was nothing about *her* that he would change, Jacob was well aware of Ann's unwavering hope that, given time, he would some day discover what he was missing.

"The potential is certainly there," she had told him when, during their courtship, they had discussed her apprehensions. "Except for my grandmother, I've never known anyone to be so unselfish and accepting."

And the night he proposed marriage, she had again revisited the subject

"My instincts tell me that you will one day share my faith. I've made it a matter of prayer"—Jacob already knew that Ann had tremendous confidence in prayer—"God answered in his usual way: there was no doubt, only a calm assurance that all would be well."

Jacob was willing to be taught. He had shared with Ann his "religion," his poetry, and it would be unprincipled not to show her the same courtesy.

Their contract was simple. Each night before bed, for five or ten minutes Ann would listen to Jacob read poetry, usually his own, but sometimes that of his favorite poets. In turn, he listened as Ann read for an equal amount of time from her grandmother's Bible. Jacob agreed readily to this compromise and always felt he got the better deal in the agreement.

Part One
Chapter Three

He loved to hear Ann read; reading was her gift. He often had her read drafts of his poems—she read them with greater clarity of feeling than he ever could—and he often made changes according to her interpretation. Watching Ann read, rather than listening alone, gave Jacob his greatest satisfaction, especially when she read the Bible. His eyes seldom left hers. Ann's eyes were a deep azure, as dark blue as his were brown, and Jacob was sure they were bluest when she read.

Eyes had always intrigued Jacob. His mother had once taught him a proverb written by her favorite poet, Antonio Machado. Its message had caused a profound change in how he saw both himself and others: *El ojo que ves no es ojo porque tú lo veas; es ojo porque te ve* ("The eye that you see is not an eye because you see it; it is an eye because it sees you"). Since then, he had made a habit of searching the eyes of the people he met, and he loved what he saw in Ann's eyes. He had studied her eyes as she read for several minutes the first time he saw her. Although he was close enough to hear her breathe, she did not notice him watching her from the opposite side of the stacks, through the space left by the book she had taken from a shelf in the university library.

Ann's eyes were truly the windows to her soul, and Jacob discovered that those windows were most open when she read. When he looked into her eyes while she looked at him, he saw only his own reflection. It was Ann's eyes when she read, and later, after Molly was born, her eyes as she gazed on Molly that Jacob loved to search most. Early in their relationship, his stare made Ann feel what she termed "comfortably uncomfortable." It made her blush, but he could tell that she loved the attention, and as their love grew and as she began to understand her young poet and the meaning of his gaze, the blushing stopped, and Jacob knew she had accepted it, looked forward to it, and cherished it.

"When I feel your eyes on me, I know that I'm loved," she explained. "It's my assurance that I hold your heart, your affection, and your devotion."

As he watched her read the Bible, he knew that *she* knew his eyes were searching hers. She never had to look up to make sure. She could sense them, and if ever they faltered—and they seldom did, and only when he was preoccupied about something—she knew. It never failed to amaze him. He could look away intentionally without cause, and she continued reading, but if something else distracted him, something significant, he could count on her questioning glance and a discussion later after Molly was asleep about what and why.

As she had done with her grandmother, Ann read to Jacob from the Old or New Testaments. The Four Gospels were her favorite text, and as time passed, Jacob came to know them well, although he had never read a word himself. Jacob had his favorite passages, too, because Ann's eyes were bluest and brightest when moist with tears. Jacob could not deny that he too felt something, something comforting and tender when she read of Christ's offering in Gethsemane or of His passion and resurrection. He attributed what he felt to his love for Ann.

Jacob had always reasoned that in addition to the chance it gave him to read Ann's eyes, listening to Ann read the Bible was an asset to his poetry. Many people about whom Jacob wrote had strong religious convictions. Ann's daily reading gave him the chance to explore the roots of the faith of some of his characters and to discover new possibilities for metaphor—an additional resource for his poetry. Any thoughts about his own spiritual feelings were immediately dismissed by his already-occupied mind. He did not allow himself to think about it. He had little time for reflection on spiritual matters as they applied to him. For him, it was enough that Ann believed. Jacob had no time for himself. Once the lights were out, his mind turned immediately to whatever poem he was working on. It was an important step in his writing process, time to clear his mind of all other concerns and lose himself in his world of words. After Ann was asleep, it was his time, yes, but not time for personal soul searching; it was his time to write.

That was before the disillusionment, before he started writing technical manuals instead of metered verse. He had tried to remain positive. Ann was obviously pleased with his good salary and her chance to be a full-time mother. He owed it to her to try to adapt. But nighttime writing sessions after Ann was asleep were now spent on projects from work. There was always a deadline to meet. He continued to listen to Ann read each night, but he had stopped both reading and writing poetry.

The truth was that despite the outward evidence to the contrary, Jacob had never stopped thinking about his writing. Ann had no notion of the plan he had been crafting. For months, he had turned it over and over again in his mind. If he couldn't publish his poetry, why not a novel? Anything was better than continuing the monotonous prosaic profession of technical writing. Jacob recognized his own gift for narrative. Novels were not poetry, but he saw the connection. He had convinced himself that it was possible, and now he was trying to convince Ann.

Jacob wished, as he searched Ann's eyes, turned as they were from his for a few moments to ponder alone his question, for some evidence of faith and confidence in *him*, in what *he* was proposing. He saw none; only fear and disappointment were mirrored there. As far as he could tell, the startling news of his desire to write a novel had awakened only doubt and cynicism, and he tried hard to ignore the feelings of jealousy that had lately found their way into his thoughts. Why so much faith in God and so little in him? Why so much doubt in his talent? Why, if Ann sensed so well his feelings, had she failed to see his pain? True, he had done his best to hide his feelings from her, but he had never been successful in hiding them before. Why could she not sense them now? Why had she not intuited during the past more than a year that he hated his job and that his happiness, "their happiness together," he corrected his thought, depended now not on her faith in God but on her faith in him, faith that he could write his novel.

As disappointed as he was in Ann's reaction, Jacob had anticipated it and prepared well. He only hoped she wouldn't cry. Ann seldom cried in front of him, but when she did, it always moved him deeply. He had prepared himself for her protests but not for her tears. But tears or no tears, there was no going back now.

Chapter Four

"Besides the Bible?" Ann repeated Jacob's question, looking once again into his eyes. "All right, I admit it, I do like to read novels. But, Jacob, you've never written one. You've only written poetry. Can you write a novel that will sell?"

She didn't mean for it to sound like it had, so doubting, so skeptical, and so materialistic. She wished immediately she hadn't said it quite that way. She feared she had hurt his feelings, but Jacob appeared to be unshaken.

"Yes, Ann, I'm sure I can. I know I can. I've weighed it all so carefully. I have the plot, the ending, everything, even the title."

Ann took his subsequent pause as her signal to ask the obvious. Now past the initial shock and defensive reaction, she would hear him out. For more than a year now, she had tried to convince herself otherwise—she had told herself that the disappointment of his book had quelled his passion for writing, and she hoped that the change in his demeanor was a sign of introspection—but she knew all along that Jacob was sacrificing for her and for Molly by enduring a job that was torture to him, and she knew he was unhappy. Even though he had done well in keeping most of his feelings from her, she sensed his frustration as his evening poetry readings slowed and then stopped all together, and she regretted now her decision not to probe the aloofness she sensed in him as he watched her read.

"OK, I give up. What's its title?" she asked.

"*A Tale of Two Poets,*" he answered with restrained enthusiasm as he again took her hand, and then paused once more for her reaction.

"I think that title's already taken," she responded matter-of-factly, trying to smile.

Despite her befuddlement, Ann was intrigued, but she wasn't about to let Jacob know it. This touch of contempt was her signal to him that she was far from being convinced.

"Exactly!" he continued undaunted. "The purpose of the title is to grab your attention, to grab the reader's attention. And it *is* a tale of two poets: one who is much like me, young, poor, talented, but unread. The other is older, extremely gifted, also unread, but by choice. They are two very different people with different lives, but who share a similar style and passion for their writing. They have no notion that the other even exists. They have never met, at least not as poets; yet, as the plot thickens, their lives become increasingly aligned. The novel will tell two stories that become one, a tale of two poets. I don't have all the details yet—no writer does until he starts writing—but I see the possibilities. And best of all, Ann, best of all"—the break in his voice said more to her than his words— "people will read my poetry. They will read it because they will know the poet, or in this case, the poets. As they read the novel, they simultaneously get to know the two poets and their poetry, which is, of course, my poetry. Don't you see, Ann? If the novel is a success, they will have to publish a collection of my poetry. People who buy and read the novel will buy and read my poetry. And if I can write one novel, I can write another. I have to write, Ann. Writing is more than what I do; writing is who I am."

It was Ann's turn to speak now. She might have asked Jacob why he couldn't write his novel and keep his job, why he couldn't write at night, like he used to write his poetry. But she already knew the answer. It was one or the other. He couldn't do both and do either justice, and he couldn't do the one and be happy. Her question was a simple and pragmatic one, but one that revealed the sum of her disillusionment, apprehension, and fears.

"And how will we live, Jacob?"

The tears glistened in her blue eyes, the eyes that now looked away from Jacob's for only the second time since the start of their conversation, but she did not close them. She bit her upper lip with her lower teeth, then pulled her hand from his and brought it to her face and covered her mouth to stop the involuntary shaking that prefaced sobbing.

Jacob sighed heavily. He reached for her other hand; she pulled it away and tucked it under her elbow.

"I'm sorry, Ann. I know it's not fair. I know you're disappointed, and I know I have no right to ask this of you. But if you could only," he searched to find the words, "if you could—" His eyes too were moist.

She knew what was coming. But how, she asked herself, could he ask her to go back to work? How could he take her away from Molly?

He swallowed hard. "Ann, you'd have to work again, but just for a year, maybe less—I hope less. I've already spoken to my boss. He's upset about my leaving. I—"

Ann looked up suddenly. "You've already quit?" she interrupted in angry disbelief.

"No, Ann, of course not. If I quit, if you agree...Ann, if you say no, I'll accept it. I'll live with it. I promise. I won't say another thing about it, not a word. But if you say yes, Mr. Hendricks has agreed to give me a year's leave of absence. I'll work part time in the furniture shop, but full-time employment is too much. If we do this, we have to do it together." His voice slowed slightly. "And if I fail this time, Ann, the job will be there after a year, or sooner...if I want it."

Molly continued to sing in the bathroom. Ann hesitated a moment before she spoke in order to get control of her emotion. She let Jacob take her hand.

"And does that leave of absence include health insurance?"

Her tone was both cynical and hopeful. They had been lucky—Ann called it a blessing from God. Neither they nor Molly had suffered serious injury or illness while they were covered by the university's student insurance nor during that worrisome year after graduation when they had no insurance. The premiums for a self-employment health plan had been higher than they could ever imagine paying. Qualifying for Ann's insurance plan through her job required a forty-hour minimum workweek. Twenty hours was the most that she had been able to handle given her less than perfect health and her need and desire to be with Molly. Jacob refused to let her work more, even though Mr. Cardona had offered her a full-time position. Would Jacob ask her to work full time now? If she did not, what would they do for insurance? She could not bear another year of being uninsured. She was so pleased with their current group plan. The thought of losing it now was almost more disturbing than the idea of working again.

"No, unfortunately it doesn't," was Jacob's disappointing response. "There is an extended plan we could carry for six months, but we pay the full cost of the premiums, and the deductible and co-payments are high. After six months we'd have to find something else. I again looked into a self-employment plan. It's still expensive, with an even higher deductible than before. The only way we could manage it would be to take out a loan now, while I'm still employed, put the money away, and use it to pay our premiums after the six-month plan expires. It would mean paying a lot in interest; it would mean going much further into debt. The best solution—"

Jacob hesitated. Ann finished the sentence for him.

"The best solution is for me to work full time."

This was the moment, the climax, when the full weight of what Jacob was proposing should have overwhelmed her. She knew Jacob expected it and would also expect her tears. But the tears did not come; instead there came a feeling inside that she had felt often before, and with it the thought, "Be still, and know that I am God." It came from deep inside her, helping her regain her composure almost instantly. It showed in her countenance. She could tell that Jacob was taken aback, even startled, by the change, and she hoped he had experienced the feeling, too. She recognized it instantly as coming from God, his assurance that He was there. She still hurt, she was still disappointed, still apprehensive, still unconvinced; but she now had the strength to discuss it rationally and with the faith that God would help her know what she should do.

"What else would have to change, Jacob?" she asked softly.

They talked briefly about life insurance, student loan payments, where they would live—they would have to find something much cheaper than the home they were currently renting in the suburbs—and how they would care for Molly. Jacob had answers for all these questions. He had written it all down. He had figured the financial aspects of his plan to the penny. Ann was amazed he had done so much planning without her knowledge. He was serious. How could she refuse? But, on the other hand, how could she agree?

By now, Molly had stopped singing, wondering why her mother was taking so long. She called out from the bathroom.

"I'm done, Mommy! Do you want to wash my hair?"

Part One
Chapter Four

When Ann didn't respond immediately, Molly added, mimicking her mother's concern, "You okay, Mommy?"

Ann smiled weakly. Molly was so perceptive.

"Yes, I'm okay. I'll be right there, honey."

But she wasn't entirely okay. She knew the decision was hers but was not prepared to make it, not yet. She stood. Jacob stood also, took her by the shoulders, and drew her close. "I'm sorry, Ann. I love you. Please, have faith in me just one more time."

"I love you too, Jacob, but it's not a question of faith in you. I need a few days to think about it," Ann said quietly. "I need time to pray," she added, looking hard into the dark eyes she had come to know so well; there was a sadness there she had not seen before that alarmed her.

"If he only knew and trusted God," she thought.

She forced another smile to reassure him that she understood.

"Just a couple of days, Jacob," she repeated, brushing another wayward curl from off his forehead with her right hand, and she turned away to wash Molly's hair.

Chapter Five

Ann waited as Molly, one by one, gently repositioned and said good night to the three porcelain dolls that smiled from the top of her dresser.

"Good night, Nancy; good night, Ruthie; good night Katie."

It was raining hard, a welcome rain after a long dry August, signaling a change in the seasons. Most of her day had been spent running errands, and tonight Ann had a slight headache and feared she was catching a cold. She had all but made her decision that morning, but several important details still needed attention. She had stopped by Cardona's Market not only to buy the week's groceries but also to talk to her former boss about returning to work. It had been over a year since she had worked there, but she was still a loyal customer, and because she and Jacob at last had a car—albeit a very used car—she did not mind driving past two other markets in order to give her business to Mr. Cardona. The sales and specials advertised in their windows did not tempt her. Besides, Mariluz Cardona ran the best Mexican bakery in the city. It was the bakery's reputation that kept the Cardonas in business. A good third of their clientele were university students who regularly drove or biked the mile from campus for a dozen *orejas, conchas,* or a loaf or two of *pan dulce.*

Mr. Cardona was one of the nicest men Ann knew. His genuine concern for his employees resulted in many lifelong friendships. After they had proven themselves, once he knew they were trustworthy and reliable and would not abuse his kindness, he moved mountains to make sure they were treated well. When Dr. Oquendo put Ann in bed three weeks before Molly was born, Mr. Cardona worked her shift until he could hire a temporary replacement. He had also insisted she take all the time off she needed to regain her strength after Molly's birth. He had told her he thought she was coming back too soon, but he also understood that she and Jacob needed the money. He was surprised now that Ann inquired about coming to work again, especially full time, and he asked if anything was wrong, if Molly and Jacob were all right.

"Has Jacob lost his job?" he asked.

"No, he's quitting. It's a long story. He's going to write again."

Mr. Cardona raised his bushy gray eyebrows in concerned surprise. Ann knew her former boss liked Jacob; he liked him very much. He had told her often that he admired his integrity and was especially impressed by the way he treated her, and he loved teasing Jacob by mimicking his Castilian accent. All the while Ann worked there, Jacob, and later Jacob and Molly, would be at the market near the end of Ann's evening shift to walk her home. Because of its proximity to the university, the neighborhood was one of the safest in the city, but Jacob took no chances. Besides, they enjoyed their walks together, and it was nice not to have to pay the bus fare— then, they had not owned a car.

Jacob would often arrive a little early. It was either that, or make Ann wait. Once he and Mr. Cardona started talking, there was little hope of leaving anytime soon. Ann inevitably had to break up their animated conversations. She spoke some Spanish but certainly not enough to participate fully. Molly didn't mind the wait at all. The longer the conversation, the longer she could spend in the bakery eating the pastries Mariluz would slip her around the side of the counter.

"I'm hungry and tired; let's go home," Ann would plead as she tugged at Jacob's arm.

"Mariluz will give you a *concha*, or Molly can share one; she has two," Mr. Cardona teased. "You'd better take her home and feed her while she's hungry, Jacob," he added. "*La pobre está muy flaca.*"

Ann was much healthier now. Molly's birth had been difficult, and she had been slow to recover. Not working at all had been good for her overall health. A worried Mr. Cardona continued to inquire.

"He has found a publisher?" he asked hopefully.

"No, he hasn't. He's going to write a novel."

"*¿Una novela?* Why a *novela*?"

Ann gave him the short version. She could do no less. Mr. Cardona was as close to a father figure as she had ever had. Jacob's father was nice, and he loved his daughter-in-law, but he never queried into personal matters, and Ann wasn't the type to offer information without an invitation. Jacob's parents lived more than five hours away. Ann's relationship with her in-laws was cordial but certainly not close.

Yes, Mr. Cardona would hire her back full time. He even agreed to a thirty-five-hour week. The records would show forty hours, satisfying his insurance carrier, and she would be paid for forty hours; but her wage would be adjusted down to cover the difference. There was only one danger in the arrangement. Mr. Cardona reminded Ann that he still wanted to retire, not because he was tired of the business—he loved every aspect of it—but after his heart attack, his doctor insisted on a drastic change in lifestyle. His market had been for sale for almost a year now, but he had yet to receive an acceptable offer.

"I'll take care of you, *hija*, as long as I'm here," he assured her. "You just tell me when you want to start. And tell Jacob I want to talk with him about his *novela*."

Ann was feeling better and better about going back to work. Mr. and Mrs. Cardona were like family. She was grateful that if she had to work again, she would at least be with people for whom she cared and who cared for her.

The store was crowded. In route to the bakery in the back to find Molly, she caught parts of a sordid conversation between two young men, obviously university students. Both the content of their conversation and the vulgarity and profanity of their language reminded her again how fortunate she was to be married to Jacob. They were waiting their turn at the end of the line that had formed in front of the bakery. Ann had stopped just around the corner to put a misplaced loaf of bread back on its shelf.

"You've been missing a lot of good action at the sorority house lately," said the shorter of the two—obviously "big men on campus." "Have you become a monk or something?"

"Nope, sorority chicks are much too easy," responded his friend, a tall handsome sort with an air of superiority. "There's no challenge. I'm into Mormon virgins now. I've got my sights on a beauty. She's somethin' else: tall, redhead. She's only eighteen, and with a body that won't quit."

"Yeah? Where did you find her?"

"I went to a dance at her church. Lance took me. I figured, why not. If I wanted to find innocence, I'd go where innocence hangs out."

Both laughed.

"You mean, where no one knows your reputation."

"Precisely, my man. I've got a lot of money riding on this one. I bet Lance five hundred bucks. I've got until Thanksgiving. It's not going to be easy; I mean, she's as innocent as they come and religious, too, but I've got it all planned out. Sometimes I surprise even myself."

Had Jacob been there, he may well have said something. Ann was not quite so bold; she wasn't sure what being a Mormon had to do with it—she had never known any Mormons—but her money was on the tall, redhead coed.

Maybe she would see them together sometime. It might be none of her business, but she would jump at the chance to make sure that this jerk lost his five hundred dollars.

On the way home, she stopped to see an apartment. Tony and Luis from the furniture shop had told her about it. Their mother, Carmen (also Mr. Cardona's cousin), lived in the same building. The apartment was vacant and immediately available. It was a nice apartment, and the price was right. Best of all, it wasn't far from the market, not really close enough to walk—although she could if she had to—but Jacob would seldom need the car; he preferred to ride his bike to and from the furniture shop. There were other advantages, too. Molly and Carmen got along famously; they would never want for a baby-sitter. The owner happily agreed to hold it until the following day for a fifty-dollar deposit.

Tonight she would give Jacob her decision. It had been a week now—she had told him a couple of days. He hadn't said anything more about it, and she knew he wouldn't until she was ready. It had been a peculiar week. Ann wanted God's answer to be "no," but each time she prayed, she felt all the more at peace, and with each new day she saw more clearly that there really was no choice. Her happiness depended on Jacob's happiness. She had decided to live by faith, confident that God would provide.

Now that she had seen to the details and her decision was firm, she was anxious to get on with it. The fact that everything was working out so smoothly strengthened her conviction that God had answered her prayers. She was even a bit excited. After all, if Jacob's scheme to write his novel worked, their initial dreams could finally come true.

The apartment she had found exceeded her expectations. They could move that weekend. With Tony's and Luis's help, it would be easy. Mr. Cardona's son-in-law, David, would be happy to help too, and Carmen, of course, would welcome the chance to take care of Molly.

Neither Ann nor Molly had seen much of Jacob that week. He was under pressure at work to finish a project and had stayed late at the office every night. He was working harder than ever. Despite the impending financial strain, Ann looked forward to returning to the "old days," to Saturday and Sunday evening strolls in the park, and to a more predictable schedule. Mornings would change for the better; Jacob, after all, would almost always be home writing. Ann would work the evening shift at the market on weekdays and the early morning shift on Saturdays. Jacob would help Tony and Luis on Monday, Wednesday, and Saturday mornings in the furniture shop. On Saturdays, Molly would stay at Carmen's. Tony's daughter, Rosita, would be there too. She and Molly were great friends— Ann had arranged for them to be in the same first-grade class—and Carmen insisted that two six-year-olds were easier to watch than one. And because Carmen spoke Spanish to her granddaughter, it would be great practice for Molly.

Things were working out beautifully; everything was in place. Insurance was still a problem but not an insurmountable one. It would be sixty days before Mr. Cardona's group plan would cover them. They had no choice but to pay two months of premiums for the extended coverage available through Jacob's soon-to-be former employer.

Ann was anxious to tell Jacob. She had made his favorite meal, lasagna, for the occasion; it would have to be reheated. Jacob had called earlier, at 6:30, to tell her he would be late again. He would be home around 10:00. He would catch the late bus. It was now almost 9:00, past Molly's bedtime.

"Where's Daddy?" she asked.

"He's still at work, Molly. He'll be home soon."

"Will you wake me up when he gets home so he can tell me a story? He hasn't told me a story for a long time."

"I know, Molly, but that will soon change. Daddy soon won't have to work so late. Kneel down now, time for prayer. It's your turn tonight."

Mother and daughter knelt at the side of the bed. Molly's prayer was simple but sincere. She had been taught well.

"Heavenly Father, thank Thee for my Mommy and Daddy. Thank Thee for our home. Thank Thee for Grandpa and Grandma. Thank Thee for my friends. Help me to be a good girl. Bless Daddy to come home safely and not have to work so hard so he can tell me stories again. Amen."

Ann kissed her daughter, then picked up her grandmother's Bible from its place of honor on the rocking chair and sat down. Jacob had surprised her with the maple rocker the day they brought Molly home from the hospital. He had made it in the furniture shop, yet another sign of his love. Molly climbed onto her mother's lap and laid her head against her mother's breast. The ritual was the same every night.

Ann wrapped her arms around her daughter and held her tight.

"I love you, Molly. Do you know your mommy loves you?"

"Yes, Mommy. I love you too."

"Do you know your daddy loves you?"

"Yes, Mommy."

"Do you know that God loves you?"

"Yes, Mommy."

"You must never forget that God loves you. You are His child, His daughter. Never forget who you are, Molly. Will you ever forget?"

"No, I won't forget, Mommy."

Ann opened her grandmother's Bible. Whether or not Jacob was there to listen, every night the family read. Usually not a lot, sometimes only a few verses, depending on their content; and when Jacob wasn't there, Ann would often pause to explain as best she could their meaning to Molly. Tonight's excerpt was one of her favorites.

"This is about when Jesus prayed for us, Molly," she prefaced.

"Then cometh Jesus with them unto a place called Gethsemane, and saith unto the disciples, Sit ye here, while I go and pray yonder.

"And he took with him Peter and the two sons of Zebedee, and began to be sorrowful and very heavy.

"Then saith he unto them, My soul is exceeding sorrowful, even unto death: tarry ye here, and watch with me."

After a few sentences of explanation, Ann continued.

"And he went a little further, and fell on his face, and prayed, saying, O my Father, if it be possible, let this cup pass from me: nevertheless not as I will but as thou wilt.

"And he cometh unto the disciples, and findeth them asleep, and saith unto Peter, What, could ye not watch with me one hour?

"Watch and pray, that ye enter not into temptation: the spirit indeed is willing, but the flesh is weak."

Again, Ann added a few sentences of clarification before continuing.

"He went away again the second time, and prayed, saying, O my Father, if this cup may not pass away from me, except I drink it, thy will be done."

Ann paused once more.

"Molly," she explained, "sometimes when something happens that makes us sad, we may not understand why God lets it happen. We must always remember that He knows us much better than we know ourselves. Before we were born, we were His spirit children. That is why we call Him our Heavenly Father, and that's why He loves us so much. He created this world so that we would have a place where we could learn things that we could never learn as spirits. We have come to this earth to learn how to be living souls. A soul is a spirit with a body of flesh and bones. There are wonderful feelings, sensations, and experiences that we can only have as souls. As souls, we learn how to love others and how to be loved. We learn too that we must take care of our physical mind and body by doing things that are good for them and that make our souls stronger."

Ann was reminding herself of the foundation of her faith as much as she was trying to build it for her daughter.

"When we die," she continued, "our spirits leave our bodies and we return again to our Heavenly Father, where we live together with family and friends. We will miss our bodies; we will miss the things we have learned. But we will be happy there because there will be no pain, no suffering, and no sadness. And there we will wait patiently until all God's spirit children have come to the earth and have experienced being a soul. Some stay only moments, some many, many years. It all depends on what we need to learn, and only God knows exactly what that is and the best way we can learn it. You see, each of us is different. That is why life is different in some way for every one of God's children. So when we die, whenever we die, we go back to our Heavenly Father where we wait for the day when our spirits and bodies will once again be reunited, when we will be resurrected, even as Jesus was resurrected. Our Father in Heaven loves all of His children. We must trust God. That is why we, like Jesus, must always say when we pray, 'Thy will be done,' because what we want may not always be what is best for our souls. Do you understand what I'm trying to say, Molly?"

"Yes, Mommy."

Ann smiled. She knew Molly would someday understand much better than she did now. Just as her loving grandmother had repeated the lesson over and over to her, she now would do the same with Molly. Ann again read from her grandmother's Bible.

"And he came and found them asleep again: for their eyes were heavy.

"And he left them, and went away again, and prayed the third time, saying the same words.

"Then cometh he to his disciples, and saith unto them, Sleep on now, and take your rest: behold, the hour is at hand, and the Son of man is betrayed into the hands of sinners."

Molly turned around in her mother's lap and looked into her eyes.

"Mommy?" she asked.

"Yes, Molly, what's the matter?" she answered, surprised. It was not at all like Molly to interrupt her mother's reading.

"Does Daddy ever pray?"

Ann felt her throat begin to swell and the tears well up in her eyes. She swallowed hard and quickly gained control. She knew someday Molly would start to ask such questions. Time passed so quickly! She always hoped and prayed this day would never come, that by now Jacob's heart would have softened, that he would have joined Ann in her faith and prayers, and thus united, they would raise their daughter. She reached up and wiped away her tears.

"I think he does. Not out loud, but in his heart."

"Why doesn't he pray with us?"

Ann had already planned what she would say, but it did not make it any easier.

"Some day he will, Molly, some day he will. You see, Daddy's mother and father didn't teach him about God. They did not teach him to pray. I've been trying very hard since before you were born to help your daddy know and love God as I do, and as you do too. Someday he will. And now that you are getting older, you must help too. You must help me, Molly. We must work together to help Daddy pray."

By now the tears were flowing freely. Molly understood. She wrapped her arms tightly around Ann's neck.

"Don't cry, Mommy. I will help you. Don't cry. We will teach Daddy who he is and how to pray."

After Molly had fallen asleep, Ann rose from the rocking chair and gently tucked her into bed. It was now almost 10:00. Jacob would be home soon. She walked down the hall into the study and locked the door. She needed to pray. She was angry, angry with Jacob, angry with herself. Molly's question had frightened her. What if Jacob never did come to know God? Never did pray? Could she bear it for the rest of her life? Could she continue to answer Molly's questions? What if the novel failed and Jacob returned again, defeated and discouraged, to a job he hated? How would he feel then about the God of love and mercy who she said was guiding their lives? Why didn't he try harder to understand? She was sacrificing much so that he could write again. Shouldn't he sacrifice too? She was tired of waiting, tired of being alone in her faith, tired of being patient.

Patience. It was hard to be patient. Sometimes, back when their dreams of Jacob becoming a published poet were still alive, when she had finished reading during their evening devotionals, she could not resist a comment or two.

"You see," she would say, "God does hear our prayers. He knows us. He is our Father. You are a father too, Jacob. You love our Molly in much the same way God loves His children."

Jacob would raise his dark eyebrows in gentle warning that Ann had exceeded the limits of their agreement—she was to read, not to preach—and then he would smile and hug her. That was usually the end of it. Ann had learned by experience not to prolong the discussion. She was being cautious and unhurried; and she knew that Jacob, who did not like conflict in any form, was not about to allow his own lack of religious conviction to become a reason for tension in their marriage. His hug was his signal to her that enough had been said and that it was time for bed.

But Ann knew that there was more to it than Jacob was aware, and she knew that like Saul of Tarsus, it was hard for Jacob to "kick against the pricks." But he continued kicking, and she was tired of it.

On her knees, she wept and pled with God. What more could she do? Should she confront Jacob with her fears? Should she change her mind about letting him write?

"Please, Father," she prayed, "help me know what I should do. Do not abandon me now." And then the words came to her, "Please let this cup pass from me."

She did not speak them. They were spoken in her mind and heart. She felt ashamed. Never before had she allowed herself such self-pity. Had not God already, several times that week and many times throughout her life, spoken peace to her soul? Had He ever abandoned her?

"Please forgive me, Father, please forgive me," she repeated. "I have no right to question Thee. I know Thy love is perfect. Thy will be done, Father; Thy will be done."

Her tears now were tears of joy, tears of gratitude. God's peace had returned. She knew what she must do.

After a few minutes, she went into the bathroom, washed her face, and then entered the kitchen. She didn't bother to turn on the lights. The table was ready, two settings with two new candles between them for the occasion. She took the lasagna from the refrigerator, put it in the oven, and then lit the candles. The flames struggled for several seconds, then grew bright, filling the room with a comforting contrast of light and shadow. Ann sat to watch the candles' flames and wait for Jacob while she listened to the rain still pouring, relentless, outside.

Chapter Six

Jacob was tired but relieved. He closed his eyes for a few moments and took several deep breaths that he exhaled slowly and completely, each time more slowly than the time before. He had left the building at 9:53 P.M., barely enough time to run the two blocks to the bus stop. He had finished his part of the project, long before tomorrow's 10:00 A.M. deadline. Staying late the last several nights had paid off. It had meant that he needn't take any work home with him tonight. Perhaps tomorrow would be his last full day, and only part of a day at that.

Whether it was or not, however, depended on Ann. It had been a week now since he had proposed quitting his job. Ann was taking her time thinking and praying about it. He had already decided definitely to say nothing more. It was up to her now. If she gave him her answer tonight, and if her answer was yes, he would give Mr. Hendricks his two-week notice tomorrow morning.

Though Jacob's immediate supervisor in the writing department had no conscience when it came to taking advantage of those under his supervision, Mr. Hendricks, the owner of the company, recognized Jacob's value and was grateful for his extra effort during the past several months. The company had been very successful mostly due to Mr. Hendricks's superb administrative and management skills. Although he had more than a hundred employees and little time to get to know them, he knew Jacob and spoke with him often.

One morning, just days after Jacob had begun, Mr. Hendricks called him into his office. He had read Jacob's résumé and asked if his newest employee might be interested in tutoring his son Dave, who was struggling in a college writing class. Jacob was enticed by the generous hourly fee and accepted readily, even though he later regretted it. Dave was not a good student. Jacob considered him a lazy, spoiled, pompous, arrogant, and calculating silver spoon, with little if any respect for others or for authority; but he managed to bite his tongue long enough to get him through the class, much to the delight of his father.

Since then, Mr. Hendricks had followed Jacob's progress in the company with great interest, and Jacob fully understood the advantage that this special attention provided. Indeed, it was Mr. Hendricks whom Jacob approached, circumventing regular channels, about a possible leave of absence in order to write his novel. It was also Mr. Hendricks who had personally noted the extra hours Jacob had spent on this latest project. He pulled Jacob aside one afternoon and told him that once the

Hamilton project was completed, as far as he and the company were concerned, Jacob had accumulated more than enough unpaid overtime to cover the two-week notice that company policy required. If he still wanted his year off, the last day of the project could be his last day in the office, even though he would continue to draw his salary and benefits for an additional two weeks.

Jacob was anxious to begin writing. All week each night, he had returned home totally exhausted from twelve or more hours of tedious technical writing and editing, but he found it hard to fall sleep. Now that the burden of telling Ann had been lifted, he would lie awake mulling things over in his mind; if he was sure Ann was asleep, he often left the bed silently to write things down. His notebook, empty for so many months—he had even stopped carrying it—was now almost full. He opened it now on the bus to jot down something he had thought of while running in the rain from his office to the bus stop.

He was the only passenger. The streets, too, were empty except for an occasional pedestrian darting for cover from a car to a house or apartment building. The storm had been unexpected, and Jacob had no umbrella, but getting wet didn't bother him. This was a warm and welcome summer shower. The colder rains would come in late November.

In the solitude afforded him by his bus journey home, Jacob's mind jumped from his novel to the circumstances that would allow its reality. He understood Ann's frustration and would not blame her if she refused to go back to work, but he knew her character and sensed intuitively that she would make the sacrifice, as she had done before, because of her love for him. He was grateful to her for that love and in turn loved her more and more each day.

The years he had spent loving Ann had changed him, matured him as a person, especially during the past year. As he struggled with a job he did not like and with the disappointment that followed his shattered life's dream to be a poet, Ann's love had never wavered. And now, now that he was on the verge of this new adventure, he suddenly saw his life—their life together—from a different perspective. He marveled that he had never before seriously pondered the questions that now perplexed him.

He wondered why it was that even though his life had not turned out exactly as he had hoped, he still had Ann and Molly's love, and he questioned: To whom should he be grateful? Certainly to Ann, and to her grandmother, who raised her, but also to something or someone else. One thing was certain: He could no longer accept the notion that he, Ann, and Molly were together by chance. The hundreds of hours he had spent over the years listening to Ann read from her grandmother's Bible had acquainted him with what had become for him, almost without him being aware, the logical explanation.

Until he had conceived the idea for his novel, he had refused to think about it, but for the last several months, and especially this week as he awaited Ann's answer, the feelings inside him had become increasingly impossible to ignore. As he again pondered those feelings now on the bus going home, his thoughts became even more troubled. Had he failed over the years to recognize the true source of his good fortune?

There either was or there was not a God. For Ann and Molly's sake, he had always hoped—somewhere in the back of his mind—that there was. He hoped it was the God of the New Testament, the loving Father to whom Christ prayed, and to whom Ann and Molly prayed with such enduring faith.

Until now, it had been enough that Ann believed, but strangely, he now reflected, Ann's faith was no longer enough. Over and over in his mind, he had considered the options. If there was a God who interceded in the lives of men, if Ann was right, he owed Him an unpayable debt and, also, a long overdue apology. From what he had gleaned from years of listening to Ann read Scripture, he was confident that he had committed no serious moral transgression, but he wondered if his sin of ingratitude had offended the God whose blessings he had failed to acknowledge.

If there was no God, then what was he to make of Ann's faith? Jacob could never concede that Ann, the finest person he knew, could continue in a faith without ample and constant evidence of its reality. He trusted her instincts and judgment in all other matters; why should he not trust her faith? And what of prayer? What of Ann's assurance and conviction that she felt God's presence when she prayed? He too had felt something from time to time when Ann read, and he could not deny the reality of what he had felt the night he told Ann about his novel.

Jacob's mind flashed back to his novel's developing plot and characterizations. He realized that one of the novel's two poets—indeed, the poet he was modeling after himself—would likely ask these same questions. He too would be a poet in search of faith, but who did not know he was searching.

Jacob had always thought he could repay Ann's love, and now Molly's love too, by providing them with a comfortable and secure life, with Ann's long-dreamed-of house in the country and the freedom that financial independence would give them to raise Molly and perhaps other children. He knew now that Ann's greatest desire had nothing to do with wealth or security. She wanted most to be united by the same faith and love of God.

If Ann was willing to trust him to write his novel, to put aside her doubt and accept his assurance that it could be done, how could he refuse to trust her? What reason had he not to join her and Molly in their prayers? But how could he pray to someone he only hoped was there?

Jacob suddenly remembered his Shakespeare: "Our doubts are traitors, and make us lose the good we oft might win by fearing to attempt." Why not give prayer a try? If Ann could sacrifice so much for what she hoped for, could he not sacrifice his pride? Tonight, he would speak with Ann about faith, about religion, about prayer. It would no doubt surprise her. He smiled. He hoped it would be a pleasant surprise. As he pulled the cord above him to signal the bus driver to stop, he sensed something he had felt before but now understood, something familiar yet also new because of his new understanding, a surge of love and gratitude for his wife, but combined with something else, something strange. It was a feeling he liked.

He decided to repeat his poem once more, to be sure it was ready to recite to Ann. He had begun its composition the day after he told her of his plan to write his novel and finished it two days later. It was his first since beginning his year and a half sabbatical with technical manuals.

Windows

I search your likewise probing eyes
in hopes that I might see
some evidence of who you are,
but I see only me.
My own reflection barricades
the windows to your soul.
I have no way to get inside,
no means to pay the toll.
It's only when you look away,
when you no longer stare,
but turn your eyes to other things
that I find passage there.
It's only when I'm not the one,
but others you perceive,
that I can know just how you feel
by what your eyes receive.
For when they look upon a child,
I there compassion spy.
Both tenderness and empathy
illuminate each eye.

The Doll in McCallaway's Store

I clearly through those windows see
delight, as long they gaze
upon a daughter as she sleeps
or as she softly prays.
There's awe and wonder mirrored there
each time they pause to see
the colors of a sunset
or the blossoms on a tree.
And something else I can't explain
that leads me to concede
that what you see can help me find
that which I also need.
Is evidence of things unseen,
is faith reflected there
each time you ponder sacred things
or testimony share?
My soul finds peace in who you are;
all doubts and fears depart
each time I enter unobserved
the windows to your heart.

Jacob got off the bus and began the five-block walk
home in the rain. The feeling persisted. He was eager to see
Ann and talk about what he was feeling, but he was also a
bit apprehensive. What would he say? He did not hurry; he
needed a bit more time to reflect. The rain had collected on
the edge of the walks that once drained to the easement but
that now, lifted by tree roots, often slopped the other way.
Jacob's feet were already wet. He ignored even the deepest
puddles. The canopy of the trees that in a light rain would

have offered protection were now, after hours of constant downpour, so heavy with moisture that they competed with the clouds to see which could produce the larger droplets.

Halfway home, Jacob abruptly stopped and looked behind him. He had the strange sensation that he was not alone, that he was being watched or followed. He quickened his pace, but after only a few steps, he suddenly felt weak and fatigued, as if he had expended all his physical strength and energy. He felt unexpectedly afraid. Of what, he was uncertain. His mind told his body to run; it did not. His chest felt heavy, his legs unsteady, as if someone, something, had him held fast so that he could not move; yet he could move, but only if he exerted a conscious, willful, and concentrated effort to do so. It was a feeling unlike any he had ever experienced, but akin to what he had felt as a child during those first moments awake after a nightmare, alone and disoriented in the dark.

Jacob had never allowed discouragement or despair to enter his mind when faced with an onerous task, with disappointment, or even with failure. His optimism, self-discipline, and stoic response to circumstance had always combined in his character to allow him to overcome the beginnings of any doubt or fear. But he had neither the mental nor the physical resources to confront the oppressive unknown force that now overwhelmed his control of both body and mind. He was entirely powerless.

After what was actually only a few minutes—but seemed to him to be almost an hour—standing motionless, confused, helpless, and trembling in the rain, Jacob's mind fixed its attention on something outside the power that surrounded him. A thought, which in the darkness seemed at first miles away, quickly approached and gently entered, not just into his mind but also into his entire being. In a voice unspoken, it told him to pray. Jacob looked up into the black sky. The rain rolled over his face and chin, then down his neck into his collar behind his loosened tie. It was time for a leap of faith.

"God, Father in Heaven," he whispered. "If there is a God, and thou art God…help thou my unbelief."

Jacob knew well the language of prayer from listening to Ann, and as he now used that language to pray for the first time in his life, he felt, almost heard, other voices speaking in chorus with his own, as if the words were not his alone. They seemed to come also from those he loved, from Ann and Molly. He felt them near, as if hundreds of prior pleas now joined with his.

No sooner had he said his simple prayer, he found himself free from the power that had subjected him. It was as if it had fled something it feared. He looked behind him again, wanting to thankfully acknowledge the new presence now with him. As he quickly walked the remaining two blocks home, he marveled at what he had just experienced. He climbed the steps to the porch of their little rental house. Ann had seen him coming from the dining room window and met him at the door. She smiled and shook her head.

"*Estás hecho una sopa,*" she said, repeating a new phrase she had learned earlier that morning in the market.

Jacob returned her smile.

"*Muy bien, vida mía,* you've been studying."

"Not really. It's just something I picked up from Mariluz. As soon as you've changed, come into the kitchen. I've made lasagna. We need to talk."

"Lasagna is a good sign," Jacob thought.

After he had changed clothes, Jacob stopped at Molly's bedroom to kiss her good night. He hadn't seen her awake for two days. She slept soundly, softly, half smiling, as if she were dreaming something pleasing. He knelt at the side of her bed and gently stroked her dark brown curls.

"Tomorrow, sweet Molly," he whispered, "I'll tell you a story for sure." He paused a few moments and listened to her breathe. "And tomorrow you can teach me how to pray."

The acid-sweet smell of scorched tomato paste welcomed Jacob to the kitchen. When he saw the candles and china plates on the table, he was sure of Ann's answer. He felt once again the surge of love and gratitude he had experienced earlier on the bus. He watched Ann as she took the lasagna out of the oven, cut it, and placed a portion on each plate, her grandmother's plates, used only for special occasions. She looked more beautiful than ever. Her eyes glistened in the candlelight. Her soft blond hair, cut just above her shoulders, playfully followed every movement of her head. Her nostrils flared ever so slightly, and her mouth, partly open, tried in vain to repress an indomitable smile.

"You're staring at me, Jacob," she said without looking at him. But missing his immediate rejoinder, she quickly looked up to see his face. She somehow seemed to understand and stepped into his arms. The right side of her face found the security of his broad chest, and he held her there as tightly as he dared for at least a half a minute, his lips pursed and pressed firmly against her hair as he struggled to hold back that first tear.

Jacob never cried. He was well practiced at controlling his emotion. Many, many times, as he sat in the quiet of the night writing his poetry, in those moments of verbal epiphany, those moments Longinus called "the sublime," when his words came together in ways beyond his ability to combine them, when the muses smiled on him, he had often felt but always controlled an urge to cry. But this time was different. His throat burned; it was hard to swallow and that first tear, although it never fell, pushed the reservoirs of his eyes to their full bearing capacity.

When at last he dared speak, Jacob held Ann a bit tighter.

"Forgive me, Ann," he said in a half whisper. "I'm not sure how to say this, but…" He paused, unsure of himself, staring at the light of one of the candles on the table.

Ann pushed herself slightly and gently from Jacob's embrace, moving her arms from around his waist to his chest, her hands resting just below his shoulders. She looked up tenderly into the flickering flame reflected in her husband's moist brown eyes.

"Please go on, Jacob; please tell me."

Jacob knew that Ann was enough acquainted with the promptings of the Spirit to sense what it was he wanted to say. She had already started to cry.

Jacob sat Ann down on one of the kitchen chairs and, as was his custom, pulled his own chair close to hers so their legs interlocked. He leaned slightly forward and took Ann's hand. She put her other hand on top of their joined hands and brought them to her lap. Jacob reached up and wiped a tear from her check with the thumb of his other hand.

"Ann," he said, "I think God's been trying to tell me something today—well, not just today, for a long time actually…" He sighed heavily. "You were right. It's wrong for me to ignore God's goodness to us. Ann…I love you, and I love Molly. I want her to be just like you. It will take me some time, but I want to be like you too." The words came easy for him now. "I want to learn to pray…I want God to speak to me as he speaks to you."

Tears of joy streamed unchecked down Ann's cheeks and dropped unashamedly onto their clasped hands.

"Tonight I felt His presence as I tried to pray. Ann, I feel He is with us now."

The candles burned on and the lasagna grew cold as Jacob recounted his experience on the way home. He told her about the fear that had overwhelmed him and about the warmth and peace that had come in response to his simple but sincere prayer. She listened patiently, lovingly, crying softly.

Chapter Seven

Although Jacob was anxious to get his novel under way, he also wanted to write a second poem for Ann, the perfect poem, something that communicated the depth of his love and gratitude. Love poems were scarce in his repertoire, not really his trade, but he came upon an idea one day in the furniture shop while pondering his novel, an idea that allowed him to combine his penchant for narrative with the touch of lyricism that the poem required.

That night after Ann was asleep, he began the task in earnest, and each night he escaped from his sleeping wife for an hour or so to continue the course of its composition. Three weeks later, the poem was complete and memorized, and Jacob had waited patiently for several days for just the right moment to recite it.

It was a beautiful autumn Sunday night. The day had been filled with worship, friends, and family. They had gone to Mass in the morning with Carmen and Rosita—not Jacob's favorite way to spend an hour—then picnicked and played Frisbee and croquet in the park. After the Sunday evening meal and animated conversation with friends in Carmen's apartment, Ann had coaxed Jacob into bed just a bit earlier than usual—and not because she was tired. As they lay in the dark and talked of their life and their love, Jacob changed the subject slightly.

"I've written a new poem for you, Ann, my best attempt at a love poem. Would you like to hear it?"

"A love poem? By all means," she replied.

Jacob sat up and put the two pillows behind him against the headboard and gathered Ann in his arms.

"Make yourself comfortable. It's rather long."

Ann snuggled in as close as she could.

"I'm ready when you are."

Peas and Carrots
(for Ann)

Late one evening after supper
when not a word was said,
I walked down to the market;
my new wife went to bed.
I made a simple purchase,
a flower and a can.
On my return I woke my wife
and placed them in her hand.
"The purpose of the rose," I said
"is penance for my crime,
but the can's much more important;
to explain, I'll need some time.

If you'll rest in my arms a while
and promise not to sleep,
I'd like to tell a story 'bout
a pledge I vowed to keep.
When I was young, my sister
and I would always fight.
It seemed that I was never wrong,
and she was never right.
Poor mother did the best she could,
but all her efforts failed.
Despite her prayers and prodding,
my stubbornness prevailed.
To give our mom a needed rest,
one summer, we were told
we'd spend a month with Grandma,
who was seventy years old.
I glared hard at my sister;
my sister looked at me.
We rolled our eyes in unison;
for once we could agree.
Our grandma, she was nice enough;
she grandma'd by the book.
Our only apprehension
was she didn't really cook.
We'd eaten with her oft before
and knew that we could plan
that most of lunch and supper would
come straight out of a can.
Our mom knew well her mother
wasn't known for her cuisine,

so she made us swear we'd not complain,
and we'd eat our platters clean.
When we arrived at Grandma's house,
she told us to unpack
while she went to the market.
We'd eat when she got back.
Before she left, she asked us each
to write down just a few
of those foods we both liked to eat,
and she'd see what she could do.
Now I was fond of carrots,
while Sis was keen on peas.
Our mom, at home, served beets or corn
or beans with grated cheese.
For if she catered to my taste,
my sister made a scene,
and if my sister got her way,
then I got downright mean.
You see, Sis hated carrots
and I couldn't stomach peas.
So peas were tops on Sis's list:
by 'carrots,' I wrote, 'please.'
Now one thing 'bout our grandma
I really should explain,
she was as wise as grandmas come
and saw right through our game.
And something else you ought to know
that played into her scheme,
we'd had no food since breakfast,
just a bowl of rice and cream.

When she called us down to supper,
we saw supper was to be
two plates with peas and carrots mixed,
one for Sis and one for me.
It was clear to see that Grandma
had not mixed them in the pan;
the proof was on the counter top;
they were mixed inside the can.
On the label, 'peas and carrots,'
and worse, we realized
that the only chance for supper
was to eat what we despised.
For nothing more was on each plate
except a piece of bread,
which vanished in a gulp or two
right after grace was said.
Now true to what we'd promised Mom,
both sat quiet in our seat;
but hunger drove us to devise
each one a way to eat.
My fork collected carrots squares.
I tried to compensate
their lack by savoring every one.
The peas stayed on my plate.
My sister, with her butter knife,
pushed her carrots in a pile,
then guided peas from plate to spoon
then to her waiting smile.
Once I'd dispatched my carrots
and all her peas were dead,

I asked if there were seconds,
but Grandma shook her head.
I glared hard at my sister;
my sister looked at me.
The solution to our problem
struck us simultaneously.
I smiled slyly at my sister;
my sister smiled at me.
We'd been so self-indulgent,
so blind, we could not see.
And as I ate her carrots
and as she devoured my peas,
our Grandma knew that she had cured
our juvenile disease.
And since I was the oldest
and bore the greater blame,
my Grandma took my hands in hers
and firmly spoke my name.
'The grief you cause your sister
because you taunt and tease
exasperates your mother
much more than you hate peas.
I want you now to promise me,
give me your sacred vow,
that while you're living in my house
you'll get along somehow.
For life is peas and carrots,
and in each can—I'm sure—
there's something she can give to you
and you can give to her.

You'll have to live with women
the most part of your life.
For now, you have a sister;
someday you'll have a wife.
The nature of most women is
to give more than their share,
while men are prone to selfishness
or think fifty-fifty's fair.
The man who would be happy,
the man who's smart and wise,
learns quickly how to consecrate
and not just compromise.
Start first with peas and carrots,
and once you've learned to share,
your love for one another
will make you both aware
that when they're mixed together,
the flavor of each one
makes them tastier than when alone
and life a lot more fun.
When two souls join together,
we make real our fondest dreams,
like cheese and macaroni,
or my favorite, pork and beans.'
I listened to my Grandma and
I curbed my selfish ways.
I haven't lost the lessons
of those can-fed summer days.
The year she died, I promised her
that some day when I'd wed,

and we'd had our first contention,
before angry words were said,
I would tell my bride the story,
after getting off my knees,
of what I'd learned when still a boy
from carrots mixed with peas."
I knew my bride had understood;
she had not gone to sleep.
The years have passed; we've made a home
where trust and love run deep,
where a dried rose and a tin can
on the mantel o'er the hearth
remind us that together
we're much better than apart.

Jacob could feel the warmth of Ann's tears on his neck.
"I love you, Ann…I'm the luckiest man alive."
"I love you, too, Jacob…but luck has little to do with it."
Jacob nodded and held her tightly. "You're right. God
had been very good to us."

Chapter Eight

"I'm not a little girl anymore, Mother. I'm sorry I worried you. Tell Dad I'm sorry." Camille kissed her mother on the cheek. "I love you. Good night."

She knew that her mother liked to keep the door that led to the attic partially open, but Camille closed it carefully behind her. How she had kept from crying, she did not know. She was angry, not with her mother for treating her like a child, but with herself.

Running up the twenty-two wooden stairs to her attic room was difficult enough without the tears in her eyes and the weight of the backpack she carried in front of her, but it was the burden she carried inside her heart that weighed most heavily. The rise on each step ran at least an inch higher than its run, and her toe caught the lip of step number sixteen. The backpack broke her fall forward, but the knuckle of her middle finger on her right hand was caught between the pack and the edge of step number twenty. Kneeling now on step eighteen, she indignantly threw the backpack through the open door to her room at the top of the stairs and brought the wounded knuckle to her mouth to stop the bleeding and check the pain.

"Are you all right, Camille?" called a concerned mother from the hall below.

"I'm fine, Mother," was her swift reply. She jumped up quickly, entered her room, and closed the door before her mother could open the door below. With her mangled knuckle still between her lips, she pulled off her glasses with her other hand, then wiped the tears from her eyes. She examined the damage to her finger and trimmed the torn skin with her front teeth. It was a nasty scrape, but returning now to the kitchen for a bandage would mean facing her mother again and maybe her father, too. If she did that in her current emotional state, she would surely confess all. She couldn't risk it. She would wait awhile until both had gone to bed and bandage it when she went down to brush her teeth, or perhaps she would not go down at all. The damage to her finger wasn't as serious as it felt. She could move it. It was a bit swollen, but it wasn't broken, and it had almost stopped bleeding.

Camille sat down on her bed. She needed a few moments to regain her composure and collect her thoughts. It was late, and she was exhausted, but she was too upset to sleep. Through the partially open dormer window, she listened to the rain beating hard against the roof of the house next door. She was glad to be alone, away from her family and especially away from Dave.

She could have had the much larger room downstairs and been much closer to the bathroom and telephone, but the countless trips up and down the attic stairs and the somewhat cramped quarters were small prices to pay for the privacy her sanctuary afforded her. The stairs were her best defense; it was impossible to climb them undetected; they squeaked with almost every step, a foolproof built-in warning system that even her pesky little brother Mark could not circumvent.

The house belonged to the university where Susan taught piano and where Camille took classes. It was a wonderful turn-of-the-century, two-story house—three stories, if you counted Camille's attic—full of charm and character. It had high ceilings and beautiful woodwork.

The neighborhood was equally enchanting, relatively safe, and quiet. Almost every morning, Camille and her mother walked together to campus along sidewalks lined with enormous, mature sycamore maples, noble giants that dwarfed everything under their patriarchal care. They grew in the center of spacious twenty-five to thirty-foot-wide grass- or ivy-filled easements between the sidewalks and the street that led to the campus entrance five blocks away.

The street was narrow to begin with, but it appeared more so given the scale of the surrounding elements, especially the trees. Their branches reached across the street to mingle with those of their neighbors in a caress that painted ever-changing patterns of light and shadow on the plantings and pavement below. Her father said they had been planted in 1918, the date documented in the oval-shaped impressions pressed by the "Wilkins Construction Company" into the concrete walks at every intersection and again halfway between them. The homes and yards, though mostly small, were generally well groomed and maintained. The neighborhood was infused with a wonderful feeling of decency, permanency, and stability.

The rain continued to fall relentlessly as Camille got up off her bed. She took the books from her backpack and put them with the others on the shelf above her desk, books she had checked out each evening that week from the library just before it had closed. It was important that the time on the checkout slip evidence, if needed, that she had indeed spent each evening at the library. Dave would drive her back to campus for that very purpose before dropping her off around the corner a block from the house. Camille felt guilty for such an elaborate lie. She may never have to speak it, but it was still a lie, even unspoken.

Her parents did not approve of her relationship with Dave. He was much too old—twenty-six; she was much too young—eighteen. More important, he was not a member of the Church. Getting serious with anyone during her first year of college was a mistake, but even more so was getting serious with someone who could not take her to the temple.

But Camille liked almost everything about Dave. He was tall and handsome, witty, generous, and confident, perhaps too confident—that had been her parents' impression—her father had used words like "cocky," "spoiled," and "smug." He was rich; that was certain. He drove a cherry-red Jaguar and had his own apartment, despite his parents' very conspicuous home located in one of the city's most exclusive neighborhoods. That he was almost twenty-seven and had not graduated was reason enough for her mother's immediate disapproval after their first date. He was still in college, Camille explained in his defense, because he had traveled widely—he skied and had tried almost every resort in the world. She loved to hear about his experiences in places she had only read about, and he loved telling them—and he was going to graduate after spring semester, before starting his career with his father's company.

"You are attracted to him because he is infatuated with you," her mother argued. "Beware of his motives. This is all new to you, Camille. Please, remember your goals and standards. Please, be careful."

Camille understood perfectly her mother's warning. Her parents and grandmother had taught her well. She knew and shared their standard of morality. There was no flexibility in the family's moral code: chastity before marriage, marriage in the temple, and total fidelity afterward. It was weaved into the fabric of their faith. She had, until now, never questioned its validity; never, until now, had she any reason for doubting its authority. But never, until now, had anyone shown so much interest in her.

Camille seldom dated during high school, and "seldom," she realized, was an exaggeration. Other than school girl's-choice dances, Camille had never actually had a real date, a date when the young man had himself acted on his own personal interest and initiative. Shyness was certainly not the deterrent; Camille was gregarious. No one could *not* like her. Neither was she unattractive, just a late bloomer, as her grandmother Annabelle often reminded her. Her height, her red hair, and that her astigmatism ruled out contact lenses were probably the deciding factors; but during the last few months of her senior year and summer months after graduation, the rest of her anatomy had quickly caught up to her five-foot, ten-inch frame. Admiring eyes now easily and anxiously overlooked the glasses, and her long auburn hair had become a real asset.

Her parents' warnings had not fallen on deaf ears. Of course she shouldn't fall for the first guy who showed interest, and she hadn't. During her three-month summer semester at the university, she had gone out with several of the young men she had met at the LDS institute or on campus. She did not discriminate in her dating between members of the Church and members of other faiths since she had no intention of encouraging any serious relationship. But Dave was different from the others. He had persisted despite her initial insistence that she was not ready to steadily date anyone, and, unlike the others, she was also very attracted to him.

They had met at a church-sponsored back-to-campus dance in late August. Camille was on the planning committee—she was involved in, and volunteered for, almost everything available. Dave had come with a friend, he bragged, to meet girls. Their first date was a walk through the Hispanic neighborhoods on the other side of campus to the bakery at Cardona's Market. By mid-October, they were seeing each other almost every night. Alarmed and increasingly vigilant, Andrew and Susan did not hesitate to voice their concerns. Camille listened respectfully. She had always relied on her parent's levelheadedness to counterbalance her impulsive nature. She loved them deeply and would never willingly disappoint them. She agreed with them that Dave was moving too quickly and promised to break off their relationship.

The day after their "family discussion," Camille tried to explain to Dave her parents' fears and reservations. He seemed to understand but persuaded her that they need not stop seeing each other altogether. What they had was real, he said, and he was perfectly willing to curb their relationship.

"I'm thinking I'd like to learn more about your Church," he added. "If we don't see each other, who will answer my questions?"

Camille was easily convinced, reasoning in her mind that this just might be her best or even her only chance for true love. What did it matter if he wasn't a member now? She was sure he would be some day.

He promised to "slow down" if she would continue seeing him at least once a week, but their compromise was soon forgotten. They never again met where Camille's parents—or anyone else who knew them—could see them, and they continued to study together in a secluded quiet place Dave had discovered in the basement of the chemistry building. But studying was more an excuse to begin their afternoons and evenings together than an end in and of itself. They were very discreet on campus, seldom meeting in public spaces and never showing their affection—Dave's suggestion. They had kept it a secret; no one they knew, knew.

Camille was convinced that she was in love, and she was sure that Dave would someday accept the gospel and join the Church. She had given him a Book of Mormon. He promised to read it during Christmas break, and that once he had read it he would hear the missionaries. Time spent with Dave meant longer nights in the attic studying to keep up with her courses, a price she gladly paid. She enjoyed their afternoon hand-in-hand walks through the park in the Hispanic neighborhood on the other side of the university—a safe place where anonymity was assured. Dave preferred their evening drives outside the city limits and their increasingly more intimate encounters in his parked car.

These secret rendezvous gnawed at Camille's conscience—she knew her parents trusted her and she loathed deceiving them—but Dave showed no sign of regret or concern and downplayed her worry and feelings of remorse. In fact, he seemed to enjoy the covert nature of their relationship.

As the October days slipped into November, Dave had become increasingly possessive and, to Camille's initial dismay, much more expressive of his affection, both verbally and physically. Though she felt uncomfortable at first with each new liberty taken, his words somehow magically changed them into further proof and confirmation of his love and devotion. Dave was very convincing—he said all the right things—and Camille began to question some of the values she had long held sacred.

She was sure Dave loved her, but she wondered why they had never really talked seriously about marriage, why somehow Dave always eluded the subject. Perhaps, she hopefully reasoned, he wanted to surprise her. She assumed their engagement was inevitable. After all, that was her life's experience, the example of her parents and grandparents. When two people were in love, they got married. Surely Dave was planning a Christmas proposal, perhaps even a Thanksgiving surprise.

Once he had asked her, then things would get complicated. How would she explain it to her parents? Impossible! She could hardly simply say, "Guess what, I'm engaged to the guy you warned me not to see anymore." She and Dave would have to continue their deception, feign reconciliation, and then finally, an "official" engagement once he had decided to be baptized. Until then, Camille reasoned, perhaps their love alone was enough to justify their increased intimacy.

That night, after Dave had dropped her off in the rain a block and around the corner from her parent's house, as she walked slowly under her umbrella toward the porch light that was always left on for her, Camille was deep in thought. Each step, taken purposely so that the bottom of her jeans would evidence the long walk from campus, was a blatant reminder to her of her deception. She began to tremble, not from the cold—it really wasn't very cold for November—but from the sudden realization of the consequences of what she had been willing to do tonight and what she had agreed to do tomorrow. It started to rain even harder. Susan was waiting for her at the door.

"Why didn't you call for us to come and get you, Camille?" her mother asked as she took Camille's glasses off her and started to dry them with her handkerchief. "I sent your dad to look for you in the library, but he couldn't find you."

"Um…" Camille organized her thoughts quickly, "I was there."

It was a big library. She had tried to find Dave there once before and knew how difficult it could be to locate someone.

"I was in the bathroom for quite awhile," she continued. "He must have just missed me. What time was he there?" She hoped she sounded sincere.

"He's been gone for almost an hour. I told him to wait in the car for you at the bottom of the hill if he couldn't find you. I don't know how he could have missed you. Oh, I forgot."

Her mother turned off the porch light, her sign to her father, five blocks away, that Camille had come home.

Camille coughed several times to give herself a few seconds to think. She wasn't sure what to say. She wasn't accustomed to so much lying. Her mother's reaction to her coughing bought her a few more precious seconds.

"Camille, you're catching a cold! Why didn't you call if you knew you were catching a cold? You must have realized we'd be worried about you."

No, she had not realized they would be worried. She had not thought at all about her parents' feelings. Her mind was on other things. Just moments earlier, up the street and around the corner in Dave's car, after she had responded without much hesitation to yet another new and bolder expression of his love, Dave had suggested they go to his apartment.

"There's no time tonight. My parents will be waiting for me because of the rain...tomorrow," she added in a trembling whisper.

Strange, she had reflected as she walked in the rain, strange how she had abandoned her principles so quickly. Dave had asked her a month before if she would like to see his apartment. She had informed him firmly about her rule never to go into a man's apartment. She continued to reflect on it now subconsciously, even as she frantically constructed her alibi.

"I'm sorry. I didn't realize it was raining so hard, and when I did realize it...and was just about to call you, Heather offered me a ride."

Her mother wrinkled her eyebrows, an obvious sign that she wasn't buying it.

"Then why are you so wet?" she asked slowly.

"She was in a hurry. I had her drop me off at the corner so she wouldn't have to turn, and I stepped in a puddle. I thought the umbrella would keep me dry. It's no big deal, Mother."

Camille knew she wasn't making a good case, but she hoped that her tone of exasperation would quell her mother's inquisitorial attitude, and it did. But it was obvious that her mother sensed something and wanted to talk. She was stroking her daughter's long red hair as she often did. Soon she would pull it back behind her ears and put her glasses back on for her, exactly as she had done ever since Camille could remember.

"Camille, we're very proud of you. We know we can trust you, but please, from now on, please call us. We're parents; we worry. You spend so much time lately at the library. We miss you. You've grown up so fast. Maybe you could humor us and do some of your studying here."

Her mother's love had cut her to the quick. Camille had wanted to cry in the street, even more so now. Deep inside, she wanted the lying to stop; she wanted to confess and ask her mother's advice and forgiveness. She wanted once again to be her mother's little girl. But now was not the time. She needed time to think. She needed to get away quickly, before the tears.

"I need access to the Web and the reference books. Next semester won't be as bad."

Susan tried to put back her glasses; Camille took them and put them on herself.

"I'm not a little girl anymore, Mother. I'm sorry I worried you. Tell Dad I'm sorry." She kissed her mother on the cheek. "I love you. Good night."

Camille sat at her desk. Through the sound of the rain she heard her father pulling the car into the garage. She quickly turned off her lamp and walked across the room and listened at her door. He might not come up to talk to her if he could see no light under the door. It was much darker in her room than it was outside. Her window looked out over the east side of the house, over the driveway that led to the garage in the backyard. What little light there was in the room came indirectly through the window from the street lamp across the road reflected off the neighbor's roof next door, light that dimly illuminated the shelf on the wall near the window where she kept Molly Ann. She felt her doll's eyes upon her.

Camille waited several minutes at the door, holding her breath, listening carefully for the squeak of the stairs. She heard the door to the attic creak at her father's touch, but nothing more. Her "chat" with her dad would come in the morning. She sat on her bed and looked up at her doll. Assured she would not be interrupted, she allowed the tears to flow freely.

"Tell me, Molly Ann," Camille said softly, "why did I tell Dave tomorrow? What must he think of me? He doesn't know any better. I'm the one who has the Gospel. I'm the one who needs to be strong. But he knows what I believe. Why would he have even suggested it? Why haven't we talked more about our future, about marriage? Why are we dangerously approaching sex when we haven't even talked of marriage? What should I do?"

As she spoke, a bolt of lightning illuminated the doll's piercing yet gentle eyes, the dark blue eyes that seemed now to probe the true feelings of Camille's heart. The sudden light also revealed an envelope lightly resting in Molly Ann's lap. Camille rose and turned on the lamp. It was her mother's custom to place her grandmother's weekly letters there. The letters always arrived on Tuesday, but today was Friday. Camille knew immediately that it could mean only one thing: a poem. Since she was twelve, it had been her right to be the first to read each of her grandmother's poems, and she had made her grandmother promise that she would immediately send her any new poem she wrote while they were apart. Camille opened the envelope quickly and read.

"Dear Camille, I have sensed from your recent letters that something is wrong. I've been working for several months on this poem. It was to be my Christmas present to you, a new tradition for us; but God's Spirit has prompted me to send it to you now. I pray it will help. Love, Grandma Annabelle."

The poem was in her grandmother's beautiful hand-writing on a separate piece of gray parchment.

Stay the Course
(for Camille)

Stay the course the Savior laid.
Trust in him; be not afraid.
Others' lights may all have dimmed.
Guard your lamp and keep it trimmed.
Drink life's water at its source.
Timeless laws are yet in force.
Other choices bring remorse.
Stay the course.

Take your time; you must not go
faster than your soul can grow.
Keep a steady prayerful pace,
like your Savior, grace by grace.
Pumps flow freely after prime.

You'll need time to make life rhyme.
Step by step, you'll upward climb.
Take your time.

There are seasons in each life,
times of calm and times of strife,
when to listen, when to talk;
do not run before you walk.
Order in all that you yearn
gives you power to discern.
Take each challenge, each concern,
in its turn.

Follow Christ; be not deceived.
Keep the faith that you received
when your heart was fresh and pure.
You knew then; be now as sure.
Shun the choices fools endorse.
Undue haste will bring remorse.
Keep your cart behind the horse.
Stay the course.

Camille didn't bother to stop the tears that fell on the parchment. The rain intensified outside. She was sorry she had lied to her mother and ashamed of what she had let Dave do. She knew she should pray. She had promised her grandmother that she would pray every day, and her parents also often reminded her after saying good night as they always had: "Don't forget your prayers." She had not kept her promise very well, especially during the last few weeks. She realized now why: She was too ashamed to pray. But now as she sobbed and pondered the message of her grandmother's poem, she knew she must pray.

She remembered another of her grandmother's poems. She pulled a hardbound, five-by-eight, dark green notebook from the top drawer. Shortly before she and her family had moved that spring, she had spent the better part of two Sunday evenings at the desk in Grandma Annabelle's parlor copying her favorite poems from her grandmother's books of poetry. She wanted them with her while she was away. It was easy to find, a short poem she had included not because it was one of her favorites, but because of its brevity: It was just the right length to fill the empty space left on the last page. It had meant little to her then, but its message now filled every fiber of her being as she read out loud.

It's Time

If you accept and bear the blame,
    if sorrow and remorse are real,
it's not the time to hide in shame;
    it's time to kneel.
If you are anxious to confess
your sin and change, but know not how,
it's not the time for hopelessness;
    it's time to bow.
When justice claims that you repair
a wrong or harm you can't undo,
it's not the time to court despair;
    it's time you knew
that Jesus Christ spared you the rod.
Accept His will; His voice obey.
It's time to humbly speak with God;
    it's time to pray.

Camille knelt at her chair by the side of the desk, and as the rain continued to pour outside, she poured out her heart to her Heavenly Father, expressing her remorse as best she could and asking His forgiveness and for strength to do what she knew must be done. She must tell Dave that the intimacy must stop, that she was determined to regain her self-respect and to keep herself pure and chaste for the man who would someday take her to the temple. If it was Dave's intention to be that man, he must share her faith, including her standards of morality; and if she lost him because he would not, she would trust in God. Camille wanted a marriage like her parents' marriage, a marriage like her grandmother's had been: two souls joined together in a sacred partnership based on love, trust, a shared faith, and absolute fidelity.

For almost an hour she prayed and pondered, and pondered and prayed. Illuminated by God's Spirit, she now saw Dave in a more telling light. The covertness of their relationship, the calculated measuring of his advances, the lack of commitment in their conversation, and finally, the invitation to his apartment—all the evidence combined to paint a clear picture she had until now been too blind to see. How could she have been so gullible?

Tomorrow was Saturday. Tomorrow would be a new start. She would ask Dave several important questions: Why had they spent so little time with his parents and with his circle of friends? Why had they seldom spoken of their values and beliefs, and of their future; what were his true feelings about religion and family? Finally, what did he hope to accomplish by taking her to his apartment? He would tell her what he thought she wanted to hear, all lies. She would be ready for them, and to say good-bye.

The day after that would be a day of reconciliation. It was appropriate that it would be Sunday. After church, Camille would confess to her parents and ask their forgiveness. She would cry in her mother's arms and on her father's shoulder. She would tell them she loved and respected them, and would thank them for their example. She would promise to do all she could to regain their trust. And finally, she would write an important letter to her grandmother.

Part One
Chapter Eight

The rain finally stopped. Camille paused again in her prayer to listen, as she had learned to do, not to sounds of the night but to the still, small voice in her heart that was acknowledging her prayer and confirming her decision. She felt warm and resolved, calm in the assurance that a forgiving Heavenly Father loved her. She prayed again, this time thanking God for her many blessings. This month of November would truly be for her a month of thanksgiving.

Chapter Nine

Camille slowly opened her eyes. Mark was bouncing up and down on his knees beside her, delighted that he had somehow entered her sanctuary undetected. The force from the legs of the bed rebounding against the hardwood floor reverberated in the raised sash of the dormer window Camille had left open. The cold morning air, fresh and inviolate after the rain the night before, filled the attic room with its promise of a new season, and the sunlight that filtered through the trees outside the window announced the end of a long but cleansing storm.

"Wake up, lazy," Mark repeated until her eyes were finally open. "It's ten o'clock. Mom says to fold the clothes in the dryer before she and Dad come home. You're lucky they let you sleep in. I had to do all your work."

A long hard stretch and yawn, then in a single motion Camille threw off her covers, sat up, and wrapped her arms around her unsuspecting little brother, pulling him down in front of her. He squealed with delight as she tickled him unmercifully. Mark was eleven, old enough and strong enough that Camille needn't worry about hurting him—he had grown at least five inches during the past year—but young, immature, and simple-hearted enough that the physical contact between a younger brother and a mature older sister remained unrestrained in its innocence.

Camille adored her pesky little brother. When he was born, she had been bitterly disappointed by her shattered hopes for a younger sister, the sister who was to be named Annie and with whom she would share a room and her deepest little-girl secrets. But from the moment she first saw little Mark in the hospital, lying in her mother's arms, or perhaps from the moment she first held her tiny new brother in her own trembling arms, she was smitten. Her own maternal instincts took flight with dreams of someday holding and nourishing a child of her own. As the years passed, her mother Susan's example had etched in her daughter's character an enduring love for children and a reverence for motherhood.

Camille understood that all too soon her little brother would flee from like displays of sibling affection. Someday the innocence with which they now wrestled in her bed would be lost forever, but she was grateful on this clear, clean, and cold morning, after the storm of experiences of the night before, that her brother was still a child. She needed the evidence that touching and being touched were still the fruits of love, pure and unfeigned, that physical human contact was still the product of relationships that were blameless and good.

"Gross! What happened to your finger?" asked Mark when he caught a glimpse of his sister's scraped knuckle.

"I fell coming up the stairs last night."

"Does it hurt?"

"No, I'd forgotten all about it."

The family followed a fairly rigid schedule on Saturday mornings. Beginning at 7:00 A.M., the entire family worked together to clean the house and do the week's laundry. It was their tradition, and no one was exempt from full participation. Camille was surprised that her parents had let her sleep in, and she wondered if they knew more than she thought they did. The weekly shopping always followed their housework. They usually went to the grocery store together at about 9:00. They had obviously left Mark behind with instructions to wake her at 10:00. They would be home in about a half hour. After their shopping, they almost always enjoyed a late breakfast of waffles or hotcakes.

Camille took a quick shower and folded the clothes. She then set the table, plugged in the waffle iron, and mixed the batter. She would start the first waffle when she heard the car in the driveway. This morning she felt happy and secure in the knowledge that she belonged to a family, and she was eager to do all she could to demonstrate her gratitude and appreciation.

At the sound of the car horn, Camille quickly filled and closed the waffle iron, and then ran outside to help bring in the groceries. Mark was right behind her.

"How's your cold, Camille?" asked her mother.

"I feel fine. I don't think it's a cold. I'm making waffles."

"Great," her father enthused as he started to get out of the car. "I'm starved. Shopping makes me hungry."

"Everything makes you hungry, Dad," Mark chided as he searched the bags in the backseat for surprises.

No sooner had her father pulled his long body out of the car and stood than Camille had her arms around her father's neck. Camille got her height from her father; he was easily seven or eight inches taller than she was. She pulled his head down and kissed him on the cheek.

"I love you, Dad, and I'm really sorry I worried you last night," she said, then grabbed two bags and headed for the house.

Andrew looked inquiringly at Susan across the roof of the car.

"What was that all about?"

"I have no idea," said Susan as she shrugged, "but she certainly seems happy."

After breakfast, Camille and her mother did the dishes while in the backyard Mark and her father raked the leaves that had fallen the night before. Very few leaves were left now on the trees; most were in the compost area behind the garage. It had been a glorious East Coast autumn, and her father had lamented several times that it would soon end. Even though they were renting, he took the same pride in their yard and garden as he always had back home. The first hard frost was late but could come anytime, and there was still much to do. The neighbors were out raking, too. As soon as the dishes were done, Camille and her mother would join them. The plan was to surprise Mrs. Jenkins across the street with a thorough cleanup of her yard.

Camille watched her father and brother through the window above the kitchen sink, while she washed and her mother stood next to her drying. She felt a surge of love that brought a tear to her eye.

"Is there something you want to tell me, Camille?" her mother asked tenderly.

"As a matter of fact, there is, Mother, but I'd like to wait until tomorrow, and I want to talk to both you and Dad."

Camille met her worried look with a smile and a gentle touch on her mother's arm. "But don't worry, Mom, it's something good, something very good," she added.

"All right. I'll tell your father to postpone the little talk he was planning."

Camille smiled broadly and then looked out the window once again. Her father, always the teacher, was pointing upward, quizzing Mark on the names of the trees. She continued to smile as she recalled having been taught the same lesson.

"You know, Mom," she said, "you and Dad have done a wonderful job as parents. You've raised us with the same care and attention to detail that you give to your music and that Dad gives to our yard. I remember how hard Dad worked on our yard back home when we first bought the house, and how hard he worked at Grandpa and Grandma's, all that attention to detail, to doing things well, the right way, and since then, all the time spent maintaining and improving. It's all paid off beautifully."

The dishes were done. Mother and daughter embraced, and it was her mother's eye that now harbored a tear.

They worked at Mrs. Jenkins until 2:30 P.M. They raked the wet leaves onto a large blue plastic tarp and then dragged it back to the compost pile. Her father and Mark also pruned and mulched Mrs. Jenkins's prize roses; it was a chance for another teaching moment between father and son.

The cleanup at Mrs. Jenkins's was another family tradition for which Camille was now all the more grateful. One Saturday afternoon each month, they devoted a few hours to a family service project. They took turns selecting and then planning the activity. It was Mark's turn, and Camille joined her parents in letting him think he had come up with the idea on his own.

About the time the maple leaves began to fall in earnest, Camille listened one evening while setting the table, to a conversation skillfully prepared to assure that Mark "overheard." Her parents often used tactics like this to indirectly convey information to their children. Her mother had noted that the Widow Jenkins was having difficulty recovering from a recent surgery. Her father's likewise casual observation as they ate that the leaves were piling up in some of the neighbors' yards was all the prompting Mark had required. He asked Camille the next morning to help him write an unsigned letter to Mrs. Jenkins.

"Dear Mrs. Jenkins," it said. "Please don't hire anyone to rake your leaves. They will disappear on the Saturday before Thanksgiving." Mark agreed with Camille that it should be a surprise, and a wise Mrs. Jenkins played her part well. Mark beamed.

Final exams were less than three weeks away. Camille had resolved to begin that very afternoon to make up for the study time she had wasted during the semester on Dave. After their late lunch with Mrs. Jenkins, she retreated to the solitude of the attic for a few hours of serious study. But before she began, she kneeled again in prayer, thanking God once more for her family and asking for strength to carry out her plan. She had practiced what she would say to Dave the night before. There was no need to think anymore about it. It was time now to concentrate on her physiology textbook.

Camille had promised to meet Dave that evening in the park at 6:00 P.M. At 4:30 she left the house for campus. This time she did not lie when she told her parents where she was going. The unread library books that had collected over the past week on her shelf were in her backpack, adding much more weight than she was used to carrying. Most of them were not due for another week, but she was anxious for a clean break, and she wanted no reminders of her deception. She planned to take a break and walk to the park after an hour at the library, not the park immediately adjacent to campus but the park on the far side of campus, past the married student housing and near Cardona's Market.

How strange that only now did she see the absurdity of it all. Why would Dave make her walk that extra mile and a half? What was wrong with meeting at the other park or at the library, for that matter? It now seemed like a long way to go for the two-minute speech and glacial good-bye she had planned, just long enough to make it crystal clear that the relationship was over. After a triumphant walk back, she would spend the rest of her evening studying alone in the library.

That was her plan. Camille was breathing hard when she reached the top of the 147 stairs—she had counted them several times—that led from the campus entrance to the main mall, that in turn led to the library. Even though it was a cool, almost cold evening, certainly cold enough for the jacket she was wearing, she was perspiring from the exertion. She smiled as she thought of what surely would be Dave's reaction when he saw her dressed in her running shoes, faded jeans, and red flannel shirt. She had always tried to dress attractively for Dave, but tonight she looked as if she were going camping. She hadn't bothered to change her clothes, let alone shower or freshen up her makeup. When she said good-bye to her parents, her father hadn't noticed anything out of the ordinary, but her mother had.

"That's a bit casual for you, isn't it?" she remarked suspiciously.

"Yes, it is." She grinned. "I'll tell you why tomorrow."

Dave too would no doubt suspect something was up when he saw her. Her work clothes were hardly apropos to the evening he had planned for her.

At 5:30 Camille left the library computer lab and locked her backpack in her locker. She was nervous. It had been difficult to concentrate on the paper she was writing. She began to wonder how Dave might react. The notion to call him instead of meeting him in the park occurred and reoccurred to her several times. But no, nervous or not, she was determined to see her plan through. Dave may be a cad, but she never suspected he would be anything but a gentleman. After all, she ashamedly admitted to herself, he had never done anything she had not consented to. He often pushed the limits but had always stopped when she insisted. She believed that he would walk away once he understood her resolve. Face to face was the only way to end it, the only way he would be convinced, and the only way she would be satisfied.

She walked slowly across campus. She had given herself plenty of time. Clouds had moved in again after what until then had been a cool, sunny day. The sun would not set for at least another hour and a half, but it seemed later. Camille was sure she would be back in the library before dark, and if it rained, this time she would call for her parents to come and get her.

When she arrived at the park entrance, Dave was already there, waiting in his Jaguar. He opened the passenger side door from the inside, but Camille did not get in. Instead, she crouched down to where she could see him through the open door.

"Let's go for a walk," she said, then shut the door.

Dave got out and looked at her across the top of the car. His eyes jumped quickly from her eyes to her jeans and then back again.

"What's up, Camille? I thought—"

"Let's go for a walk," she repeated assertively, trying to dominate her nervousness.

"All right. Let me get my coat."

Camille walked to the front of the car and waited. Dave sensed something was wrong and did not try to kiss her. He touched her arm as a signal that he wanted to take her hand, but both hands remained buried in her jacket pockets. She turned and started walking. He followed.

They walked slowly for several minutes in uncomfortable silence. A few people were still in the park. An older couple approached from the opposite direction, walking arm-in-arm. They smiled and nodded a greeting as they passed. Once they were well behind them, Camille was the first to speak.

"Tell me, Dave." She stopped and looked into his eyes. "Do you believe in God?"

"Of course, Camille." Dave only half suppressed his snicker. "Everyone believes in God. What's that got to do with us, with tonight?"

"Have you ever prayed to God?"

"Yeah, I guess, when I was little. Why?"

"Because I pray, Dave. My father prays, and my grandfather prayed. I want to marry someone who prays."

Dave's sardonic smile was all the evidence Camille needed. It was time to end it.

"I'm not going to your apartment, Dave. It's not right. I don't think you really love me. If you did, you would have asked me to marry you by now—"

"Whoa! Stop right there," he interrupted. "What's gotten into you? How can you say I don't love you? It's precisely because I do love you that I can't keep my hands off you. It's my way of expressing my love. Camille, surely you see that. Sexual intimacy is a wonderful and natural thing. God himself created it. When two people are in love, they are physically attracted to each other. Sex is a way to consummate that love, the only way. You'll see, Camille. Once we've consummated our love, then we'll know for sure that we're right for each other. Then we'll start to talk about marriage."

He tried to put his arms around her, but she stepped away.

"No, Dave. Don't touch me. You're wrong. Marriage is the way two people consummate their love, and sex is the way they consummate their marriage. If you don't believe that, I can't see you anymore. Good-bye, Dave."

Dave followed Camille and grabbed the wrist of the hand she had taken out of her pocket. She tried to pull it from him, but he held it tight with both his hands.

"Wait, Camille. I'm sorry. Please, don't walk away. I can't lose you, Camille, not like this. Give me another chance. Please don't say good-bye, not yet. I do love you, Camille, and it's not just about sex. Please, Camille…I promise. If I'd known how you really felt, I'd never have suggested my apartment. You may be right; we may not be right for each other, but don't throw away what we have. Please, Camille, let's not end it this way. I'm begging you. Let's go back to the car where it's warm and talk this out."

Camille was unprepared for such an uncharacteristic show of remorse and humility. She was moved but far from convinced. Perhaps she had judged him a bit too harshly, and perhaps he deserved a better explanation.

"All right," she nodded, "but not in your car. Let's keep walking."

She put her hands back into her pockets, and they walked on. Dave asked a lot of questions, seemingly sincere questions, about her faith, her values, her family, her dreams for the future. She answered all of them as frankly and honestly as she could and wondered why they had never talked like this before. Dave listened attentively, submissively, perhaps too submissively. His answers to her questions were equally forthright and candid, perhaps too candid, almost contrived. Dave seemed like a stranger, completely out of character with what she was used to. It was as if he were following a script, saying everything that she wanted him to say.

Camille felt uneasy, but then Dave admitted that his interests were more physical than spiritual. When he also agreed that perhaps she was right, that perhaps they weren't meant for each other after all, and that it would be better if they made a clean break of it, Camille felt much better. She was glad they had talked it all out and could now part on good terms.

They had walked around the entire park and were back at the north entrance, standing once again in front of Dave's car. It was getting late. It would be dark in a few minutes.

"I've got to get back to campus," she said.

"I don't want you to walk back in the dark, and it might start raining. Let me drive you," Dave offered. "It's the least I can do after making you walk all the way here. I'd really be a jerk if I didn't see you safely back. Let me do at least one thing right."

"All right," she said, but no sooner had she spoken than something inside her told her she should walk away. But Dave had already opened the door for her. It would be rude not to accept. Once inside, and as Dave walked around the back of the car, the feeling was magnified. Darkness was only seconds away. The only other car in the parking lot had backed away from the curb and would soon pass by them en route to the exit. That same something inside that had urged her not to get in the car now told Camille she should flee, that she should run to the safety of the approaching car. But Camille suppressed the feeling, and the moment of decision was lost as the other car sped away.

"Don't forget your seat belt." Dave smiled.

"A strange thing to say," thought Camille. She always fastened her seat belt and often lectured Dave for not fastening his. The tone of Dave's voice seemed strangely cold to her. His hand was anxiously on the ignition, waiting for the familiar "click" before starting the car. She felt his eyes watching her as she pulled the seat belt across her body. Her quick glance caught a trace of ironic satisfaction in his smile.

The road from the parking lot led down a steep hill to where it crossed the northwest and lowest corner of the park. It then made a sharp turn before ascending another hill where at the top it intersected with the boulevard leading northeastward to the university. Camille and Dave had driven it many times. At the bottom of the hill was a small one-way turnout where Dave had often taken Camille to "talk." It was a secluded spot, isolated from the rest of the park by the huge London plane trees that surrounded it and by the thick grove of hedge maples that separated it from the main path some one hundred yards away. The bitter memory of the place amplified Camille's uneasiness. She tensed as they approached the turnout but relaxed again when the Jaguar did not slow down to make the turn. But her relief turned instantly to terror as Dave braked suddenly and turned sharply into the turnout.

"Whoa! That was dumb. Force of habit," he laughed sarcastically as he brought the car to a sudden stop and turned off the lights. Camille struggled to unfasten her seat belt, but it would not unlatch until Dave had released the brake, and he knew it. When he released it to turn toward her, she hit the release button and reached desperately for the handle on the door.

"You're not going anywhere," he said, as he grabbed her by the top of her jeans with one hand and the collar of her shirt with the other. He pulled her back into the car and reached over her to close the door. The door hit her hard on the top of her head and did not completely close. He pushed her face down hard against the seat, sending her glasses to the floor.

In an instant, he opened the other door and pulled her legs out from under her so that she was lying face down, her ribs painfully pressed against the emergency brake between the bucket seats, her legs below the knees sticking out the door.

Camille had never screamed as a child, and the terror of her circumstance did not allow it now. She was horrified beyond anything she had ever experienced or could ever have imagined. Not even in her worse nightmares had she dreamed of anything like this ever happening to her. Dave was lying on top of her. The harder she struggled, the more he pressed against her. She couldn't move; she could hardly breathe.

"Dave! I can't breathe! Please don't! You're hurting me!" she cried, not knowing what else she could say.

In sordid contrast, Dave had plenty to say.

"Shut up and hold still. You owe me this," he snarled.

His language was insipid and foul. Every fifth or sixth word was an obscenity or a profanity. He had already pulled her coat off and was now pulling at her flannel shirt. The buttons gave way one by one, and Camille stopped pleading and began to pray.

"Help me, Heavenly Father; please help me," she sobbed over and over.

"I told you to shut up," he growled in her ear, but looked up after the passenger door suddenly flew open.

Chapter Ten

Jacob switched off the lathe and examined his work. "Perfect," he said out loud. He enjoyed making furniture, and he liked the men who worked with him. After Ann and Molly, he considered Luis and Tony to be his best friends.

"*¡Bien hecho*! That looks great!" said Luis, looking over Jacob's shoulder at his work.

"*No está mal*," replied Jacob with feigned humility.

"You were born to work in wood, Jacob," added Tony, who had come over to join the conversation. "My offer still stands. When you're ready to go full time, just say the word."

Jacob smiled. Little did Tony know how close he was to taking him up on his offer. Jacob was as good with his hands as he was with his words. His woodwork reflected the same search for perfection that motivated his poetry, and now, his novel. Tony saved all the delicate jobs for the three mornings each week when Jacob worked in the shop. For several weeks now, he had tried to tempt Jacob with extra hours and had sometimes succeeded. Tonight, for example, a Saturday night, Jacob had worked a full day. The shop was two weeks behind on its orders, and Jacob knew that Tony was grateful for the extra help, but it wasn't friendship alone that motivated him.

It had been less than three months since he had quit his job to write his novel, and money was already tight. With Christmas a little more than a month away, the extra money would come in very handy. He had tried to secretly put a bit of cash away for a new porcelain doll for Molly—Molly loved dolls—and something nice for Ann, but something always came up that depleted his reserve.

The hours he spent in the shop served another important purpose. The novel was progressing nicely, but writing, although invigorating, also exhausted him. At times he would write for five or even six hours at a sitting, but he normally needed a break every few hours to let his imagination settle, to ponder the direction his writing was taking, and to make sure he hadn't neglected anything. On Tuesday, Thursday, and Friday, a hard run in the park before lunch, just before Ann went to work, in addition to giving him the exercise he needed, allowed him to ponder what he had written that morning. Also, many of his best ideas came to him while running. The time was especially useful for working out and adding details. An hour every afternoon walking and playing with Molly after school in the same park provided a similar time for reflection.

On Monday, Wednesday, and Saturday mornings, Jacob started work at 7:00 A.M. in the furniture shop. Writing all day every day was counterproductive. He had written enough to know that it was better in the long run to leave his writing all together for several hours every other day or so and concentrate on something else. He had learned that it was after these periods of "rest" that he was most productive, but because he was so driven to write, it was difficult for him to find meaningful distraction.

The furniture shop offered the perfect solution. Here, his attention was directed to something entirely different from writing, but something he enjoyed. Changing his physical surroundings provided a new atmosphere where ideas often popped uncoaxed into his mind. His notebook was never closed for very long. In the furniture shop, he could both rest his mind and refine his writing, while at the same time supplementing Ann's salary.

Two weeks earlier, Ann's job at the market had taken a turn for the worse. Mr. Cardona had suddenly received an offer to buy the market, an offer, he said apologetically, that he could not refuse. The store's new owner was a corporation with plans for expansion, and the new manager had made several unwelcome changes. To start with, the store suddenly lost its Hispanic flavor and family atmosphere. Several of Ann's coworkers, all of them Hispanic and most of them related to the Cardonas, were let go to make room for the friends and relatives of the new management. Second, any prior personal "arrangements" made with existing employees were null and void. Mr. Lambert, the new manager, told Ann that her thirty-five-hour workweek was a luxury the store's new business plan could not afford. Either she moved to a forty-hour week, and at the wage shown by the store's records, or she must take a reduction in salary and lose her insurance. The new insurance carrier required a higher co-payment and deductible but was still better than anything Ann and Jacob could find on their own. The changes, unfortunately, meant that each of Ann's weekday afternoon shifts was now an hour longer but with no increase in her total salary.

There was another even more important disadvantage to the store's change in ownership. Ann had been feeling increasingly fatigued during the past several weeks. A concerned Mr. Cardona had interrupted her six-hour cashier shift with an hour in the office—sometimes longer—to allow her to get off her feet for a while, and it had helped a great deal. Her new seven-hour shifts at the checkout counter, with only the usual breaks, were now almost more than she could bear. She had spent a couple of hours every morning during the past week looking for another job, but had thus far been unsuccessful.

Jacob and Ann had discussed it all one evening, and Jacob had insisted that she go see her doctor for a thorough checkup, but Ann, who miserly managed the family budget, had hesitated.

"The co-payment can be better spent elsewhere. I'm just tired from standing all day," she assured him. "I'll be fine once I get used to it. Mr. Cardona was so nice to let me sit every day. I'm just used to being pampered."

But Jacob was not entirely convinced. He suspected something else was wrong and had made an appointment—his Christmas stash would pay for it, if necessary—but it would be almost two weeks before Dr. Oquendo could fit her into his schedule.

He would reason later that Ann's spiritual euphoria and general happiness had helped her easily, and unfortunately, ignore what her body was trying to tell her. It had clouded his judgment, too. Jacob had never seen her happier.

Except for Ann's declining health, life was very good. They had little extra money, but they again had a dream that helped them easily tolerate their poverty. Jacob had settled into his routine, writing methodically but enthusiastically, and he too had never been more content. He was glad that his new spiritual attitude had made Ann so happy, and her happiness was contagious. Though his mind was focused on his novel, he was keenly aware that he was not the man he was before, that his budding faith was making him a better husband, a better father, and yes, a better writer, too.

He was now able to portray the spiritual dimension of the characters in his novel much better than he had done in his narrative poetry. Because he now saw many of the characters of his poems in a much different light, he was tempted to rewrite them, making the changes necessary to communicate that difference. Once he had finished the novel, he would have much more rethinking and rewriting to do.

Jacob's understanding of himself as a writer had changed direction. He no longer thought of himself as a voice from the outside that described the emotions and feelings of others. He felt instead that he was a part of a chorus of feelings and emotions. His voice was unique, to be sure, but he was singing the same song, in tune with the voices of others on equal spiritual ground, others with whom he shared a common spiritual heritage and purpose. He felt he was communicating something that his readers already knew and felt, but of which they needed to be reminded, and in a way only his voice could convey.

Everything was going as he had planned, even better. He was only sorry that the Cardonas had sold their market and that Ann now had to work so much harder. He hoped she would soon find another job, but if she could not, and perhaps even if she could, he had all but decided to accept Tony's offer and go to work full time at the furniture shop. The insurance plan there was every bit as good as their current plan, and his salary would be much higher than Ann's. Their overall income would be only slightly less but could actually be more if Ann found something part time, something for ten or twelve hours a week. Jacob could write at night, after work, and on weekends. It might take him several months longer to finish, but Ann's health was more important than any delay it might cause him. If he had to work full time, making furniture had it all over technical writing.

Jacob had followed Ann's example and made his decision a matter of prayer. He hadn't received the direct inspiration that he had half expected, but each day the idea became more and more agreeable to him; perhaps this was God's answer. He would love to tell Ann on Thanksgiving Day that she would no longer have to work. He imagined her reaction, and it made him smile. He wasn't sure if God had answered his prayers, but he had pretty much determined what he would do. He decided to wait until Ann saw her doctor on Tuesday. Regardless of what the doctor had to say, he was ready to surprise her with his new plan, and he took some time off thinking of the novel to orchestrate and rehearse his speech during his run in the park. It reminded him of how he had practiced another speech he had made a few months before. This speech would be much more pleasant to deliver, he was sure; and as he felt again that familiar surge of love, he lengthened his stride and quickened his pace.

"That's enough for today," barked Tony. "It'll be dark soon. Let's clean up...and by the way, Jacob," he added, "great work. If you can give me another full day on Monday, I'd be very grateful."

"You've got it, Tony," Jacob committed.

Fifteen minutes later, Jacob was on his way home. It was less than three miles from the furniture shop to their apartment, ten or fifteen minutes by bike past Cardona's Market, through the park, and through the corner of "Little Mexico." Jacob's bicycle had precious little tread left on either tire, so it did not surprise him when the rear wheel went flat soon after he entered the south entrance to the park. It was a cool, cloudy evening, cool enough that he did not expect to see another living soul as he walked his bike toward the opposite entrance.

Jacob knew every inch of the park. It was here he jogged and here he played with Molly almost every afternoon on the playground. Here he, Ann, and Molly had enjoyed many Saturday picnics and Sunday morning strolls, now and during the years they lived in the married-student housing nearby. They had flown their homemade kites in the open grass in the spring and played in piles of yellow and orange leaves under the trees in the fall.

Two main walkways diverged shortly beyond the south entrance and rejoined again across the park at the north entrance. Jacob would normally have automatically taken the shorter, safer, and more level east-side route between the open grass and tennis courts, but tonight he suddenly found himself on the west pathway, puzzled and even a little angry at himself for not paying closer attention to where he was going. It wasn't too late to turn back, yet he continued down through the grove of hedge maples that sheltered countless metal benches and tables where, in the summer, throngs from the surrounding neighborhoods— especially those without the luxury of air-conditioning— gathered for cool refuge from the afternoon heat.

The grove was deserted and it was now dark. A one-way road traversed the north corner of the park just beyond the grove. A narrow turnout at the road's lowest point permitted cars to drop off passengers. As Jacob began his descent into the trees, a single flash of light to the north betrayed the presence of a car approaching the turnout. Without that flash of light, Jacob would never have known the car was there. The road was a good hundred yards from the main path, and the grove was so thick there that even without the leaves on the trees, during the light of day cars could enter and exit entirely unobserved. It was a very secluded spot, and Jacob well imagined the car's purpose in being there.

As he continued along the path into the grove, Jacob felt himself strangely drawn to the idea of the car parked in the turnout. He could not imagine why he was so curious. It was totally uncharacteristic and illogical. He was eager to get home. He had called from the shop to let Ann know he was on his way. The flat tire meant at least a fifteen-minute delay. It wasn't the first time the old bike had failed him, and Ann would assume the obvious, but any further delay would certainly worry her. It was therefore totally irrational, even absurd, to now find himself off the path walking fast—almost running—toward the turnout.

The ground was still damp and soft from yesterday's rain. The car's lights went out. The sense of urgency that impelled him was frightening. He felt his heart pound in his temples as he leaned his bike against a tree. He ran the last fifty yards as fast as the darkness permitted through the thickest part of the grove. From his angle of approach, he could easily see the car without himself being seen.

As he stepped from behind the trunk of one of the massive plane trees that lined the turnout, Jacob recognized the red Jaguar immediately, even without the HENDRICKS spelled out on the personalized rear license plate. He also knew instantly who was inside. In the afternoons, while watching Molly play on the park's playground, he had occasionally seen his former boss's son, Dave, strolling hand-in-hand or arm-in-arm with a tall, attractive, and well-proportioned redheaded coed. They were a striking couple. Even the most happily married man could hardly help but admire the anatomy of the smiling, slender, auburn-haired beauty who was obviously very much in love with his former pupil.

Jacob had at first been surprised to see them there since there were two other parks in the city much more convenient to the university and much more befitting the Hendricks's social station. But given Dave's Don Juan reputation, Jacob understood easily the reason for the otherwise irrelevant choice.

Something else about the girl was particularly unsettling to him: her modest manner of dress, temperate use of make-up, and the unassuming way she carried herself betrayed a wholesomeness that seemed uncomfortably out of place with what Jacob imagined were Dave's intentions. But it seemed now, given the context of the current circumstances, that Jacob had wholly misjudged her.

He stood about twenty feet behind the car, slightly to the passenger side. He could see that the driver's-side door was wide open. There was a dim light on inside the car, and he thought he could make out the outline of one head protruding above the seats. The car moved slightly on its springs, reflecting a changing in position of the occupants inside.

It was now crystal clear to him that he had no business being there. He felt silly, embarrassed, and angry with himself for giving in to his curiosity. Yet, he knew that it wasn't curiosity alone that had drawn him there. He was confused and frustrated, and hoped he could quickly find his bike in the dark, but he now realized that he had no idea where he had left it. Ann must be frantic by now. He turned to leave but had taken only a few steps when he recalled that the door on the passenger's side was slightly open. An idea of what that partially open door might mean now entered his mind in the same way he had experienced the night of his first prayer. Like then, it had come from outside himself and not from within, as if it were not his own thoughts but something that was being communicated to him from somewhere or someone else.

He turned again, ran quickly to the car, and without thinking flung open the passenger-side door. The first thing he saw, illuminated by the dim light of the door panel, was one of the girl's eyes looking up at him through a mass of long red hair that had been pushed over her head, an eye filled with terror and tears, pleading for help.

Dave had reacted to the open door by reaching to close it. In an instant, Jacob had him by the hair and had pulled him over the girl through the door. One blow from his knee to Dave's face was all that was needed. Dave lay face down and unconscious on the ground. Jacob had reacted without thinking and had both of Dave's arms cocked behind his back. He was almost sure he had broken one of them.

It had all happened in a matter of seconds. Jacob remembered something he had seen once in a movie and quickly took off Dave's shoes, pulled out the laces, and used one to tie Dave's arms together behind his back and the other to tie his feet together. The girl had left the car and put on her jacket and her glasses. One lens was broken. She was standing a few feet away from them. Jacob looked up at her. She was crying. Despite the darkness, he could also see that her lower lip was bleeding. When he stood up, she instinctively took one step backward. She was shaking violently, and Jacob realized that he was shaking, too.

"Are you all right?" he asked, not knowing what else to say.

"I don't know…I think so…thank you so much. If you hadn't come—" she quickly put her hands over her mouth and nose and took a very shaky, deep breath.

Dave was coming to and had turned on his side.

"I wouldn't move if I were you," Jacob warned, "and keep your mouth shut."

To Jacob's surprise, the girl stepped forward and kicked Dave hard in the stomach. "That's for breaking my glasses," she said.

Jacob's weak smile prompted a like response.

"I'm sorry. That wasn't very ladylike…I'm not feeling much like a lady. But thanks to you," she paused and took another deep breath, "thanks to you, I'm still something else."

Jacob nodded. He was pleased he had not misjudged her after all.

The girl sighed hard again, fighting to control her shaking so she could better speak. Another two deep breaths through her nose did the trick.

"I've seen you," she said, "in the playground with a little girl. My name is Camille, Camille Harrison."

"I'm Jacob," he answered, stepping toward her and awkwardly offering his hand. "Jacob Kikkert, and my daughter's name is Molly."

"Really?" Camille answered. "Molly's a great name. Are you married? I'm sorry," she quickly added. "I'm much too nosy, but you did save me from a fate, well, a fate worse than death. I think God sent you."

Jacob pondered for a moment. "Yes, I guess He did," he said thoughtfully. "My wife's name is Ann."

"Really?" she said again. "Um…that's a pretty name too."

There was a long uncomfortable pause.

"What do we do now?" she asked.

"Well," sighed Jacob, "I suggest we roll lover-boy Dave here over and—"

"You know him?" Camille interrupted, surprised.

"Yeah. I used to tutor him. It's a long story. I suggest we put him in the backseat and take a ride down to the police station. I've always wanted to drive one of these things."

Camille hesitated and then looked at him hopefully.

"Please…Jacob, I trust you. You were listening to God when I wasn't, but I'd rather not get back into that car if it's all the same to you."

Jacob was impressed by how quickly she had regained her composure.

"I've got a better idea," she continued. "Why not lock him in the trunk and tell the police where they can find him. We can call from the pay phone at the entrance."

Jacob smiled and nodded. This young lady was proving to be as clever as she was beautiful.

"All right, but I've got to call my wife first," he added, both because it was true and because he thought it would reassure her that she was safe with him. "She's probably worried sick. If she hasn't loaned the car to the neighbors, she can come and get us."

It was no easy task, but once Dave was locked in the trunk of the car, they quickly found Jacob's bike and hurried to the park's north entrance. Their haste did not allow for much conversation, but by the time they reached the pay phone, Camille had persuaded Jacob not to call the police. Doing so, she convinced him, would precipitate a series of inconveniences that would unnecessarily complicate her life. She suggested instead that they call Dave's parents. Jacob half grinned as he imagined the possibilities. Who better than Mr. and Mrs. Hendricks to open the trunk of their son's car? He readily agreed.

The call to Dave's parents would have to wait. They had only one quarter between them and no phone card. Jacob's call home found Ann worried but still calm. She had not come looking for him because she had loaned the car to Carmen.

"It's a very long story, Ann," Jacob said. "I'm bringing someone home with me. She'll help explain."

"She?" asked Ann.

"Her name's Camille, and she needs a little first aid and a ride home."

"Do you want me to call Luis to come and get you?"

"No, it'll be just as fast if we walk. We'll be there in twenty minutes."

During those twenty minutes, Camille and Jacob became fast friends. Jacob remembered something Ann had told him once, something her grandmother had told her: "If you want someone to be your friend, you must let him or her do something for you." Well, he had certainly done something for Camille. Perhaps this was why he felt so comfortable with her, as if they had been friends for a long time. She was bright, gracious, wholesomely principled, and much like Ann in other aspects of her character. He wasn't sure why it was so important to him, but he genuinely hoped that she and Ann would become good friends so their association might continue.

A very curious Ann greeted them at the door, with Molly standing shyly behind her. After the necessary introductions were given and received, Ann offered to take Camille's jacket. Her perplexed reaction to Jacob and Camille's mutual quick glance and smile prompted Jacob to forgo any further formalities.

"Camille needs to make a phone call right away," he explained, and then he turned his attention to Camille. "You can use the phone in the kitchen."

"Do you have an extension?" Camille asked, hopefully. "You don't need to say anything, but I'd feel better if you listened in. You, too, Ann."

"Of course. We have a portable phone in the bedroom." Jacob nodded. "If you're sure you want us to."

"I do, please," Camille responded.

"Molly," Jacob crouched down to face his daughter. "I'm afraid this call that Camille is going to make is for grown-up ears only. If you'll go play in your room for a few minutes, I'll take you and Mom with me when I take Camille home, and we can stop for ice cream. Maybe you can show Camille your dolls. Why don't you go get them ready?"

Molly was clinging bashfully to her mother's leg, but her eyes had been riveted on Camille from the beginning. Her large dark curls bounced up and down as she nodded her agreement. Camille's wink prompted a timid smile, and Molly ran into her bedroom and closed the door behind her.

"She's not normally so shy," explained Ann.

"She's beautiful," Camille responded.

The Hendrickses were home. Camille was polite but unambiguous and to the point, with just enough expression of emotion in her voice to maintain the gravity of the situation. Jacob felt sorry for Mr. Hendricks. He was a good man who deserved better.

Ann listened wide-eyed and open-mouthed, glancing often at her husband and squeezing his hand as she heard of his hero's role in the adventure. She bit her lower lip so as not to laugh out loud as Camille explained that Dave was locked in the trunk and that the keys were under the front seat, and she smiled with pursed lips and nodded her accord when Camille insisted that Dave never try to contact her again.

Dave's parents were understandably concerned for their son's safety but also properly apologetic and grateful that Camille had not called the police and would not press charges. They promised she would never see him again.

As Camille talked and they listened, Jacob pondered the amazing coincidence of it all. It seemed even too far-fetched for fiction. He would never dare suggest anything so improbable in his novel. He thought only momentarily about possible repercussions, but they really didn't matter. He could never go back to technical writing, so any possible enmity that might come from all this between him and the Hendrickses was irrelevant. He had done the right thing, and he would live conscience-free with the consequences.

Jacob watched Ann gently dress Camille's cut lip and scraped cheek with antibiotic cream, and then, while the two women chose a T-shirt for Camille to wear under her buttonless shirt, he escaped with his notebook into the bedroom to write down a few things while they were still fresh in his mind.

Chapter Eleven

"I think you oughtta go," Jed urged. "Don't be worryin' 'bout the window. You can finish whenever you get back, and I'll be happy to teach your lesson next Sunday."

"I'll be back on the twenty-eighth," Annabelle assured him, "but if you think it needs to be up before then, I can come back Friday night and work on it all day Saturday."

"No, no, Annabelle. There's no rush. You take all the time you need. I'll put up a sign. The kids'll understand. You enjoy yourself and give everyone my love."

It was decided. The Thanksgiving display in the store would stay up a few days longer this year. The Christmas display would have to wait until she came back. Annabelle was sure that Susan would be ecstatic when she learned she was coming. She had tried to convince her for weeks, but Annabelle had insisted she couldn't. She had always spent the greater part of the Friday and Saturday after Thanksgiving in McCallaway's store; the children expected to see the new display when they walked to school on

Monday, and she had told Susan that she could not let them down. But Annabelle ached to see her family, to be physically in their presence, to delight with them in their family holiday traditions, and had decided she could not wait until Christmas. She debated for several days and had finally called Jed. She had the money. There was really no reason for not going, except the store. The children would just have to be patient; that was all there was to it. She had already checked on flights. There were plenty of seats on the late flight on Monday. Tomorrow, she would give Susan the good news when she called.

Annabelle wasn't much for talking on the phone; she preferred writing and receiving letters. Still, Susan called her every Sunday night just so they could all hear her voice and she theirs. But important discussions, like the ongoing dialogue between Camille and her grandmother, were reserved for weekly letters.

Annabelle read Camille's letters over and over, and for several weeks she had noted a change in her granddaughter's mood. She seemed uncertain, distracted, and at times even distant; and Annabelle believed that there was meaning hidden between the lines that could only be uncovered through good old-fashioned face-to-face communication. Missing her family was the reason she had given Jed for her Thanksgiving trek east, but her real motivation was the nagging feeling that Camille needed her.

Annabelle did not worry without good reason. Though she was by nature inclined to vigilance, she had long ago concluded that fretting over those things she could not control was a waste of valuable mental energy, and had learned to replace worry with faith and trust in God. Susan was the worrywart of the family, a trait inherited from her father. Andrew had much the opposite inclination, and it was at his request that Annabelle once wrote a poem on the subject. Andrew memorized its repeated refrain and used it often to let Susan know when she was pushing the limits. Annabelle recalled its verses now as she wondered if perhaps she was being overly concerned about her granddaughter.

Worry, Worry, Worry
(for Susan)

Worry, worry, worry:
prosperity's disease.
Those who fret and worry
are so difficult to please.
Some call it depression,
others say it's stress.
Call it what you want to,
it's worry nonetheless.
It seems, in their abundance,
some soon begin to fear
that all that makes life happy
may change or disappear.
Who gives you all your blessings?
From whence your gain or wealth?
What is your source of happiness?
Who grants you strength or health?

The opposite of worry
is faith in God above;
it's confidence that He is there
and guides your life with love.
What cause have you to worry
if you are in His care?
Or do you doubt His wisdom
or His power to answer prayer?
Perhaps you think what's best for you
is not within His plan.
The truth is He will guide you home;
just do the best you can.
Now, I don't think that worry
will drag you down to hell;
but if you're full of worry,
you'll never do as well
as when your soul is full of faith,
your heart contrite and meek.
To minds bogged down in worry,
God's Spirit cannot speak.
And if because of worry
His message can't get through,
how can you know your purpose
or the good that you can do?
Worry, worry, worry;
it's prosperity's disease.
Those who fret and worry
are impossible to please.
Some call it depression,
others say it's stress.

Call it what you want to,
it's worry nonetheless.

Annabelle seldom changed her poems once she had inked their final version on the gray cotton parchment paper she had ordered especially for that purpose. She had taken several classes to learn calligraphy and had her own unique style. But with "Worry, worry, worry," after several weeks of gathering dust in the parlor desk drawer, waiting for Susan to move it to its place in the collection, she discovered an important error as she recited it one morning in the garden, a single three-letter word repeated in the second and fourth lines of the fourth stanza, an oversight that gave rise to possible misinterpretation. The original version read:

> Who gives you all your blessings?
> From whence your gain and wealth?
> What is your source of happiness?
> Who grants you strength and health?

She scolded herself for being so careless and wondered why she had failed to note the discrepancy during the long process of its composition. She rewrote the verses to read:

> Who gives you all your blessings?
> From whence your gain or wealth?
> What is your source of happiness?
> Who grants you strength or health?

Life had taught her over and over again that God does not always give material wealth to those who follow Him, but He blesses them in other ways that are not so self-evident. As they strive in faith to live their lives by the example of His Son, each day brings spiritual gain and growth, even though that growth sometimes comes through adversity.

In like manner, God sometimes withholds blessings of good health from those who love and serve Him; yet He never abandons them. He gives them the strength necessary to overcome or endure life's disappointments and challenges. In the process, they grow a little here and a little there, precept upon precept and line upon line. By humbly accepting and striving to do God's will, their weaknesses eventually become strengths. Living had taught her that bad things often happen to good people, but Annabelle believed and taught her children and grandchildren that there was purpose in all things, and it was her faith that God's view was perfect, broader and higher than her own, that had sustained and would sustain her in whatever burden she was required to bear.

Annabelle's faith had passed the test of life. She fervently believed that all men and women are spiritual children of God, sent to earth to grow, to experience mortality, and to learn how to love and find joy in personal relationships. In short, all are here to prepare for a happy and glorious resurrection that will once again unite body and spirit, husband and wife, and parent and child in an eternal world where the reasons for why things are as they are and happen as they do will at last be made manifest. She trusted that a loving Heavenly Father knew her far better than she knew herself. This was the bedrock on which she had built the foundation of her faith, and her desire to communicate that faith with those she loved was the catalyst for all that she did and the primary motivating force behind her poetry. For this once shy, bashful girl who had seen much of living, poetry was the missing ingredient, the component that refined and organized all the other aspects of her personality.

Before she discovered her penchant for poetry, Annabelle's inability to assert herself in conversation often left her at a disadvantage in social circumstances. But she had come to terms with and adapted to the limitations imposed by her personality. She was reservedly but congenially conversant with her neighbors, the good people of her ward congregation, and the parents who came with their children to pick pumpkins. Congeniality was enough. Intimate friendships and personal relationships outside her family had never really interested her. Still, before she discovered her gift for writing poetry, she was often frustrated by her inability to communicate in candid conversation with those she loved. God had given her a life of experience and a depth of faith and understanding that she longed to share with those whom He had placed within her influence. She was most troubled when her shyness kept her from acting on what she knew were the promptings of Deity, the whisperings of the Spirit urging her to say what she intuitively sensed others needed to hear.

It always seemed, in her conversations with those closest to her, that she was always the designated listener. It had always been that way, ever since she was a child. Even her maiden name was a reflection of her unassertive personality: Samantha Annabelle Gray, Anonymous Annabelle, her father affectionately called her. Others talked and Annabelle listened, and though she filled her passive role well—Annabelle was an extremely good listener—she wanted to do more. She knew she was capable of a much more active and vocal role in the lives of her family. Her Primary classes were concrete proof. There, she was expected to do most of the talking, and she was an excellent teacher, but her family expected something different, and try as she may, she could never break out of the mold that had been cast for her. Never, that is, until her family discovered that their mother and grandmother was a gifted poet.

Now things were quite different, and Annabelle no longer wished she could be more like her daughter and granddaughter: gregarious, confident, and assured even among strangers. She was grateful to be who she was and that God had given her a medium by which she could circumvent her weakness and be a force for good in the lives of those He had given her. Poetry was the medium of her faith and her access to the minds and hearts of her family. Her greatest joy was watching Susan or Camille at the parlor desk reading and pondering one of her poems, and she felt her heart leap in her chest each time Camille asked her to recite a particular poem during their walks in the canyon or their chores in the yard and garden. As the years passed, her poetry gained for her an ever-growing respect and credibility in the minds of her family, and they not only listened intently when she had something to say but also regularly sought her opinion and counsel. Her poetry had also increased her confidence that she could be more than just a good listener, and she was.

Annabelle sang softly as she meticulously wrapped the box containing the red satin high-collar dress that might well be the last she would make to adorn Camille's Molly Ann. She could wait and bring it with her when she came for Christmas, but its rightful place was under the family tree, the tree that tradition dictated would go up the day after Thanksgiving. The dress had been ready to box and wrap since the end of August but had lain undisturbed—except for the weekly dusting—on the piano in the parlor for any visitors to praise and admire. The piano now seemed naked without it—how she wished Susan were there to play—and she placed the wrapped package exactly where the dress had been before.

Her original thought was to put the poem she had written for Camille in an envelope and tie it with the same silver ribbon that garnished the glossy green and red wrapping paper, then put it on top of the dress inside the package. But Annabelle was glad she had sent the poem early, and she was eager to hear Camille's response when she saw her on Monday. Still, she would have liked to have included a poem with the dress inside the same package, and the thought struck her unexpectedly as her fingers played with the ribbon: perhaps there was still enough time; perhaps she could write another in time for Christmas.

"Perhaps I'll begin right now," she said aloud.

It was still early and she had nothing better to do. Her Primary lesson was prepared. She had promised to make cookies for tomorrow night's fireside, but she would make them right after meetings so they would be as fresh as possible. The novel she was reading had turned out to be a disappointment—Jed had picked a real loser this time. She was reading it now only to finish what she had started.

Annabelle sat down at the parlor desk, opened the drawer, and took out a clean sheet of paper and a pencil. With the eraser end of the pencil firmly between her lips, she gazed for a few moments at the package, at the piano, and at Paul's photograph of the church steeple on the wall above. Annabelle often used ordinary objects in her poetry to communicate spiritual truths. Perhaps the wrapped package on the piano had something to teach her. She recalled nostalgically the memory of four-year-old Susan kneeling at the piano bench, wrapping objects she had gathered from around the house. She smiled as she recalled the hope in her daughter's eyes as she proudly presented her gifts in anticipation of the expressions of surprise and patronizing "thank yous" always given in exchange. She began to write.

The words flowed almost effortlessly through the pencil to the white paper parchment. Only twice before had she completed a poem in one sitting. She labored over most for days, even weeks, allowing the verses to come at their own pace, in their own time. But tonight was different, and as the ideas became words and the words became poetry, Annabelle knew that the words she was writing were not entirely her own. She knew God's Spirit was with her and that this poem had a special purpose.

Only once did she pause with the thought that she should stop and go to bed, reasoning that an old woman needed her sleep, that tomorrow was going to be a busy day. But she dared not break the wonderful spell, and on she mused and on she wrote, propelled by a sense of urgency she could not explain. Eight hours later the writing was complete. She marveled at its length; she marveled at its message. Not in her wildest dreams had she imagined she could write with such passion and with such remarkable ease. She read it over and over again but changed nothing.

Not Mine, But Thine

My youngest daughter just turned four,
and from her party gained much more
than gifts received from guests and host;
the joy of giving touched her most.
So now to earn my praise she sits
and wraps for me all sorts of gifts:
crayons and ribbons, toys that wind,
most anything that she can find.
Trinkets, pencils, pens, wrench sockets,
keys and coins fished from my pockets,
all wrapped in newsprint, tied with twine,
she gives me what's already mine.
Her picture book, her pretty doll,
and other things I well recall,
hoping my favor to assure,

she gives me things I've given her.
I keep them on my shelf awhile.
My lavish "thank yous" bring a smile
of faith in my parental knack
for knowing when to give them back.
Quite oft the things our small ones do
remind us we are children too.
Our gifts to them help us recall
that Heavenly Father gives us all.
When to the Lord I give a tenth
of all the blessings He has sent,
my time, my wealth, what ere it is,
I give Him what's already His.
And every gift I have to give
is likewise given me. I live
each day and praise Him who in love
metes out His blessings from above.
If I of my abundance share
or of my lack my tithe still spare,
through heaven's windows, He will pour
a bounty far beyond my store.
The alms we leave at heaven's door,
in time, return to us with more
than we can ever hope repay;
our debt to Him grows day by day.
And those of us who vainly boast,
because we think we give the most,
should sore repent, for in His sight,
He treasures more the widow's mite.
My children's gifts, in time, mature;

their trust, their love unfeigned and pure,
their gratitude for lessons learned,
they give, but still, it's all returned.
What have we then to offer Him
who fills our cup far past its brim?
What can I give? What does He lack
that He can never give me back?
It must be something He desires,
a gift to which a God aspires,
a priceless pearl, so fine, so fair,
He'd never let it leave His care.
Dear Father, that one gift I own,
one thing that's mine, and mine alone,
I freely give, as Thou to me,
for Thine to keep eternally.
That gift for which Thou dost most yearn,
an offering Thou canst not return,
I give Thee, Father, God divine:
my free will Lord, not mine, but Thine.

Annabelle took her calligraphy pens and inkwell from the middle drawer, then several sheets of the gray cotton parchment that held the ink so well. She copied the poem carefully. While the ink dried she knelt at the piano and said her evening prayer. She had much to be grateful for. When she finished, she stood slowly. Old age had been very good to her; she hoped she could always kneel in prayer. She only then glanced at the clock on the shelf. It was 3:50 A.M. She would have guessed it was no later than midnight and again marveled at what she had done. She had never written continuously for such a long period. She folded the sheets of parchment carefully, sealed them in a matching envelope, and tied it with the same silver ribbon that garnished Camille's Christmas package. If she was careful, she could remove the tape and not tear the glossy green and red paper—the paper she had ordered from the children raising funds for the PTA (Annabelle's meticulously wrapped packages showed no tape on the outside). A few minutes later, she gently placed the envelope inside on top of the red satin dress, then carefully rewrapped the box and placed it back on the piano. Camille's gift was now complete and ready for Christmas.

Chapter Twelve

Ann glanced stealthily at her watch. Mr. Lambert might well be spying from the one-way window he had had installed in his office above the checkout aisles. She did not want to give him further reason to censor or insult her.

During her last break, she had climbed the stairs to ask if she could leave an hour early. She had felt dizzy several times that afternoon and evening, her head hurt, she was constantly thirsty, and she was taking frequent mini-breaks to go to the rest room—she wondered if she had a bladder infection. Tomorrow she would see Dr. Oquendo. She was glad Jacob had made the appointment, even though she had objected. Mr. Cardona would have sent her home immediately, probably even driven her himself; but Mr. Lambert showed her no sympathy.

"If you'd concentrate on your work instead of watching the clock all the time and thinking about your next break," he scolded, pointing his pudgy little finger at her, "maybe you wouldn't have a headache." His breath was nauseating, and Ann took a defensive step backward toward the door and brought her hand to her nose, an obvious affront that only fueled his anger.

"I have a lot of customers in the store tonight," he continued indignantly. "If I let *you* leave, *they* have to wait in line longer. My customers are more important than your silly little headache. Take some aspirin. You can leave when your shift is over."

"I'll take some aspirin if you'll use some mouthwash," she had been tempted to say, but had not. She had also been tempted, as she angrily descended the stairs, to keep on walking right out the door; and she had spent the last fifty minutes wishing she had. She felt awful. Her mouth was dry, she ached all over, and her light-headedness continued, but with only ten minutes left on her shift, she was glad she had stuck it out. She was sure Dr. Oquendo would find nothing seriously wrong with her—it was probably a minor virus or infection—but whatever it was, she planned to ask him for a note that she could present to Mr. Lambert. He had behaved badly, and she wanted vindication.

Ann placed Mr. Andrade's bag into the shopping cart. He was a regular customer, a smiling, frail, elderly gentleman who always made it a point to go through Ann's checkout line, even if it meant waiting a few extra minutes.

"Thank you, Ann," he said cheerfully.

"Thank *you*, Mr. Andrade. Have a nice evening, and say hello to Mrs. Andrade for me. I hope she feels better soon."

As soon as Mr. Andrade had turned away from her toward the exit, Ann pressed her middle fingers hard against the inside corners of her closed eyes then moved them in unison across her eyelids to her temples and pressed even harder. Just five minutes to go, and luckily, there were no other customers in line or anywhere near the front of the store.

"Are you okay, Ann?" asked Ramona from the next check stand. "You really look awful. Go ahead and leave. I'll take the next one."

Ann quickly scanned the store for possible customers and then glanced up involuntarily at Mr. Lambert's window.

"Thanks, Ramona. You're an angel. I owe you."

As quickly as she could, she pulled the cord across the aisle, turned off the light, closed her cash register, took off her apron, and grabbed her coat and wallet from under the counter. She was supposed to wait until Monica came to relieve her, and she was quite sure Mr. Lambert was watching, but she was too ill to care. Maybe she could be out of the store before he had time to get his fat little body out of his chair and down the stairs. She was wrong; he met her at the exit. His mood hadn't changed.

"And where do you think you're going? How dare you? You haven't been relieved yet!" he panted. The trip down the stairs had winded him.

"I'm sorry, sir," Ann explained as she veered around him, with a trace of contempt in her voice she could not hide, "but I'm just too sick to care."

"Then don't bother coming back!" he called after her, the higher pitch in his voice betraying his anger. "You're fired! Did you hear me? You're fired!"

Ann didn't stop to argue. Though she thought the words she wanted to say, she did not say them. She only wanted to get home as quickly as possible. The fresh and cooler outside air felt good in her sinuses and lungs as she hurried to her car. It had stopped raining, and even though it was cold, she had not bothered to put on the coat that she now tossed on the seat beside her. When the seat belt failed to respond to her first pull, she let it go and turned on the ignition, the windshield wipers—but only briefly to clear off the remnants of an earlier downpour—and then the lights.

"Okay, so I'm fired. What are we going to do now?" she mumbled to herself as she pulled out of the parking lot.

"We'll figure out something," she thought, as she accelerated into the left lane. The market's insurance was obligated to carry them for thirty days. Surely she would find another job before then. She was surprised at her own lack of emotion. She actually felt relieved to be free of that awful place and vowed never to go back, even to shop. Strange how a place that had once felt like a second home had become so loathsome to her. It wasn't worth her tears.

Her mind turned quickly to more pleasant matters. Just that morning, Jacob had offered a wonderful prayer. Each time he took his turn, it was all she could do to keep from crying with joy. Her experience and her instincts told her not to rush Jacob's spiritual growth. He was, after all, only a child spiritually, so she tried hard not to overly manifest the emotion she felt. His character required a calmer and more disciplined approach. She knew that he would someday face a trial of his faith—all who love God do—and she prayed that he would be prepared.

Ann knew he was content with how things were progressing with his novel, and she did not want to distract him by any undue concern for her health, so she had done all she could to keep her increasing fatigue and lack of energy from him. After all, she was sure it was nothing serious. In the evening, after her shift at the market, she did everything possible to conceal her weariness while the three of them held their evening devotional before tucking Molly into bed. Jacob took his turn reading from Ann's grandmother's Bible, and Ann's heart was full. But while Jacob told Molly her bedtime story, Ann, totally exhausted, would quickly get herself ready and climb into bed; it was a struggle for her to stay awake until Jacob came in to kiss her good night before resuming his writing.

Tonight Jacob was working late again with Tony and Luis. He had fixed his bike last night, but Luis would bring him home because of the rain. They might already be there. Carmen was staying with Molly. She knew that Ann wasn't feeling well and had insisted that she let her fix dinner.

"But we've invited our new friend over," Ann had told her.

"All the more reason I should do the cooking," joked Carmen. "Besides, with all the work at the shop, I know Tony won't let Jacob off any earlier than he has to. Don't you worry about a thing. I'll have it all ready by the time you get home so you can eat right away," she promised, "and if your guest arrives early, Molly and I will be the perfect hostesses. *¿No es verdad, Molly?*"

The bounce of Molly's curls could not keep up with her rapid-fire nodding. She was very excited.

It had been Molly's idea to invite Camille for dinner as they drove her home Saturday evening. Camille did not hesitate in accepting. She and Molly had genuinely taken to each other, and Ann was glad they had.

"Don't forget to bring what you promised," Molly reminded Camille as they dropped her off in front of her house.

"I won't, Molly," Camille pledged.

It was to remain their secret. Neither Ann nor Jacob had been able to coax Molly into telling.

Although she felt weak and tired, Ann was looking forward to the rest of the evening. She had had mixed feelings about Camille. There was no denying that she liked her; she liked her very much. Neither was there any doubt that God had purpose in their meeting; what that purpose might be, only time would tell. Ann was thrilled that Jacob had been led to save her. She knew that every experience he had with the Spirit would make him stronger and increase his faith. If Camille became the family friend it seemed she was destined to be, she would be a welcome reminder to Jacob—to all of them—that God indeed watches over and intercedes in the lives of His children.

Camille would also be a wonderful influence on young Molly. They could not have asked for a better role model. Yet, in spite of all the apparent good that had come and could come from this new relationship, in spite of the evidence that God himself had willed Camille into their lives, Ann could not ignore the fact that Camille was stunningly beautiful, young, and vibrant. The truth was that Ann's declining health had left her feeling much the contrary and vulnerable to occasional thoughts of connubial inadequacy.

Saturday evening, as she and Jacob lay in bed and she listened to him recount the details of his adventure with Dave, Camille, and the Spirit from his perspective, Ann chided herself sharply for harboring even the slightest of suspicions. She did not doubt Jacob's faithfulness. Natural feminine inclination was no excuse. The seeds of jealousy and rivalry that she was sure Camille's beauty would sow in even the most confident of feminine egos had fallen on infertile ground. Ann, however, had nevertheless allowed them to fall, and she scolded herself for letting it taint her opinion of someone whom she otherwise much admired and who she hoped would become a cherished friend.

Ann had always wanted a sister. Since her grandmother's death, she had been without the comfort of close female companionship and conversation. Jacob's sisters were pleasant, but not one of them believed as she did, and all were wrapped up in their own lives. The discovery that Camille's religious beliefs and moral values were so much like her own had awakened in her a repressed longing for female friendship. She imagined that had her own parents lived, her family experience would have been much like Camille's.

Camille had been the main topic of conversation last night at the Rodriguezes. Sunday evenings were the highlight of the week for the Kikkerts and for the Rodriguezes too, whose large extended family had adopted Jacob, Ann, and Molly. These weekly Sunday get-togethers had taken place as long as any of the current Rodriguez clan could remember. Luis and Tony, their mother Carmen, Tony's wife Laura, and their three children—including Molly's best friend, Rosita—Raúl and Mariluz Cardona— Raúl was Carmen's brother—their daughter Angela, and her husband David were almost always there too. Others came, but less regularly. For the first several Sundays, they took turns interpreting for Ann, and they politely spoke to her in English, but no one bothered to interpret now. They had quickly discovered that she understood almost everything they said, and although she was hesitant at first to say much, the love and friendship she felt there soon erased any language or cultural differences that might have discouraged her. Now, whenever she had something to say, she would say it in a spontaneous mixture of English and Spanish that delighted everyone, especially Jacob, who was proud of his wife's uninhibited efforts to learn Spanish.

Ann had never known the joy and pleasures of having parents and siblings, let alone cousins, aunts, and uncles. She had always longed to be part of a united and loving extended family and had been disappointed by the relative restraint and ceremony of her relationship with her in-laws, and especially with her sisters-in-law. So it hadn't taken her long at all to fit right in with the amicable Rodriguezes. She reveled in the candor and integrity of their conversation and in their good-natured teasing. She was charmed by the deference, even chivalry, shown by the Rodriguez men and by the reverence and respect willfully given to patriarchal and matriarchal authority. There were no generation or gender gaps when it came to their kindness and courtesy. These were good people in every sense of the word, and the Kikkerts thanked God each day in their family and personal prayers for the love and positive influence of good friends.

Ann was feeling much better now that she was on her way home and had replaced her ill thoughts toward Mr. Lambert with kinder ones. Just one more intersection ahead on the main road—the light had turned yellow and she would have to stop—a turn to the left, then four blocks on to their apartment. Her brisk walk to her parked car and the adrenaline her anger had primed had combined to mask the warning her body was sending her. It started to rain again, very hard. She turned on the windshield wipers and the left turn signal, and then reached across her body for the seat belt that in her haste and anger had remained unlatched.

There was no warning, no chance to stop and pull to the side of the road; only a sudden sense of numbness, then a total loss of consciousness, and Ann fell forward against the steering wheel, her foot still heavy on the accelerator.

Chapter Thirteen

"I don't think you know where you're going," accused Mark wryly from the passenger seat. "I hope we find it before it starts raining again."

"I know what I did wrong," answered Camille. "I should have turned at the last light, that's all. We'll just go to the park and start from there."

She had not paid close attention to their route two nights earlier when Jacob, Ann, and Molly had driven her home, but she knew she could retrace the route she and Jacob had taken on foot from the park entrance. As they drove past the pullout, she smiled as she imagined what might have happened when Dave's father opened the trunk of the Jaguar, but her smile was short-lived as she also pondered what might have been had God not seen fit to intercede by sending Jacob to her rescue.

She glanced at her doll—she had dressed her in her favorite outfit, the green dress with off-white lace—and then at the carnations she had purchased for Ann, both lying on the seat between them, and she forced her reflection to the more pleasant events of that memorable weekend. Her smile returned.

Camille had been quite taken with her handsome rescuer. Her knight in shining armor was everything she hoped the man she would someday marry might be: chivalrous, handsome, kind, devoted to his family, and, best of all, prayerful and receptive to the promptings of the Spirit. It was just her luck that he was already married. Not only had he saved her virtue but he had also restored her faith in manhood in the moment that faith had been most vulnerable. She needed the assurance that there really were good men in the world, and Jacob had given it to her.

She had also been delighted with the other members of the family. She was particularly captivated by Ann's deep blue eyes. They were her doll's eyes, and although she did not understand why, she hoped desperately that Ann would accept her as her friend. She had likewise marveled at another similarity, by how much little Molly's hair was like the doll's, whose name both she and her mother shared

Carmen had returned with the car shortly after she and Jacob had arrived at the apartment, but since Ann had loaned the car to Carmen to use both that evening and the next morning, she had to go upstairs for the keys. This gave Camille a few minutes alone with Molly, who was thrilled with the chance to show off her dolls. They sat together on Molly's bed.

"This one is Ruthie; she's the oldest. This one's name is Katie; she fell and broke her arm. And this one is my favorite. Her name is Nancy. *La abuela* gave her to me."

"They're wonderful, Molly," Camille exaggerated. She was totally smitten. "Maybe someday I can introduce you to my doll."

"What's *her* name?"

"Well, strange as it may seem, her name is Molly Ann."

"Really? I like that name." Molly laughed. "What does she look like?"

"Well, she has beautiful dark curly hair like yours, and a pretty smile and blue eyes like your mother's ("astonishingly like your mother's," she thought). Someday I'll bring her by, if you'd like."

"I'd like that very much," said Molly, nodding excitedly, and she gave Camille an unexpected hug. "You promise?"

"I promise."

Camille hugged her back. She was now even more determined to further foster this new friendship with Jacob, Ann, and Molly, good people who personified her dreams for her own future, and she was glad she now had an excuse to return. Perhaps Molly would be the little sister she had always hoped for. Perhaps the similarities between Ann and Molly and her Molly Ann were far from coincidental.

Her parents had not expected her home from the library so early, and she had made it almost halfway up the squeaking attic stairs before being detected.

"Is that you, Camille?" her father called from the study where he and her mother were reading.

"Yeah, it's me. I'll be down in a minute," she called back.

She changed her clothes, put on her other pair of glasses, gathered her thoughts, and then slowly descended the stairs to talk with her parents. She had wanted to wait until Sunday, but her cut lip and scraped cheek were more than reason enough to not wait. It was the right time too for other reasons. It was late enough that Mark was in bed asleep but early enough not to infringe too much on her parents' bedtime. Besides, she was anxious to have it done with. She would sleep much better with her burden lifted. She took a deep breath and entered the study.

She started crying even before her glance found her mother's eyes. She embraced each of her perplexed parents for several moments before finally controlling her emotion. She signaled for them to sit back down on the love seat under the window, and she moved one of the chairs from the front of her father's desk so that she sat facing them, her knees almost touching theirs.

"Mom and Dad, I love you very much. I know I have your love also," she began. "And I know there's nothing I could do that would cause you to stop loving me. But tonight I need something more than your love; I need your understanding and your forgiveness. I need you to listen. You mustn't interrupt. I've a story to tell you, a story that begins badly but that has a very happy ending."

She told them everything; they listened intently and tenderly. Tears flowed unrestrained down the cheeks of both mother and daughter while masculine eyes held most of them back, but obviously only through great effort. Love was expressed, forgiveness given, and a kneeling prayer of gratitude offered together with her father as voice.

Part One
Chapter Thirteen

Camille slept well that night, free at last from the secret guilt that had alienated her from those she loved, grateful to again be a daughter who had learned well and applied the lessons her parents had tried to teach her, and all the more certain of a Father in Heaven who hears and answers prayers and guides the lives of his children.

Sunday had dawned bright and beautiful. Camille had always found great strength and comfort in sitting with her family in church, and that morning those feelings were intensely magnified. The sacrament was especially meaningful to her, and she listened carefully to the talks and found personal significance in almost everything that was said.

Her father called Jacob early that afternoon and thanked him profusely for what he had done for Camille. Jacob extended Monday night's dinner invitation to the whole family, or to as many as could come. Her father regretfully declined due to an engagement he and her mother were committed to attend. The director of urban forestry was retiring, and a dinner was being held in his honor.

Camille knew that her father was anxious to both meet Jacob and further demonstrate his gratitude, so a date was set for brunch the following Sunday—Thanksgiving leftovers at the Harrisons'. Jacob accepted. That same Sunday evening they would also all attend her mother's concert, the last and most important of the three that the university had scheduled for her. Camille, who was in the study with her father during the call, hanging on his arm and his every word, was thrilled.

"You'll fall in love with all of them from the moment you see them," she promised, "especially Molly. She's so cute, and she and I are practically already sisters."

"Who's Molly?" asked Mark, feeling unfairly left out.

Her family's Sunday-night call to her grandmother ended with great news: She was coming for Thanksgiving—Camille had already dropped the letter she had written that afternoon in the corner mailbox. Although their two separate dinner appointments and only one car required a bit of strategic planning, the whole family would be free to welcome Annabelle at the airport at 11:30 P.M.

So far, all had gone as planned. Camille had dropped her parents off at the restaurant for their dinner at 7:30 so she would have the car. She and Mark were now on their way to the Kikkerts' apartment. They were not expected until 8:30, but they had left early both to buy flowers and to be sure they could find the way. The plan was to leave the Kikkerts' place just before 10:30, then pick up their parents on the way to the airport.

From the park's entrance they continued down the hill along a street lined for several blocks by tidy, well-kept bungalow houses and large mature ash trees, the edge of the large Hispanic neighborhood known to the locals as "little Mexico," even though there were probably more Hispanics of Puerto Rican origin than Mexican living there.

Camille turned to the right and then continued for another three blocks to where the road intersected with the main connector that, if followed to the left, eventually led back to the university. It began to pour again, very hard;

the sound of the rain against the car echoed and amplified inside.

"Wow! Cool!" enthused Mark. "It never rains like this back home."

"Cool, nothing," retorted Camille. "I can hardly see… here's where I should have turned the first time," she explained, as she waited for the light to change. "Another five blocks straight through this intersection and we're there." She looked quickly at the clock on the dash. "And right on time," she added.

The light turned green. She glanced again at Molly Ann and smiled in anticipation—she could hardly wait to see Molly's face when she showed her—then accelerated through the intersection.

Chapter Fourteen

Jacob's mind was seldom idle in the furniture shop. Unlike the sterile, controlled, and unvarying environment of the offices where he had written and edited technical manuals, the converted warehouse where Tony and Luis had set up shop offered an ideal setting for his imagination, an ever-changing stage on which to play out the musings of his creative mind. When it rained, as it was raining now, the sound of the drops beating hard against the metal roof combined with the chorus of electric lathes, saws, presses, planes, and sanders, making it next to impossible to hear anything less than a full shout. The fluorescent lights dimmed slightly at every power surge, and the color of the wood was darker and the grain much less pronounced.

On clear days, natural light poured into the shop from all directions through the multitude of panes partitioning the enormous windows surrounding in serial succession an interior space four times larger than actually needed by its occupants. The grain of the wood seemed to rise to the light, and the lamps that hung low on rusted chains from the ceiling thirty feet above became little more than jealous, useless ornaments.

During the course of the day, Jacob had made copious notes in the spiral notebook that now lay open on the table behind him, but at the moment he was giving his full attention to his work on the lathe. The table leg he was crafting would serve tomorrow as a model for the other three. It was almost finished, and the slightest slip of the gouge could mean starting all over again.

It was near time to close the shop for the day. Tony enforced his hard-and-fast rule: No matter how far behind the shop was in its orders, he never asked nor allowed his employees to work more than four hours of overtime per day and no more than a total of twelve hours overtime per week. Accidents were many times more likely when workers were tired, and in the twelve years the shop had been in operation, there had never been a major mishap—some close calls, yes, but never the loss of life or limb—not counting fingers.

For Jacob, the day had been extremely productive. Ann kept close tabs on the hours that he worked at the shop, but she did not know about the extra cash on top of his hourly wage that Tony had insisted on paying for his unscheduled hours. This cash would go a long way toward the surprises he had planned for Christmas—Jacob had sworn both Tony and Luis to secrecy. But more important than the extra cash was the progress he had made on his novel. Jacob had filled several pages in his notebook with a steady flow of ideas and details. Indeed, the muses had decided that day to take up residency in the underused space of the busy shop. If he had any doubts before about full-time employment there hindering his ability to complete the novel, the success of the day had laid them completely to rest. It confirmed the decision he had already made. It was, he concluded, an answer to his prayers, and he had given Tony the good news as they shared the *empanadas* that Carmen had sent with Jacob for lunch.

The hours had passed quickly. Jacob was in a very good mood. He could hardly wait to tell Ann that her days at the market were over—regardless of what Dr. Oquendo might tell them tomorrow—and he had interrupted his mulling over the novel with occasional reflection on the events of the last several months, and especially those of the last few days. He marveled at their good fortune—their blessings, he corrected himself—he must learn to give credit where it was due.

If not for his concern for Ann's health, life would be just about perfect. Last night Ann and Molly had left the weekly gathering at Carmen's an hour earlier than usual, long before Molly's bedtime—Molly was obedient but not at all happy about leaving.

"I'm not feeling very well. I think I'm catching a cold or something," Ann explained cheerfully. "I'd better get to bed early tonight."

Jacob followed a few minutes later. It was not like Ann to let a little cold take her away from the festive atmosphere that always characterized their Sunday evening get-togethers. He had suspected for several days that Ann was feeling worse than she was letting on, and he watched her eyes even more carefully than usual that evening during their reading and as she prayed and again the following morning for signs of pain or discomfort, but he had seen nothing, and when he asked how she was feeling, she insisted that she felt fine, only a bit tired.

"I think it must be anemia or something," she told him. "I just don't have any energy."

She was probably right. She had had anemia shortly after Molly was born. Though Jacob continued to be troubled by Ann's declining health, he was somehow confident that there was no cause for great alarm.

"Surely," he thought to himself, "God would not have shown us such favor only to now allow Ann to be seriously ill. Of course He'll take care of her. How could He not? Surely no one deserves His blessing more than she."

Ann wanted him to have more faith. "Okay," he thought. "I'll have faith that she will be all right."

Jacob concluded also that their new friendship with Camille and her family must also have a divine purpose. Sunday's call from Camille's father had been an unexpected surprise and pleasure. Although it was only a phone conversation, he had been impressed by Andrew's manner and sincerity. Time would tell, but obviously, the two families had been brought together for a reason. Jacob looked forward to meeting the rest of the family and to seeing God's will take its course.

"Let's close up shop," shouted Tony.

It was no longer raining, but outside it was still dark and overcast. The lights grew progressively brighter as, one by one, the machines slowed and stopped.

Part One
Chapter Fourteen

Jacob put his bike in the back of Luis's pickup. Luis had invited himself to dinner when he heard that Carmen was cooking. He could use a good meal—or so he said. The real reason was obvious. He had heard so much about Camille, especially from Molly, who talked of little else, that he just had to see for himself if anyone could be that beautiful. He fancied himself quite the lady's man.

"Do you think she'd be interested in a handsome Latino carpenter?" he asked, winking at Molly.

"I'm sure she would, but Tony's already married," teased Ann in her improving Spanish.

The route from the shop home by car or truck was much different than by bike. Luis preferred to take a more indirect but quicker route on the boulevard that veered several blocks from the park and then joined the main connector at the intersection by what was once Cardona's Market. Jacob looked at Luis's watch. Ann's shift would end in a few minutes. He smiled; it would be her last. He was glad that he would be making it home before she would, and he checked the parking lot as they approached. He was only a little surprised not to see their old Chevy in its usual spot.

"Isn't that your car?" asked Luis, pointing ahead at the tail lights of a dark green sedan about a hundred yards in front of them in the left lane.

"Yeah, it is," replied Jacob. "She either left early or your watch is fast. Let's see if we can catch her before we turn."

Luis accelerated. They were only a few car lengths behind her when it started to rain again, very hard.

"I can hardly see," complained Jacob. "You could use some new wiper blades."

The light in the intersection where they would both turn left had turned yellow, and Luis eased off the accelerator, but the distance between the two cars lengthened.

"Whoa. Slow down, Ann," said Jacob under his breath.

"She's going to run the light," warned Luis.

Jacob leaned forward to better see through the small area on the windshield that the wiper blade was keeping clear. The light was red, and the distance between the cars continued to grow. He glanced quickly, first to the left, and then to the right. A small white Toyota had started through the intersection.

Jacob strained to judge the distance. His voice trembled as he spoke.

"Please, God, no!"

Chapter Fifteen

Annabelle sat motionless, staring forward through her tears and the rain that had fallen heavily and steadily since they had left the airport. The wiper blades were working furiously, but it was still difficult to see the road ahead.

"We've had a lot of rain lately," Mrs. Jenkins told her. "I'm sorry I can't go any faster. It won't be long now, another five minutes or so."

"This is very kind of you," said Annabelle, glad for Mrs. Jenkins' efforts to break the solemn silence. "I'm grateful Susan and Andrew had someone they could send."

"They've been wonderful neighbors to me. It's the very least I could do. Just Saturday, they cleaned up my yard…we had lunch together, too…they speak of you often. They've shared some of your poetry with me. It's beautiful…you are exactly as I imagined you'd be. I recognized you right away from their description. I made a sign with your name on it, but I didn't need it."

Annabelle had sensed immediately that something was terribly wrong when she saw no familiar faces among the small crowd that had gathered to meet the passengers on her plane. Moments later, a wrinkled and arthritic hand had gently but firmly taken her arm. She looked down into a timeworn but compassion-filled face that confirmed her premonition.

"Mrs. McNeely?"

Annabelle nodded.

"I'm Abigail Jenkins. Andrew asked me to come for you. I'm so sorry. There's been a terrible accident. It's Camille and Mark. I'll take you to the hospital. I've arranged for the airline to deliver your luggage later."

Mrs. Jenkins answered the unspoken question in Annabelle's fearful eyes.

"Mark is going to be fine, but Camille is hurt very badly."

Mrs. Jenkins knew little more about the accident. Andrew had called her from the hospital. She had asked only what she should tell Annabelle.

The remaining few minutes of their drive in the rain passed in silence. Both women were satisfied that enough had been said. Mrs. Jenkins pulled under the covered drop-off area in front of the hospital's emergency entrance.

"Thank you, Abigail," said Annabelle, gently touching her arm before opening the car door.

"God bless you, Annabelle," replied Mrs. Jenkins.

The woman at the information desk directed her to the surgical recovery area on the third floor, where through the series of glass walls behind the nurse station she could see Susan and Andrew together at the side of Camille's bed. Susan was sitting on the bed holding Camille's hand and stroking her arm. Andrew was standing beside her, his right arm wrapped around his wife's shoulders and his left hand holding Camille's doll. Molly Ann was wearing the green dress with the off-white lace, the first of the many Annabelle had made for her. Andrew had left word with the nurse to bring in Annabelle as soon as she arrived.

Susan and Annabelle wept in each other's arms while Andrew sat on the bed in Susan's place, holding his daughter's hand. He too was crying unashamedly.

Camille lay motionless, her head wrapped in bandages; her long red hair had been tied together and lay over her right shoulder. The rest of her body was also covered with gauze and bandages. Only her right arm from her shoulder down had escaped unharmed. Internal damage and head trauma had been extensive. The doctors could do nothing more. They had already informed Susan and Andrew that if Camille lived, she would be paralyzed from the neck down, and there would be extensive brain damage. The decision to remove life support had been made moments before Annabelle's arrival. It was now only a matter of time: a few hours, at most a few days.

As she embraced her daughter and joined her in her sobs, Annabelle thanked God in her heart that she had been prompted to come. She could not imagine not being there for her family when they needed her most. Though she had little to say, her presence alone gave them the strength and comfort of her faith and the assurance of her love and God's love. The trial of her faith twelve years ago at her husband's sudden death had prepared her to now help those she loved through their own trial of faith, and she understood her purpose.

Twenty-five minutes later, Andrew and Susan left the room for a few minutes to check on Mark, who was on the second floor in the intensive care unit, and to allow Annabelle to be alone one last time with her granddaughter. Andrew had laid Molly Ann on the bed beside Camille. Her green dress was spotted with dried blood. The room fell silent as they closed the door. Camille's faint breathing was the only sound to be heard. Annabelle's tears began again as she took Camille's hand and held it first to her lips, then to her breast.

"I love you, Camille. I will miss you terribly...Molly Ann says she'll miss you, too. She and I will comfort one another while you're away. I'll keep her with me always to remind me that we will both see you soon. I always believed it would be me who would go first, and that we would have to endure many years of separation. I'll come along soon; I won't be long, I promise. And I also promise to continue to read you every new poem. You'll be the first to hear. I know you'll be listening. And I'll write one every Christmas just for you, beginning with the one that I've written this year to start our new tradition."

Annabelle never wrote a poem that she did not also immediately memorize. She now recited the poem that lay in her luggage inside the Christmas package containing the red satin dress with the gold and silver lace. The last two stanzas were her prayer to God as she held Camille's hand to her tear-stained cheek:

"Dear Father, that one gift I own,
one thing that's mine, and mine alone,
I freely give, as Thou to me,
for Thine to keep eternally.
That gift for which Thou dost most yearn,
an offering Thou canst not return,
I give Thee Father, God Divine,
my free will, Lord, not mine, but Thine."

And as her voice failed her and she struggled to finish the last few verses, she felt God's Spirit confirming to her that, indeed, His will would be done. It did not remove her sorrow, but it strengthened her resolve to endure it and to be a comfort to her family.

Susan and Andrew returned a few minutes later.

"I'll go see Mark now," Annabelle said.

"He'll be so happy to see you, Mother," said Susan. "The bishop and his wife are with him, but he's very frightened. We haven't—"

"We haven't told him about Camille," interrupted Andrew, "and I don't think we should until...until it's time and we can be with him."

Andrew walked with Annabelle out into the hall.

"How is he?" she asked.

"He was in quite a bit of pain, so they've drugged him pretty heavily. He has a broken collarbone, a badly broken arm, and a broken leg. He lost a lot of blood from where the bone of his arm severed an artery. If not for the quick action of someone who stopped right away to help, he'd surely have bled to death. But the doctors say he'll be fine.

Bishop Lundberg and I gave him a blessing. He and his wife, Marilyn, have been with him for the last hour or so."

Annabelle took Andrew's arm and squeezed tightly.

"Thank you, Andrew, for loving my daughter," she said, her voice trembling. "I'll find my way from here. You go back to her."

The hospital halls were empty and silent. As she left the elevator on the second floor, she noted the sign on the wall directing her to the intensive care unit to the left. An elderly Hispanic woman passed between the open elevator and the sign. She too had been crying. A second arrow pointed to the hospital chapel in the opposite direction to the right.

"She must have come from the chapel," Annabelle thought subconsciously.

The impression that she too should pray before going in to see Mark was enough to turn her to her right, and she soon found herself at the end of the hall at the chapel door. It was slightly open, and she could hear the faint voice of a child above the silence that surrounded her. Annabelle entered quietly, gently pushing the door only enough to allow her to slip silently inside. Two heavy pale green and gray curtains separated the eight pews, four on each side of a center aisle, from the entrance behind her. This was a non-denominational chapel. Only one picture graced its walls hanging above a small altar at the end of the center aisle, a beautiful oil painting of a grove of olive trees, so large that it almost covered the entire wall.

Annabelle walked a few feet to her left and peered around the far side of the curtain, discovering the source of the voice. She was a little girl, perhaps six or seven years old, with large dark curls—curls much like Molly Ann's—kneeling in prayer behind the first pew on the right side, next to the outside aisle. Her tear-stained face was lifted toward the ceiling, her eyes closed, and her little hands clenched under her delicate chin.

Now that she was inside, Annabelle could hear the child's voice clearly, even though she was speaking only slightly above a whisper. She was surprised that such a small child had been left alone, and even more surprised, as she listened, that so small a child knew so well the language of prayer.

"Heavenly Father," the little girl continued, "Mommy says that I must always trust You. She says that I should tell You how I feel and ask for what I want, but that I need to always say 'Thy will be done,' like Jesus said." She started to cry again, her sobs interrupting each phrase. "Heavenly Father, Mommy is hurt bad...I don't want her to die...please don't take my mommy away. We love her and we need her...she and I are teaching Daddy to pray and to love You...I can't do it by myself. Please, make Mommy better...Daddy's so sad. He's crying—and Daddy never cries—please, Heavenly Father...please don't take Mommy away."

Annabelle immediately understood. This was the daughter of the woman in the other car, the woman who had run the red light and hit Camille's car on the driver's side—Camille's side. Annabelle felt a surge of compassion, and with it the conviction that the child's mother was not to blame. She did not yet know the details of the accident, only that for no explainable reason a car had run a red light at a speed far exceeding the posted limit and the conditions imposed by the torrential rain. Whatever the reason, she was once again assured, as she listened to both the voice of the little girl and to the familiar voice she often sensed inside, that God's will had been and would be done, and that there was something here that she had been sent to do.

As the little girl continued to cry, Annabelle pondered for several moments what exactly she should do. There was something besides the dark curls that seemed very familiar about this beautiful child. She longed to approach her, to hold her, to assure her that her Father in Heaven loved her and had heard her prayer. She may well have acted on that impulse—she wondered often since if she would have—had the door not suddenly opened behind her. At the sound of the opening door, she stepped quickly around the curtain and knelt down on the back pew, all the time continuing to look at the little dark-haired girl. The child turned toward her, and for a brief moment—two or three seconds, maybe more—their tear-filled eyes met before she turned the other way to the sound of the voice of the woman—the same woman Annabelle had seen in front of the elevator—who had entered and was now walking down the right aisle toward the front of the room.

"Molly," the woman called out urgently, and Annabelle's heart leaped at the sound of such a familiar name. *"Ven. Dicen que tu mamá pronto se despierta."*

As the little girl disappeared out the chapel door, Annabelle knew that she must follow. Something urged her to action, action that she did not take.

"What can I do?" she thought, trying to justify her hesitation. "She doesn't even know me. I might frighten her," she reasoned.

Annabelle's prayer was for Mark, Susan, and Andrew, but she also prayed for forgiveness and for another chance to help the little girl with the powerful prayer. One thing was certain: She knew she would never forget the little girl's face, her eyes, and especially her prayer.

Part Two

I live for those who love me,
whose hearts are pure and true;
for the heaven that smiles above me,
and awaits my spirit too;
for all human ties that bind me,
for the task by God assigned me,
for the bright hopes yet to find me,
and the good that I can do.
-George Linnaeus Banks-

15. And now, O all ye that have imagined up unto
    yourselves a god who can do no miracles, I would ask
    of you, have all these things passed of which I have
    spoken? Has the end come yet? Behold I say unto you,
    Nay; and God has not ceased to be a God of miracles.
16. Behold, are not the things that God hath wrought
    marvelous in our eyes? Yea, and who can comprehend
    the marvelous works of God?

17. Who shall say that it is not a miracle that by his word the heaven and the earth should be; and by the power of his word man was created of the dust of the earth; and by the power of his word have miracles been wrought?

18. And who shall say that Jesus Christ did not do many mighty miracles? And there were many mighty miracles wrought by the hands of the apostles.

19. And if there were miracles wrought then, why has God ceased to be a God of miracles and yet be an unchangeable Being? And behold, I say unto you he changeth not; if so he would cease to be God; and he ceaseth not to be God, and is a God of miracles.

-Moroni 9:15-19-

Chapter One

"Molly, are you home?" Jacob called out hopefully.

The room was cold, and there were no schoolbooks on the kitchen table. Of course, Molly had again stopped on her way home from school to admire the doll in the window at the department store. It had appeared there suddenly last Tuesday afternoon, between the toy trolley station and the green and red Christmas patchwork quilt, the porcelain doll that reminded Molly of her mother, and Jacob of his guilt.

Jacob took off his coat and hung it on the hook behind the door, then crouched down and opened the stove. Several embers still glowed from that morning's fire. With the small shovel, he cleared away the ashes and scooped them carefully into the metal bucket, where they would spend the night cooling. He would throw them out with the trash in the morning. He constructed a small teepee of kindling and smaller pieces of firewood over the warm embers, then crumpled a half-sheet of newspaper and placed it inside under the kindling. The paper smoldered briefly, then burst into flame. He waited until the flame rose from the wood before adding two larger pieces, then he pulled a chair away from the table and sat in front of the stove to warm himself and wait for Molly. He would wait ten minutes, and then would go looking for her. He knew exactly where she would be.

Just over a year had passed since Ann's death, but time had not dulled the memories that haunted him. Neither had their recent move accomplished its purpose. Although he and Molly were now far away from the physical reminders—the objects, places, and people—that constantly rekindled those memories, his guilt and anger still smoldered, and the doll in McCallaway's store, the doll Molly now wanted for Christmas, a doll whose eyes were the same deep blue that Jacob had once read and loved, had ignited again the fire of his suffering. Both the stoic nature of his character and the practiced discipline of his mind had failed him—and running away had failed him, too. He could neither forget nor forgive, and as he sat in the cold quiet of the garage apartment—his and Molly's home for the past four weeks—he pondered once again the travesty of events that had propelled him into the past year, a year from Thanksgiving to Thanksgiving, but without thanksgiving; a year of constant memories of Ann, but without Ann; a year alone with his self-blame and self-pity; a year without faith and without prayer.

His last attempt at prayer had fallen on deaf ears. From the moment he saw Ann's car speeding toward the intersection in the rain, he had prayed that she might be spared. He had continued to pray as he lay half inside and half outside the window of the overturned car, trying desperately to stay the bleeding until the ambulance arrived. He had continued to pray at her bedside in the hospital as she languished between life and death. He had put all the faith he could muster in God's goodness; he had pled for His mercy and His love. But Jacob's prayers—all of them, he now reasoned—had been in vain.

Ann had awakened for a few brief minutes before she died, unable to speak, unable to move any more than to feebly squeeze Jacob's hand. All that she could do was to look into his eyes and faintly smile, the same eyes and faint smile that haunted his memory, the same eyes and smile he now saw mimicked by the doll in McCallaway's store.

Then Ann closed her eyes forever, and Jacob felt life leave the hand that he held and the faith he had so desperately clung to leave his broken heart. Molly was there, too, standing with Carmen on the other side of the bed. She had asked Carmen to take her somewhere she could be alone to pray, but had returned. Ann had looked and smiled at Jacob, then at Molly, and at Jacob again. And when her eyes closed, Jacob looked across the bed into his daughter's eyes. He would never forget the confusion and fear that he saw reflected there as his eyes met hers, eyes that questioned, as he did, why, why Ann had died, why there had been no answer to prayer.

So Jacob had stopped praying. Ann had been wrong. There was no God in heaven, no loving Father who watched over His children. If there was a God, He was someone, something else, not the God of compassion and mercy whom Ann had loved and trusted so faithfully.

Ann's God would not have allowed her to die—not only to die but also to suffer and die. Ann's merciful Father in Heaven would not have ignored a little girl's trusting plea that her mother might live. Why would he leave a child without her mother's love and care?

And what of Camille? He had seen Camille's long red hair through the broken window of the other car as he ran past its wreckage in the rain to Ann. Luis, who was only a few yards behind him, had stopped to give Camille and her little brother first aid. No loving God would have led him to save Camille's life, only to take it from her in such an absurd way, killed by the wife of the man who had rescued her. If Camille and Ann were meant to die, why in such bizarre and unbelievable circumstances?

No, Jacob had reasoned over and over again during the past year, no God had led him to save Camille. It had been his own instincts, a happenstance, something else—he wasn't sure—but it was not the will of the loving God of the New Testament whom he thought he was learning to know and understand. Not the God Ann had assured him would bless them and reward their faith with peace in this life and the life to come. It was a lie, all a horrible and fantastic coincidence.

And because there was no God, Jacob was left with only himself to blame. The autopsy had shown that Ann had type-2 diabetes and that her loss of consciousness in the car was certainly the result of an excessive level of blood sugar. To Jacob, it was all too simple. Had he not been so selfish, they would have known. Had he not insisted that he had to write to be happy, had he not asked Ann to work again, had he kept his promise and stayed with his good-paying job and insurance plan, had he been the husband and father he should have been and sacrificed his own selfish desires for his family's sake, had he paid more attention to Ann instead of filling his mind with his worthless fiction, Ann's diabetes would surely have been detected and measures taken to ensure her health and safety. Had he not been so selfishly foolish to think he could write a novel, Ann would still be alive, Molly would still have a mother, and he would still have the love of, and purpose for, his life. Yes, he alone was to blame, but subconsciously he also blamed Ann's faith. Her faith that they were in God's care had made her careless, and his faith in her faith had perpetuated the series of fantastic events that had taken her life.

Jacob wept bitterly and unashamedly during the first few hours following Ann's death, but on the following day, he showed no outward emotion. If not for Molly, he may have reacted much differently—how differently, he did not allow himself to speculate. For Molly's sake, he stoically went through the motions, accepting the gestures of sympathy and condolence offered by family and friends while the hurricane of guilt and self-blame raged within him. He politely acknowledged all expressions of love and sorrow and bit his tongue as he nodded in feigned agreement whenever anyone spoke of heaven, God's will, or Christ's mercy. Inside, he refused to be comforted, finding neither relief nor solace in anything anyone could tell him.

It was for Molly's sake too that the day after the burial—Thanksgiving Day—he began working full time with Tony and Luis in the furniture shop, determined to do for Molly what he had failed to do for Ann. He was determined that she would never want for comfort and security, that she would never have reason to doubt his total devotion. No sacrifice he could make would be too great; no selfish desire would ever keep him from discerning and meeting her needs. He would think only of Molly; Molly would be his sole purpose in life. He would not make the same mistake twice.

Jacob still wanted Molly to be like Ann, but with one important difference. He and Molly would live without God. He would continue to teach her to be honest and kind and morally grounded, but he would erase the delusion of the faith that had failed them. He would spare Molly the disillusionment he had experienced and found so distasteful. God's love was a fairy tale. Jacob's love was all Molly would need.

This, his resolve, passed its first test that first night he tucked Molly into bed alone, without Ann. Jacob struggled to rule his emotion.

"I love you, Molly. Do you know your daddy loves you?" he asked. These were the same words he had heard Ann say to Molly hundreds of times.

"Yes, Daddy."

"And…do you know your mommy loved you?"

There was silence.

"Daddy?"

"Yes, Molly?"

Part Two
Chapter One

"Did you say 'loved' when you meant to say 'loves'?"

"No, Molly. I meant to say 'loved.' Your mother is gone now." His voice trembled, but he did not allow the tears that moistened his eyes to fall. "All we have now is each other and our memory of your mother, the memory that she loved us and that we loved her. Do you understand that, Molly?"

Molly did not respond.

"Your daddy loves you and your mommy loved you," Jacob explained, "and that's all you need to know, Molly. We will love one another and be strong, and remember that Mommy loved us."

Molly did not argue, but her eyes turned from her father to the rocking chair in the corner. Jacob's eyes followed. Ann's grandmother's Bible lay defiantly in its accustomed place. Jacob did not like what he saw when he looked again at his daughter's eyes, and he removed the Bible later that night while Molly slept and placed it in a box in the back of his closet.

Jacob worked long hours in the furniture shop, often ignoring Tony's hard-and-fast overtime rule.

"I don't know how we ever got along without you," Tony often told him.

When he wasn't working, he devoted his full attention to Molly; bicycle rides and walks in the park, reading together, errands to the market, countless trips to the library, meals, and bedtime stories; they did everything together. And whenever Molly was near, Jacob feigned a smile and a cheerful heart. He was resolved that Molly would never see him sad or despondent. He had promised himself that she would never again see him cry. Together, they continued to join Carmen and her family at their Sunday-night gatherings, but their friends soon learned which topics of conversation to carefully avoid. No one spoke of religion, and whenever someone forgot him or herself and mentioned Ann, Jacob would fall uncomfortably silent, and someone would quickly change the subject.

Jacob's decision to leave the East Coast came as no surprise to his family and friends. Tony paid his most valuable employee as much as he possibly could, but Jacob was determined to eliminate his debt and provide Molly with opportunities unavailable to her in their current financial circumstances. For several months, he had been content to work in the furniture shop, but he knew that for Molly's sake, he must soon return to the profession that offered them much greater financial security and the chance to begin saving for Molly's college education.

In July he approached his former employer about returning to his technical writing job. To his credit, Mr. Hendricks harbored no enmity toward Jacob. On the contrary, he had been very gracious, going beyond common courtesy in offering Jacob his personal condolences at the funeral service. However, both agreed that it was unwise for him to return to his former position— Dave was now employed in his father's company—but Mr. Hendricks offered to write Jacob a highly favorable recommendation, and he kept him informed regarding opportunities in other companies.

Part Two
Chapter One

The best opportunity came early in the fall. Mr. Hendricks called late one night to tell Jacob that an old friend who owned a small but growing writing services company was looking for an experienced bilingual writer to head his translation department. Jacob inquired immediately and interviewed on-site a few weeks later.

The mountains surrounding the Western valley where the company was located were dressed in their finest fall colors, and the peaceful college town promised Jacob far more than fresh mountain air and scenic beauty. It offered him new hope, hope that a change of surroundings might allow him to begin to forgive himself, for Molly's sake, he reasoned.

Jacob had discovered that living for Molly alone was not enough. He could not endure another year like the past one. He was tired of his anger, tired of feeling guilty, tired of blaming himself, tired of living a lie. He longed for a new start, and he hoped that by removing himself and Molly from the constant reminders of the past, they might make a good life in a new place.

Jacob started his new job the Monday after Thanksgiving. He and Molly began the three-day trip just one week before the anniversary of Ann's death. While interviewing, he had found a beautiful old home that had been abandoned for several years, a fixer-upper to say the least. He had whittled away all year at his debt but was still unable to qualify for a mortgage. The arrangement made with the home's owner was ideal. Instead of paying rent, Jacob would use the rent money to restore the home, and after a year, when the work was complete, the owner would finance its purchase, with any extra money Jacob had spent on the project being applied to the already determined purchase price. Meanwhile, he and Molly would live in the garage behind the house, a garage that had been converted into a studio apartment that, at one time, had housed the owner's widowed mother. There was a swing in an oak tree out back and a fertile spot once devoted to a large vegetable garden—Ann would have been pleased.

They were not far from the grade school Molly would attend—she could walk easily—just down the hill a few blocks and then through the last two blocks of the town's commercial section and into the residential area that surrounded the school. From the living room window of the house they could see to their right both the school and the adjacent park, and to their left the mouth of the canyon that framed the white steeple of a nearby church.

Jacob had abandoned his writing. The well of his inspiration had run dry. The characters he had created and developed were strangers to him now, shadowy reflections of abandoned dreams, misguided men and women all living the same lie, supposing that life had meaning beyond the limits of mortality and time, clinging foolishly to the childish hope of a purpose larger than life. A few weeks after Ann's death, he deleted his files and sold his computer; he had no need for it at the time. Neither had he any use for his poetry. The year had passed, and he had not written a single verse. Anything creative he had ever written, including his poetry and one paper copy of his unfinished novel, lay cloistered with Ann's grandmother's Bible in a cardboard box, sealed with duct tape and pushed to the back of the closet shelf. As he and Molly had packed Ann's rocking chair and other belongings five weeks ago, he had come close to leaving the box behind but had changed his mind—why, he wasn't sure.

Today was Thursday, December twenty-first. Until Tuesday, things had gone well. Jacob enjoyed his new job. He had a talented and friendly staff, and he was given great freedom to set his department's policy, standards, and schedule, and he had had the last say in hiring two new writers. He and Molly had settled into a comfortable routine. His flexible schedule allowed him to see Molly out the door on her way to school each morning before he biked the short mile and a half to work, and she was seldom alone for more than ten or fifteen minutes before he too arrived home in the afternoon. Leaving work early meant bringing work home every day, but he did not mind. He and Molly would settle in right away next to the stove at the kitchen table.

While he completed the day's editing, Molly labored on her homework. She was a good student and asked for Jacob's help only on rare occasions. At about 6:00, sometimes a little earlier, they would bundle up and take the walk down the hill to explore some new corner of town, then walk partway back up the same hill to the cafeteria for supper. Jacob wasn't much of a cook, and they had gotten into the costly habit of eating out every evening, but he justified the extra expense: He could afford it now, and he would much rather spend his evenings working on the house than cooking meals and doing dishes. Sometimes, however, just for a change of pace, they ordered their food to go, and then ate together in the quiet of their cozy apartment. After their meal, they worked on the house until Molly's bedtime, when Jacob stopped just long enough to tell a bedtime story and tuck her into bed before returning to work a few hours alone.

Saturdays and Sundays were spent almost exclusively on the house, except for Jacob's daily morning run several miles up the canyon while Molly slept in. Even though it was often very cold, Jacob was set on staying physically fit, again, for Molly. His return route took him past the redbrick church with the white steeple. Work on the house was proceeding nicely. Molly worked too, seldom leaving her father's side—handing him tools, sweeping, and cleaning away debris—except to read or sometimes play upstairs with her dolls in the dormer window of what was to someday be her room.

Until Tuesday, Jacob had believed that their move was working the magic he had hoped for. His heart often felt genuinely light as he listened—while sanding a staircase or stripping a casing—to Molly relate her adventures in school, or as, hand in hand, they explored their new town during their late afternoon walks.

Last Christmas, their first without Ann, had been almost unbearable for Jacob. While he worked overtime in the shop with Tony and Luis, Molly had spent her time after school with Rosita either at Tony's house or in Carmen's apartment. Consequently, Molly was naturally included in the Rodriguez family's many holiday traditions, most of which were deeply rooted in their Catholic faith. Jacob participated on Christmas Eve and Christmas day, for

Molly's sake, but refused to be anything more than a silent observer, watching Molly's eyes resentfully as she played with the Nativity or as she listened intently to Carmen tell or read the stories of Jesus' birth. He did not like what he saw in his daughter's eyes—the same faith he had seen in Ann's eyes—and he painfully forced a smile whenever her eyes found his. Even the Christmas *villancicos* he had sung all his life were painful reminders, as he watched Molly sing them, of the lie that had taken Ann away from him.

This Christmas would be different. They would have a tree and lights in the window, though no Nativity. Jacob had promised that, on the coming Friday, they would decorate their place. They would have music too, festive songs like "Jingle Bells," "White Christmas," and the other more secular songs of the holiday—Jacob had purchased several discs in McCallaway's store after carefully scrutinizing their content. He was even going to attempt to cook a small turkey, and for presents, he had picked out a beautiful and expensive porcelain doll and a bicycle to replace the one Molly had outgrown and they had left back East—both purchased from McCallaway's store and now wrapped or assembled and ready for Christmas day. They were well hidden in the attic of the house, along with the packages Carmen had sent. This holiday season they would begin their own family traditions, part of their new life.

In their changed surroundings, Jacob hoped also to change the way he remembered Ann. He longed to be able to remember her without the regret, the guilt, and the blame that tormented him. He believed that he was making progress, but suddenly, the doll had appeared in

McCallaway's store, the doll whose eyes brought back all those feelings and memories he had fought to erase. It had appeared, as if from nowhere, last Tuesday afternoon.

Molly always stopped to admire the Christmas display with the other children who paraded past the store every day on their way to and from school. Stepping into McCallaway's store was like stepping eight or nine decades back into time. The entire building had been nostalgically made over to resemble the small-town main-street store of a simpler time, a marketing strategy that worked very well, judging by the number of customers inside and the cars in the parking lot at the back of the store. The building occupied the last block of the east end of the town's business district, a block that extended awkwardly past where the main road turned abruptly left before making its gradual curve and climb north and then east again between two hills, then descending once more on the other side of the hill before making its way toward the canyon. A pedestrian tunnel funneled schoolchildren and shoppers under the road just after it made its ninety-degree turn and brought them up again onto the sidewalk that passed in front of the street entrance to the store.

Whoever had designed the building and site had integrated it beautifully into the surrounding residential zone, a neighborhood dignified by beautiful homes on large, well-cared-for lots, scattered sparingly along winding streets lined with mature, stately trees. One house in particular, the one directly across the street from the store, was famous for its flowers and gardens. After admiring the display in the store window for a few moments and before continuing on their way to or from school, many of the children would turn and wave to the elderly lady who sat watching them from her parlor window.

The store's large display window tastefully sampled McCallaway's wares without price tags or signage of any kind. Some highly artistic hand had placed them just so in a busy Santa's workshop, where a giant toy trolley moved along its track in and out of the reindeer and the hard-working elves who were putting final touches on the toys and other items for sale inside. A pensive Santa sat behind his desk, checking his long list of good little girls and boys that draped over his desk and onto the floor, and the children outside pointed excitedly to their names. Molly's name coincidentally headed the long list, and Molly was thrilled. She had excitedly brought her father to see the display the Monday after Thanksgiving during their late afternoon stroll, and Jacob had been impressed. Any store that would go to such lengths to welcome the season would certainly have his business.

But on the Tuesday before Christmas, Molly saw the doll. And like today, Jacob had come home to an empty apartment. Alarmed, he had retraced Molly's route from school—down the hill and through the tunnel—and found Molly standing in the cold, gazing transfixed through the window of McCallaway's store.

"Look, Daddy," she pointed excitedly. "It's Camille's doll."

"What do you mean, Camille's doll?" Jacob asked.

"It has to be, or one just like her," Molly continued. "See, she has dark curly hair just like mine and eyes just like Mommy's. The doll was our secret. Camille told me she had dark curls like mine and eyes like Mommy's. Don't you remember, Daddy? Please, Daddy, can Santa bring me her for Christmas instead? I know I asked for the other one, but I'd really, really love to have Molly Ann."

Jacob looked at the doll, confused. It was true; the doll's eyes were exactly the same piercing blue as Ann's, and her faint smile was the same smile Jacob had seen a thousand times over in his memory.

"Molly Ann?" he asked impatiently.

"Yes, Daddy. Molly Ann. That is her name. It's the name Camille gave her. She is Camille's doll. I know she is. Isn't she beautiful, Daddy? Isn't she wonderful?"

That was Tuesday. He had scolded Molly gently about coming straight home from school. Her teacher's note on Wednesday informed him Molly had arrived late that morning, and he scolded her again.

"Santa doesn't like it when little girls are late for school," he warned.

As Jacob now waited and watched the fire inside the open stove, his mind's eye saw Ann's eyes and smile again. He had tried for more than a year now to replace the memory of Ann's face with some other, with her eyes and smile as she had read or as she had played with Molly. He had spent hours looking at photos and portraits, but no image could supplant it for long; it always returned. And now, for Molly's sake, he must buy a doll that now stared mockingly at him in his memory as he stared into the fire, a doll with Ann's name, Ann's smile, and Ann's eyes.

Chapter Two

Annabelle sat in her parlor chair embroidering, patiently waiting, listening for the sound of the school bell and wishing it were not so cold outside. Colder weather meant that few of the children would stop for long, or not at all, to look at the display window. Yesterday, only a few had paused long enough to count the seconds it took the trolley train to return from its rounds through the display inside, and today was much colder. She suspected that, like yesterday, all would again scatter within minutes of their arrival; all, that is, except for the little girl in the gray coat and green hat.

Annabelle had watched the children for so long that she recognized all of them, even when they were bundled in their winter clothes. She knew them by their size and shape, by their walk, and by their wave. And she knew their names—all of them, even the name of the new little girl who always wore the gray wool coat and green stocking cap. She had quizzed the children in her Primary class the week before Thanksgiving.

"Her name is Molly," they told her. "She lives on the avenues in the old Porter home.

"Molly," Annabelle repeated. She began to look for opportunities to meet this new little girl with such an important name. She watched for her every morning and afternoon. She had also seen her several times from her window in the early evening, walking with a tall handsome dark-haired man—her father, she assumed, the same man she had twice seen running in the canyon during her early Saturday-morning walks, precisely the two Saturdays after Thanksgiving. The Monday following Thanksgiving they had come, as had many others, to see the new display, and it was no coincidence that Molly's name appeared on the top of Santa's list.

Annabelle had worked very hard on the display this year to make up for the previous year's disaster. Jed had hired someone else. Annabelle had not returned on the twenty-eighth as she had planned. She had all she could do with the funeral, looking after her family, helping with their move back from the East Coast, and nursing Mark back to health. She had worked so hard on the display this year that she had spent the first two weeks of December confined to her bed or the parlor chair with the flu. She was feeling much better now.

The year had passed quickly—one year for someone who has lived seventy-one is not a long time—and not a day of that year had gone by that Annabelle had not thought about her granddaughter. Camille's portrait on the parlor wall and her doll, Molly Ann, watching her from her places of honor atop the piano or her bedroom dresser, reminded her constantly. Susan had insisted that her mother take the doll and all her clothes.

"Camille would want you to have her," she had argued.

A drawer in the parlor credenza was immediately reserved for the dresses Annabelle had made, one for every Christmas for twelve years running. She changed them periodically during those times when nostalgic musings were better managed by busy hands. Dress number thirteen was in her lap now. Only the embroidering remained. She wondered how it would look on Molly Ann, and she glanced at the empty piano, at the spot from which the doll's deep and searching blue eyes had watched over her every day of the past year, and she reflected again on the strange series of events that had moved those eyes from their usual place to the corner of the patchwork quilt in the display in McCallaway's store.

Those events began Monday night—just three days ago—the night Annabelle finished her most recent poem, only her second since Camille's death. During the first eleven months after the accident, she had written nothing. She was not sure why. She had made no conscious decision not to write, but she had always relied on the associations that had randomly popped into her mind, associations between concrete objects or experience and the notions and feelings that made up her understanding of life, and those associations were somehow not being made. Perhaps it was because she had made no room for them. All her attention had been centered on others: on her family first, doing all she could to strengthen and comfort them, but also on any other soul who would accept her kindness.

Susan and Andrew had been amazingly strong, especially Susan, a legacy given her by her mother, she said. Camille had lived another forty-eight hours after the life support had been removed. She had died just minutes before Thanksgiving Day. A funeral service was held in their ward on Saturday, and Susan had played her concert Sunday night.

"Camille will be listening," she insisted. "I'm doing it for her, and God will help me."

She had never played so beautifully, never so masterfully, never with greater love and feeling. A long-standing ovation followed, a unanimous gesture offered by orchestra and audience—there wasn't a dry eye among them. All had read the tribute to Camille inserted in the program. All appreciated and marveled at a mother's resolve and sacrifice. Only during the ovation did Susan, unable to stand, allow the tears to fall on the keys that had responded so perfectly to her touch, a touch that all present knew had been guided by a power beyond her own.

Annabelle had not forgotten the confirmation of the Spirit she had received during the concert. Its memory had displaced for a time many other more painful ones. She had decided not to tell her family about her encounter in the hospital chapel with the daughter of the driver of the other car, but the prayerful, tearful face of the little girl named Molly had returned again to haunt her memory.

It had returned with the serendipitous discovery of yet another Molly, a little girl she had yet to meet, yet to see up close, a child hidden by a gray coat, a olive-green stocking cap, and the distance between her parlor window and the window across the street in Jed McCallaway's store.

It never once occurred to her that the two Mollys might be one and the same. There were several other Mollys in town, one in her Primary class, and thousands, she supposed, between her and the little girl who lived back East. But somehow, the sudden appearance of this new Molly had rekindled the memory of the first, of the tenderness and empathy Annabelle had felt as she listened to her pray, and of the unambiguous impression she had been given that she could and should help, an errand from the Spirit she had been unable to fulfill.

Rekindled too was Annabelle's need to write, and the possible correspondences between ordinary things and eternal truths, the metaphors tying life's experience to life's purpose, once again found their way into her thoughts.

Always the early riser, Annabelle seldom missed her morning walk. She and Tom had begun this tradition several years before Susan was born. Six days a week and fifty-two weeks a year, rain or shine; only the fiercest of storms or the gravest of illness curbed their enthusiasm. Annabelle's favorite route took her over the bridge, through the park, past the church, and then through the cemetery, where she always paused for a few moments to rest and remember, then on up the canyon to where the groomed pathway changed abruptly to a narrow, rocky mountain trail. At the head of the trail, Annabelle always turned to retrace her route, and it was there that she first saw Molly's father. It was on a clear cold Saturday morning, the Saturday after Thanksgiving. He was running down the trail onto the path when he tripped on a rock and scarcely kept from falling headlong to the ground in front of her. He smiled his embarrassment and said, "Hello." Despite the cold, he wore no hat and had taken off his sweatshirt, which he had tied around his waist.

"What a pleasant-looking young man," Annabelle thought as she watched him disappear around a bend, and it was as she rounded that same bend that the idea came to her. As soon as she returned home, she began to write what she hoped would be her promised Christmas gift to Camille, to Camille in name but also to the rest of her family, a poem that, like the year before, would be trimmed in the same ribbon that garnished the box containing Molly Ann's new dress. The poem would again be lovingly placed inside. Mark would again serve as proxy and open the box. Susan would again read the poem with Andrew sitting beside her holding her hand. All would once again be comforted by the sense that Camille was listening. Yes, last year's gift opening and reading would be repeated again this year and become their tradition, an observance in Camille's memory and honor. Even the time and place would be exactly the same, in the parlor just before their Christmas dinner, and would be followed by a kneeling family prayer and blessing on the food.

Annabelle spent every available moment at the desk in the parlor. The poem occupied her thoughts constantly. Sleep was a burden, and she owed her bout with the flu more to the hours of precious sleep sacrificed for the poem's sake than to the exertion exacted by work on the display. The time she had spent recovering from her flu, time confined to her bed and to her chair in the parlor, allowed her to finish the poem ahead of schedule, a full two weeks before Christmas.

With her flu in check and with the poem finished, Annabelle was ready to enjoy the remaining pleasures of the season: school and church parties and programs, plays and concerts—both Susan and Mark had parts in the community theatre's production of *A Christmas Carol*—her Primary children's school play and music recitals, visits to the retirement home, the women's shelter, and the hospital, and most important, the family gatherings around the perfect fir tree that Andrew and Mark had brought from the canyon.

Annabelle's life and heart were full. She had filled the voids left there by Camille's death with service to others. She often counted her blessings. She had her health, her loving family, her comfortable home, her poetry, the peace and assurance of unwavering faith, and the companionship of the Spirit. And something else: She was no longer an unsung poet, no longer Anonymous Annabelle.

Camille's body had been returned home to be interred in the family cemetery plot near her grandfather. The members of their home ward had insisted that a second service be held before burial, and Bishop Beckstead had asked Annabelle to speak. She had agreed and had prepared a script of what she wanted to say, but while she spoke, she responded to the promptings of the Spirit and shared two of her poems.

"They are two of many," Susan explained in answer to those who inquired.

It did not take long for the word to spread. Now that the cat was out of the bag, Susan did not hesitate to share copies of selected poems with any who requested them. Before long, Annabelle McNeely had made a name for herself in the community. With Susan's help, an enthusiastic Bishop Beckstead prepared and bound a collection of fifteen poems to give as the bishopric's annual Christmas gift to the ward members. A second collection appeared at Easter, and all were anxiously waiting this Christmas in hopes of yet another.

The warmth and sincerity of people's response was gratifying, but for Annabelle, the greatest advantage that her new reputation now gave her were opened doors, the opportunities to further serve those who she sensed needed what she had to give. Annabelle was no longer merely the nice elderly lady who grew pumpkins for neighborhood children and who designed the display in the window of McCallaway's store; she was suddenly someone whose opinion mattered. She gave an impromptu tri-stake youth fireside one Sunday evening after the scheduled speaker cancelled only minutes before it was to start. Andrew quickly offered a solution. Annabelle had made the hour drive with them to hear Susan play the special musical number. Because she had memorized all of her poems, she had no trouble filling the time. By the following Sunday, she was scheduled to speak at two other firesides.

She often suppressed an ironic smile when people she had observed all her life, but who had never even given her the time of day, now went out of their way to greet her or inquire after her health. These people, however, were not the souls she was most interested in serving. The shy or neglected child, the aged and forgotten, the questioning youth—these were the major recipients of her encouragement and kindness. Her poetry gave her not only the necessary measure of credibility in the minds of those she served but also provided access to places and circumstances that greatly expanded her circle of influence. Friends and neighbors knew her willing heart and did not hesitate to entreat her.

"Would you be willing to speak to my fourth-grade class about your poetry?" "Might you consider visiting my mother in the hospital? She loves your book." "I wonder if you might help me. Could you talk with my daughter? I don't know what else to do."

Annabelle was happy and grateful to say yes. Her second poem was a reflection on the many opportunities to help others that God had given her during the past year. It had its beginnings one cold afternoon as she sat in her parlor chair, watching the children across the street. It was a Thursday, exactly one week ago. The new little girl, Molly, was there, as always, hidden by her coat and hat. Annabelle thought it strange that she felt so drawn to her, and she strained to see her face when the children turned and waved. There must be a reason, she thought. Perhaps someone, somewhere, was praying for her, and perhaps Annabelle would be privileged to be part of the answer to that prayer. She recalled a phrase from the Bible: "Father, here am I; send me." She smiled and rose from her chair. It was time to write once again.

This time, she would go slowly; she would let it happen at its own pace. She was in no hurry; she could not afford to get sick again. Bedtime would be strictly observed, she promised herself; but it wasn't, and by Monday night, the poem was complete.

"Perhaps my best yet," she said aloud as she made the final draw from the inkwell. She read it again as the ink dried. It was short enough that she already had it memorized.

A Disciple's Prayer

Father, when Thy children pray
and ask that Thou wouldst intercede,
Thou callest others in their way
who on Thine errand fill the need.
I've stores enough to last a year;
hear both my gratitude and plea:
if someone Thou wouldst feed be near,
Father, here am I; send me.
Should others need a bit of cheer,
a gentle touch, a kindly smile,
a helping hand, a listening ear,
a visitor who'll stay awhile,
my talents I would not conceal,
my brother's keeper I would be;
if there's a soul that Thou wouldst heal,
Father, here am I; send me.

Part Two
Chapter Two

If Thou a lamb who's lost and cold
wouldst bring back to the ninety-nine,
I'll leave the safety of the fold;
please, let the task and joy be mine.
I've kept my lantern trimmed and bright;
if Thou the blind wouldst cause to see,
give me the chance to share my light;
Father, here am I; send me.
Father, help me do today
whatever Thou wouldst have be done.
All I can do will never pay
the debt I owe Thy Firstborn Son,
who knowing well He must provide
the offering in Gethsemane,
when asked to do Thy will, replied,
"Father, here am I; send me."

Annabelle was very happy and grateful. This poem defined her promise to God, the promise she had made just over a year ago, soon after Camille died. Never again would she fail to do what He asked of her. The incident in the hospital chapel had not been and would never again be repeated. When He called, when He made it known to her what she was to do, she would never again hesitate.

That night, as she had done every night for more than a year, Annabelle gently lifted Molly Ann from the piano, carried her into her room, and carefully sat her down in her place on top of the dresser beside her bed. There, as always, she would spend the night between two framed photographs, one of Tom, the other of Camille. That night, as always, kneeling alone in the dark, Annabelle repeated her promise to God: If He needed her, she told Him, she would obey. But unlike any other night, that night, a strange yet wonderful night, Annabelle dreamed a dream. Annabelle seldom dreamed, but that night she did.

She was sitting behind Santa's desk—in Santa's place—in the display window of McCallaway's store. The cuckoo clock ticked loudly above her head. On the other side of the glass—although, in her dream, there was no glass—stood a beautiful and spacious olive grove. The trees were heavy with fruit, but no one was there to harvest it—no one, that is, except a small girl with large dark curls who, although she tried mightily, could not reach the fruit. As Annabelle watched, the little girl knelt and tearfully prayed: "Please, Father," she said, "please send someone to help me...I'm just too little...I can't do it by myself."

Annabelle jumped out of her chair to help, and the little girl turned at the sound. Only then did she recognize her face. It was little Molly, the daughter of the woman driver of the other car, and the olive grove was the painting in the hospital chapel. Their eyes met again as they had over a year before, only for a moment, and then Molly turned her glance suddenly toward the trolley station and smiled. Annabelle looked too as the little girl ran forward out of the grove, past the pews, and into the display. She knelt in front of the red and green Christmas patchwork quilt to admire something Annabelle could not see. The motionless trolley was in the way. What was it that had made Molly so happy? What was it she was admiring?

The cuckoo in the clock began its hourly song, and Annabelle walked toward the quilt so that the trolley no longer obstructed her view. It was Molly Ann, Camille's doll, sitting on the corner of the quilt smiling at the little girl. Her dream continued, and Annabelle found herself instantly in her bedroom as the cuckoo continued to sing behind her. The doll was not on her dresser between the two photographs. She next found herself in the parlor. The piano too was empty. She walked to the window and saw at a telescopic glance Molly standing in the cold, her dark curls blown by the wind, staring through the corner of the display window and smiling at Molly Ann, who sat on the edge of the patchwork quilt.

Annabelle awoke long before dawn. She seldom dreamed, and when she did, she never remembered her dreams. But this time, it took several minutes to convince herself that it hadn't really happened. Only after she turned on the light and saw Molly Ann in her usual place on the dresser was she completely sure. It had been so real, and one image remained clear—she could not displace it—the image of Molly Ann sitting on the corner of the quilt in McCallaway's store.

The air was cold and clear, and it was still dark as Annabelle began her morning walk, the first since she came down with the flu. The trees had long since lost their last leaves. It was cloudy and would probably snow. Hopes for a white Christmas were high all over town. Last year, it hadn't snowed until midway through January. She lingered a little longer than usual at the cemetery. On her way home, she crossed the street to look into the window of the store to be sure Molly Ann was not there, so strong was the impression left by her dream.

Later that morning, as it snowed lightly on the children who passed by the store, she looked for the little girl in the green hat and gray coat. Of all the children, she seemed most excited about the falling snow, trying to catch the flakes with her tongue.

Annabelle had no trouble understanding what it was that she must now do, though she did not understand why, but it was clear that God wanted her to put Molly Ann in the display. So, after a light and late breakfast, she phoned Jed and asked him to meet her inside fifteen minutes before he opened the store—she had her own key. She dressed Molly Ann in her green dress with the off-white laced hem, the same dress she had worn in her dream.

She told Jed nothing of her dream, but she made him promise to follow her instructions to the letter.

"No one must know where the doll came from," she explained, "no one must touch her, and, of course, she is not for sale."

She looked both ways, down and up the street, before placing the doll carefully on the corner of the patchwork quilt, then quickly left the store and returned home to make sure she could see her from the parlor window.

Susan stopped by on her way to play practice later that morning and noticed immediately the empty piano.

"Where's our Molly Ann?" she asked.

Annabelle pointed out the window and recounted part of her dream, though she did not tell her about her first encounter with Molly in the hospital chapel. Susan was very interested.

"Something good will come from all this," she assured her mother as she kissed her good-bye, "something very good. Keep me posted."

That afternoon, Annabelle anxiously waited in the parlor for the sound of the school bell. Molly was not the first child to appear at the display window, but she remained long after the others had come and gone. Annabelle knew that she was looking at Molly Ann. Five minutes, ten, and then fifteen passed, and she did not move despite the bitter cold. Annabelle could stand it no longer. She walked to the closet by the front door to put on her coat and hat. She just had to get a better look at the little girl. When she opened the door to leave the house, however, the little girl was no longer alone. Her father had come to find her, and Annabelle wished she could hear the conversation that lasted for several minutes before they turned to leave the store.

The following morning, Wednesday morning, the little girl arrived early and remained at the window until the second bell. Annabelle again put on her coat and had halfway crossed the street when the bell rang, and the little girl scampered off. She was again the first to arrive after school that afternoon—she must have run all the way—but she stayed only a few minutes after the other children had gone; neither did she remain long the following morning. Annabelle abandoned the idea of going out to meet her. She simply could not leave her chair until all the children had waved.

233

And now on this cold and windy Thursday afternoon, the last day of school before Christmas vacation and the coldest day of the season so far, Annabelle sat in the parlor chair stitching the final letters above the hem of Molly Ann's Christmas dress. The little girl in the gray coat was again the first to arrive, securing her usual place at the corner of the window. There was no doubt that she was looking at the doll and, this time—after the other children had gone—talking to her, too. Five minutes, then ten, and then fifteen passed. Annabelle wondered if her father would again come looking for her.

Then it happened. Despite the biting wind and the bitter cold, she took off her green stocking cap and shook her head. Her large dark curls bounced from side to side. Annabelle leaped to her feet, and the dress and embroidering ring fell from her lap to the floor.

Chapter Three

"And if Santa brings you to me for Christmas, I'll keep you on my dresser next to my mother's picture. Nancy is there now, but she can go on the shelf with Ruthie and Katie. She won't mind."

Molly stood as close as possible. Any closer, and the condensation from her breath on the glass would obstruct her view of the porcelain doll to whom she spoke. The doll sat on the corner of a green and red patchwork quilt, next to the trolley station. The trolley passed within inches exactly every ninety-six seconds as it slowly made its way around the display before disappearing into the station, only to emerge again, after traveling through another display inside the store. Molly had watched a few days before as some of her classmates counted out loud the thirty-four pendulum swings of the cuckoo clock above Santa's desk as they anticipated its return. But this time, she wasn't interested in the trolley; her eyes were riveted on the doll while she patiently waited for the other children to leave.

The children didn't stay long. It was freezing cold outside. What little snow had fallen on Tuesday had been plowed from the street onto the sidewalk's edge. The north wind blew in chilling gusts. Molly wore the gray wool coat and green stocking cap and gloves Carmen had given her last Christmas. The doll was dressed in a green satin dress trimmed at the neck and hem in white and silver lace.

"You do have Mommy's eyes and her smile, too," Molly continued, "and your hair looks just like mine. See?"

She pulled off her hat and shook her head so that her curls swung playfully back and forth across her face. The doll continued to smile her approval. It had been over a year—a year to a seven-year-old is an eternity—but Molly remembered her mother's eyes and her mother's smile, her last smile before she died, a smile that had a message that Molly had understood perfectly: "Don't forget who you are, Molly. Don't forget who you are." And Molly had not forgotten. She continued to talk to the doll.

"If Santa brings you to me for Christmas, you can help me teach my daddy. Daddy is not happy. He's forgotten how to pray. He didn't understand Mommy's smile. I tried to tell him with my eyes, but he didn't understand."

Molly's mother had taught her well. Just as they had once prayed without her father, Molly now prayed by herself. She seldom missed a day. Before their move, each night after her father had told a story, kissed her good night, and closed the door, she would slip quietly out of bed and kneel at her mother's maple rocker. She prayed as her mother had taught her. And now, in their new home, she pretended to sleep as she waited for Jacob to leave their garage apartment to work on the house, and as the door closed behind him, she would faithfully roll out of her bed to talk with God.

"...and Heavenly Father," she prayed, "tell Mommy I'm trying hard to take care of Daddy, but I'm just a little girl. I can't do it alone. Please send someone to help my daddy remember who he is."

Molly continued to talk to the doll she called Molly Ann, oblivious to the cold and the occasional car or pedestrian that passed behind her. Neither did she see her father until he crouched down beside her and took her hand.

Her father glanced involuntarily at the doll and then stroked his daughter's curls with his gloveless hand. He was not angry, not this time.

"Molly," he began softly, "you'll freeze out here. Put on your hat and let's go home."

"I'm sorry, Daddy. Am I very late?" she asked. "I just stopped for a little while. I was coming right home. I was on time for school this morning, and—"

"It's okay, Molly. It's okay," he assured her. "I understand. Let's go now. What do you say we eat a little early tonight? If you like, we can look for a tree after dinner. Would you like that?"

Molly nodded, then put on her hat and again took her father's hand. As they turned away from the display window to walk home, Molly waved to the white-haired lady standing at the window across the street; it was the first time she had seen her out of her chair. When she looked up again at her father, his eyes were turned the other direction. It seemed he could not resist another glance at the doll.

The room was invitingly warm. Her father added a log while Molly hung their coats and her hat on the hooks behind the door.

"So…where do you think we should put the tree?" he asked.

"It depends," she answered. "Is it going to be a big tree or a little tree?"

"Well…" he countered, "it all depends on where we put it."

Molly laughed. Molly's laugh always made her father grin, even when she knew he was not happy inside. They had walked home in uncommon silence. Molly was the queen of chatter, but she also had the uncanny knack for knowing when to defer to silence. Her ability to sense her father's mood despite his efforts to act the contrary was equally remarkable. For a seven-year-old, she read people extremely well.

"Then it's going to be a big tree," she said decidedly, "because we're going to put it in front of the window."

"Then a big tree it is," he laughed. "We'll see if we can find one after supper."

Their conversation stopped there. Molly understood that her father was still on the job until supper time, so when he slid a stack of papers out of his backpack and onto the table, she pulled a book out of hers and assumed her usual position on her father's bed under the window: belly down, her elbows extended, her delicate chin cradled on the top of two tiny but perfectly stacked fists, and knobby knees bent. Her shoeless feet seemed to defy gravity as they precariously teetered back and forth in the warm, dry air.

It didn't take long before she had completely immersed herself in her storybook, her tongue slowly moving clockwise around her lips. She had been reading for nearly three years now and devoured books like the stove devoured firewood. When she had finished it, and before getting off the bed to fetch another, she glanced toward her father. He had stopped working and was looking sadly at the family portrait that hung on the wall above her. He did not notice her eyes on his, and she watched them for several moments before she spoke.

"Daddy, are you all right?"

"I'm fine, Molly," he said softly, then pursed together his lips and forced a smile. "I was just thinking."

"About Mommy?"

He pursed his lips again and nodded several times before he answered.

"Yes, Molly…about Mommy…how could you tell?"

"I could see it in your eyes."

Chapter Four

"Not too bad for a junior high band," Andrew proudly observed, leaning sideways toward his mother-in-law as the audience finished its applause.

Annabelle smiled and nodded. Indeed, the seventh-grade band's rendition of "Good King Wenseslaus" was a vast improvement over the sixth-grade medley they had just endured. Annabelle sat up as tall as she possibly could. She could see Mark's trumpet but not Mark, except now between numbers, when the flute player in front of him leaned forward toward her music stand to turn her pages. Satisfied that she had seen him, she sat back again to continue pondering her dilemma as Mark and the band began their second number.

She had been mulling it over in her mind for several hours, ever since the shocking discovery that her prayer had been answered. The little Molly that was so taken with Camille's doll was indeed the little girl in the hospital chapel whom she had felt prompted to help but had not. God had given her the second chance she had asked for;

although it was not as crystal clear just exactly what he wanted her to do.

She also wondered how to tell Andrew and Susan that the husband and daughter of the driver whose car had killed Camille now lived just blocks away. Andrew had been so careful to avoid the burden of knowing even the name of the driver that Annabelle had never told her family, or anyone else, of her experience in the hospital chapel, and she now questioned the wisdom in doing anything that could possibly reopen old wounds. Surely sooner or later their paths would cross, she reasoned, but why run the risk of spoiling everyone's holiday by saying anything now?

No, she decided as the band stood and bowed after their final number, she would say nothing just yet. She would be patient. If she must do something, God would make it known; of that she was sure. On the way home, however, she asked Andrew to drive up into the avenues.

"I'd like to see the lights," she lied. "Turn up past the old Porter home. I hear there's a house nearby that is very tastefully done."

The old Porter house was dark and lifeless, but as they rounded the corner, Annabelle strained her eyes at the light coming from an open window in the garage where someone was putting colored lights on a Christmas tree.

Annabelle's promise in her prayer that night to God was the same as always: "Father, here am I; send me." She wondered how it would all play out. Before going to bed, she bundled up and walked across the street to McCallaway's store to say good night to Molly Ann.

Although the inside lights were switched off, Jed kept the Christmas lights in the display window on all night.

"Well, Molly Ann," she began in a half whisper, "it looks like another little girl has fallen under your spell. I wonder if her father has tried to buy you."

The possibility had not occurred to her until she had stated it, and it was quite unsettling. Once back in the parlor, she immediately phoned Jed.

"Yes," he said, "several people have asked me if she is for sale, several women and one elderly gentleman, but nobody like you've described. He may have talked with one of my clerks. I can ask them tomorrow if you like. I—"

"No, no. There's no need," she interrupted, "but I think I'd like to bring her home right away. I don't want him to be disappointed if he comes in tomorrow. If you'll turn the alarm off, I'll use my key and come over right now."

Since his wife's death, Jed had lived in an apartment behind the store, so it was no bother to turn off the door alarms. In ten minutes, Molly Ann was back on the bedroom dresser. Moments later, before she got into bed, Annabelle opened the top drawer and took a pastel green envelope from the wooden box she had had specially made for Camille's letters. It was her last letter, written the day before the accident. Annabelle had read it every month exactly on the day of the month it had been written, the twenty-first, coincidentally also the day of the month she had written her first poem, as well as the day of both Camille's and Susan's birthdays.

"Dearest Grandma,

Your poem arrived just in time. I needed it desperately. I'm so very glad you didn't wait until Christmas. I've come to one of those crossroads in life that you always used to talk about. You remember, don't you? Those times when life sort of slaps you in the face to get your attention, when things don't go quite as you'd like or you'd planned, when you think you have all the answers, but you suddenly realize that you're not nearly as smart as you thought you were. Well, something has happened to remind me once again of just how little I really know about life and how much I depend on what others have taught me and have yet to teach me. I'll tell you the whole story when you come for Christmas. It's too long and complicated to write.

I just want you to know now how grateful I am for my wonderful grandmother. Your poetry continues to inspire me and bless my life, but your very best poem is one you'll never write. Words could never do it justice. Your greatest work of art is your exemplary life, your willingness to do whatever Heavenly Father asks of you. Thank you for all that you've taught me. I know so much of what I want in my life by watching you and my mother. Thank you for teaching my mother to pray, and for helping her teach me to pray. I've learned once again that God hears me. His door is always open for me. He heard me when I called, and He sent someone to help me. It's a long story; I'll spoil it if I try to tell it all now. It will just have to wait until the holidays.

I must tell you just one thing about it. We have some new friends. They have a strange last name, even stranger than McNeely. It's a young family, Jacob and Ann and their beautiful little girl. You'll never guess what her name is. I'm not going to tell you yet. It will spoil the story. I want you to guess. Jacob is the one God sent to help me. Mark and I are going to their apartment tomorrow for dinner, and I'm taking Molly Ann with me to show to their little girl. I'm so excited. And they are coming next Sunday after church to brunch and to Mother's concert. There is something very special about them. Jacob is a carpenter and a writer—a poet, like you—and he's writing his first novel. I can't wait for you to meet them.

Molly Ann says 'Hi' and wishes you a happy Thanksgiving. She loves you and misses you very much.

Love,
Camille"

Annabelle put the letter back in its box, turned off the lamp, and climbed into bed. Although she was exhausted, she lay awake. As was her custom, she recited a poem and then reviewed in her mind the events of the day and her plans for the next. Tomorrow after her walk, she would spend the rest of the morning at the church helping prepare for Saturday's annual ward Christmas party. There was much to do. Because school was out, the children would be coming at 2:00 for a final practice for Sunday's Christmas Eve pageant—Annabelle was in charge of the choir of angels. Many in the ward had lobbied to end the tradition of a Christmas Eve service—it was such a busy time. Annabelle was among those who insisted that the tradition continue. She did not mind being busy if it did someone some good, and she was sure it had in the past and would in the future. If she found the time later in the afternoon, she and Susan would do some last-minute shopping. That evening, the widows and widowers of the ward were getting together for a light supper and white-elephant gift exchange. It would be a full day!

"Father," she whispered and smiled as she turned on her side to go to sleep, "if you have something more for me to do, I hope I can fit it in."

Chapter Five

The tree was in place in front of the window but was only partially trimmed. It was much taller and wider than Jacob had pictured it would be earlier that week when he bought what he was sure would be more than enough strings of small colored indoor lights. He had grossly underestimated. The top half of the tree was now lit, and Molly had carefully draped the colored-paper chains, a descending spiral of alternating links of dull red, brown, and green, that she had made at school. She too had miscalculated and had fallen asleep while they constructed additional chains, using the extra sheets of the colored construction paper her enlightened teacher had sent home with her. The dry, warm air smelled of popcorn, pizza, and pine. Molly had convinced her father to forgo their usual meal at the cafeteria in favor of a pizza at home with everything on it. After all, school was over for the holidays, and Molly insisted that the beginning of their Christmas vacation was more than ample cause for celebration.

She had already put on her pajamas, so after he had pulled the sheet and blankets back to the foot of her bed, he carefully lifted his daughter from her chair at the table, gently laid her down on the bed, and lovingly tucked her in. He sat on the edge of the bed and watched her sleep for several minutes, lightly stroking her soft brown curls. She was amazing. How he loved her. What would he do without her? If not for Molly, Ann's death would have surely destroyed him, and it was Molly now who would save him once more, he was equally sure.

Jacob had come to a crossroads. He had realized his error. He could not continue living with the guilt and self-blame he had sustained and nurtured for more than a year. He knew that it was time for a change of heart, his heart. But how, how to soften a heart that had been hard for so long? He turned his eyes from Molly to the family portrait on the wall above her bed. It was a beautiful picture, especially of Molly and Ann. Why couldn't its likeness be his memory of Ann? What must he do to replace the image in both his mind and his heart, as clear today as it had been every day for more than a year, the image that would not let him forget the burden of his guilt?

Faintly, from a distance, perhaps from the house up the hill, the melody of a familiar Christmas carol broke the otherwise total silence. Jacob listened attentively as the measured legato of a lone cello, possibly a recording but perhaps not, stirred in his memory the words he had not forgotten. The cello played the carol a second time, and tears rolled slowly down both cheeks as he gave in to the urge to sing, softly, almost in a whisper, so as not to eclipse the music nor awaken Molly:

"God rest ye merry gentlemen; let nothing you dismay. Remember Christ our Savior was born on Christmas day to save us all from Satan's power when we were gone astray. Oh, tidings of comfort and joy, comfort and joy. Oh, tidings of comfort and joy."

He had not known comfort and joy for more than a year. He longed for it now, the comfort and joy that he had felt when he believed. And he still believed. He knew now that he had always believed, but only now after a year of anger and guilt, now that he could bear it no longer, had he humbled himself sufficiently to break his hardened heart. As he watched his beautiful, precious daughter sleep, the feeling returned, the same inner surge of love and gratitude that he first came to know that rainy August night not so long ago when he first recognized the Spirit, that same warm, rainy night when he first attempted to pray. He had spent the year since Ann's death angrily denying what he had felt, but he could deny it no longer. It had come again. How could he have ever forgotten? How could he have ever doubted?

How could Ann possibly have ceased to exist when he felt so strongly her presence now? She believed that the human spirit was the offspring of Deity, but that the essence of who we are is eternal, as eternal as God himself. Jacob again pondered the possibilities as he had often done before with Ann. How could it be otherwise? How could human intelligence have a beginning and an end? He felt Ann's vitality and love, as strongly as if she were there with him now. How was that possible if she no longer existed? He shook his head in shame. How could he have been so foolish, so blind?

The room was full of shadows cast in all directions behind the light of the solitary Tiffany lamp that hung from the ceiling above the table. The lights on the tree reflected their tiny greens, blues, golds, and reds in the glass that covered the family portrait. Jacob stood and cleared a place on the other side of the table where he could work and still see both Molly and the tree. He took a pencil and several sheets of paper from his backpack and began to write. It had been more than a year since he had written poetry, but the urge to write now was as strong as or stronger than it had ever been.

Jacob pondered and wrote, pondered again and rewrote. What in many years of past experience had always been a painstaking process covering several days or longer was this night compressed into what seemed to Jacob only moments. In reality, the effort had taken him most of the night, but for more than six hours, it was as if time had stood still.

When it was finished, Jacob fell to his knees and offered his poem to God.

A Sinner's New-Year Prayer

Time passes not for all alike;
for children lost in play and song,
a year compared to four or five
seems oh so long.

Part Two
Chapter Five

For heads grown gray or silver white,
a year augmented sixtyfold
is but a fraction of a life
now growing old.
And once our death removes the veil,
all memory of our past retrieved,
much like a dream, a year will pass
scarcely perceived.
A thousand years is but a day,
one age an hour, one life a sigh;
a year next to eternity,
a twinkling eye.
And yet another year of sin,
of guilt and anger unrestrained,
may leave my unrepentant soul
forever stained.
God, grant that when I come to Thee,
the memory of this coming year
may bring a twinkling to my eye
and not a tear.

It was late in coming, very late, and he was ashamed it had taken him so long. But as he wept, Jacob promised God that he would pass his test of faith.

"Father, I don't deserve Thy mercy, but please, show me the way, and if Thou wilt…"

Jacob paused. He wanted to ask God to take from his mind the image that had haunted him for the past year, but he did not. He would first prove worthy, and then he would ask.

The alarm sounded from the clock at the head of his bed. It was 5:00 A.M., time for his run up the canyon. He was astonished to realize that he had written all night, yet he wasn't tired. He felt as though the weight of the world had been taken from him. In less than five minutes, he was on his way toward the canyon. He had never run so fast, nor felt so strong.

It was much warmer today than yesterday. The cold spell that had begun just after Thanksgiving was at last over. There was no wind, and the snow that had fallen the morning before had melted. Only small soft patches remained on the lawns on the north sides of houses, garages, and large trees. Another storm was forecast for Sunday, Christmas Eve. As he ran past the church with the white steeple, he resolved to take Molly there for the Christmas Eve pageant advertised on a sign on the front lawn. He determined also that after work, he would buy the doll in McCallaway's store. It would be the symbol of his repentance, of his submission to God's will.

Because there was no school, Jacob took Molly with him to the office—they took the car. Her backpack was full of books. She would read them while he finished some work that had to be completed before the holidays, then return them to the library on their way home. No one else was in the building except Valerie, one of the writers under Jacob's direction. Valerie had dark hair, dark eyes, and was as delightfully cheerful as she was beautiful—Jacob had felt an irrepressible pang of disappointment when she was introduced to him as Mrs. Valerie Lawson—but that wasn't why he hired her. Her portfolio showed her to be well qualified. After just three weeks with the company, Jacob considered her to be his department's best writer and certainly its most conscientious. She came in early almost every morning and often stayed late, so Jacob was not surprised to see her there, but he was surprised and alarmed to see that she had been crying.

"Is there something I can do for you, Valerie?" he asked.

"No, no...*niñerías...cosas de mujeres*," she said. "Just something...silly. I'm sorry. I didn't think I'd see anyone in today. What are you doing here anyway?" she continued in an obvious attempt to change the subject. "I thought the day off was for everyone, including you."

"I lied," Jacob said, forcing a smile. "I got just a little behind on the Lofton project. Are you sure you're all right? Do you need a good listener? I'm a pretty good listener."

Valerie's slight pause told him much more than the assurances that followed. "No, really. I'm fine. How are you Molly?" she asked. She and Molly had met just after she had been hired—Molly always came to work with Jacob on days when school was out—and a week before, they had gotten to know each other while sitting together at the company's family Christmas party. Valerie was married and had a son just a few years older than Molly, but she had come to the party alone. "Are you excited for Christmas?"

"*Sí*, Valerie, *¿y tú?*" Molly answered. Molly was always glad for the chance to use her Spanish.

"*Claro que sí, hija, claro que sí,*" she nodded.

Jacob read the contrary in her beautiful dark brown eyes. There was something very sad there, and he genuinely did want to help.

"Hey, listen," he broke in. "Why don't you and your husband and your son join us for Christmas dinner? I'm going to attempt to cook a small turkey. There's just the two of us, and we'd love to have you. Molly could use some female company."

"That's kind of you, Mr. Kikkert, but…we already have plans. Are you going to be here long?"

Jacob decided not to press her after this, her third attempt to change the subject

"A few hours, maybe longer. How about you?"

"I was just leaving. I've got some Christmas shopping yet to do. I just stopped by to pick up a few things, gifts I've been hiding in my office. Merry Christmas, Mr. Kikkert. *Feliz Navidad*, Molly."

She left quickly, and empty-handed.

"I've already taken them…the gifts, I mean…out to my car," she turned and added on her way to the door. "I'll see you next week."

"She wasn't telling the truth, was she, Daddy?" Molly observed thoughtfully.

"Nothing gets by you, does it?" he answered. "Sometimes people lie when they hurt inside, so no one knows they're hurting."

Jacob noted the trace of irony in his daughter's look and smile. She really did know how to read people.

"Daddy?"

"Yes, Molly?"

"Valerie's pretty, don't you think?"

"Yes, I guess she is."

"Does she always wear the same dress to work?"

Jacob thought for a moment.

"I'm not sure. Why do you ask?"

"Today she's got on the same dress she wore to the party and the same dress she wore when I first saw her."

The morning passed slowly. Jacob's ability to set his personal life aside to concentrate on his work was severely tested, especially now that he was trying hard to direct his thoughts in an unfamiliar, positive direction. Every now and again, he allowed himself the luxury of letting his mind wander to what he had planned for after work and the days to come. He was eager to buy the doll. He glanced over at Molly and smiled as he imagined the glee that would flood over her face when she opened the package.

He was sure that McCallaway's store would take back the other doll on exchange. The need to buy more strands of lights for the tree would be his excuse for running to the store while Molly cleaned up after the meal he had promised they would prepare that evening at home. He also wanted to buy a Nativity and another music disc or two—there was one song in particular that he wanted very much.

They took time out from Jacob's editing and Molly's reading only to eat the sandwiches they had brought for lunch, and by 3:00 were on their way home, stopping at the library to exchange Molly's books and at the grocery store to buy everything they would need for the next three days. They were tired of eating cafeteria food. Every meal from now on would be home-cooked, at least until Tuesday. By

4:30, they were back home trying to follow one of Carmen's "famous" recipes.

"Well, what do you think? How does it taste?" asked Jacob after Molly had taken a few bites of her Spanish rice and quesadilla.

"It's good, not exactly like Carmen's, but very good," Molly answered. She was being kind.

After supper, Jacob made his excuses.

"If you'll clean up the dishes and mop the floor, I'll run down to McCallaway's store and get some more lights for the tree, after I first check on something in the house."

"Can't I go with you?" she pleaded.

"Not this time. I'll be back in less than twenty minutes. Time me."

Chapter Six

Molly quickly cleared the dishes from the table and pulled the stool Jacob had made for her from the cupboard under the kitchen sink. After she was sure her father would not return, she left the dishes soaking and knelt at her mother's maple rocker to pray.

"Heavenly Father, I'm sorry I didn't pray last night. I fell asleep, and I probably won't get to pray again tonight. Daddy doesn't leave to work on the house, and I'm never alone. That's cuz it's almost Christmas. Thank You for Daddy. He's much happier, I think. I think he's ready to remember who he is. Please send someone soon to help him. Thank You for Mommy who is in heaven with You. Tell her that I love her and I'm trying hard to be a good girl and be like Jesus. Bless Grandma and Grandpa, and my teacher, and Carmen and Rosita, and Sandy, and all my new friends. Help them to have a merry Christmas. Also, please bless my new friend Valerie so she doesn't cry. And please remind Santa to bring me Molly Ann for Christmas if he can. Amen."

As soon as she had finished her prayer, she went back to work on the dishes. As they dried in the dish rack, she swept and mopped the floor, then took a book from her backpack and started to read. After reading several pages, she stopped and listened for her father's return. She had expected that he would be back before she finished her chores and wondered what was taking him so long. According to the clock on the dresser next to her mother's picture, it had been much longer than twenty minutes, more than thirty, she calculated, sufficient grounds in her mind to justify leaving the house to look for him.

She put her coat and hat on quickly. She was glad for the chance to see Molly Ann and hoped she wouldn't meet her father until she reached the store. She would wait for him there from a spot next to the mailbox from where she could see both the display window and the front door. On her way, two of her friends from school were walking with their parents in the opposite direction, one near the shops and another in the tunnel. It seemed the whole town was in the streets. Many carried bags or boxes, and almost everyone was smiling and wishing each other a Merry Christmas.

"*Buenas noches*, Molly," said a familiar voice behind her. "Where are you going in such a hurry?"

Valerie had just come down the west side of McCallaway's store along the walk that intersected at the corner of the building with the walk coming up from the tunnel. Molly noted that she was wearing the same green dress under her fleece coat.

"*Hola*, Valerie. I'm going to find my father."

"Is he lost?" she asked playfully.

Molly liked Valerie. The way she talked to her reminded her very much of her mother.

"No," Molly laughed, "he's in the store. I think he's buying a present for me. Carmen says that sometimes parents buy presents and give them to Santa to bring. That's why some kids get more presents than others."

"Carmen could very well be right. And what do you think your father might be buying for you?"

She took Molly's hand, and they continued along the sidewalk together.

"I hope he's buying me Camille's doll, the doll in the window. Have you seen her?" Molly asked.

"Yes, I have. She's very pretty, and I hope he buys her for you. Should we go in and see if we can find him?"

"No, I'll wait for him here. Are you going in to buy something for Joseph?"

Valerie shook her head. She continued smiling, but her eyes lost much of the radiance that was there before.

"No, Molly, I'm afraid Santa is pretty much on his own this year. *Adiós, guapa.* Merry Christmas."

"Merry Christmas, Valerie."

Valerie entered the store while Molly continued a few steps along the sidewalk toward her planned vantage point next to the mailbox. Several boys were watching the toy trolley make its rounds, and several mothers were pointing out things in the window to even younger children, some in arms and some standing in front of them with their faces very close to the glass. Before she could survey the display, Molly recognized her father standing in the telephone booth about twenty feet further down the sidewalk. He was facing away from her. She glanced into the display—Molly Ann was no longer there—then again into the telephone booth at the large wrapped box at her father's feet.

Her logical assumption triggered a spontaneous smile of delight, suppressed almost in the same instant as she realized her father might see her. She turned away and ran as fast as she could into the crowd of people who were exiting the store, and then down the sidewalk toward the tunnel. She hoped her father had not seen her. It would not do to spoil his surprise.

Chapter Seven

In the attic Jacob found the receipt in the bottom of the sack. He thought it best to leave the doll wrapped in its box, proof positive that it had never been opened. If they liked, they could use the same box and the same ribbon when they wrapped the new doll.

His heart was light as he walked briskly down the hill, past the several shops that lined the sidewalk, and finally through the tunnel that led to McCallaway's store. It was already dark, and the lights on the facades and on the trees lining the streets, the well wishes of passersby, and the good-natured hustle and bustle of the season were reflections of his own good cheer. With only this and one other shopping day until Christmas, McCallaway's store was busier than ever.

There were so many people in front of the display window that he did not stop to see if the doll was still there. Had he done so, his conversation with the girl at the customer service desk would have been different.

"May I help you?" she asked politely from behind the counter.

"Yes," Jacob began cheerfully, "I'd like to exchange this porcelain doll I bought a couple of weeks ago for the doll in the display window out front. The one that's sitting on the edge of the patchwork quilt."

"I'm sorry, sir, but the doll is not for sale. It's for display only."

Jacob's smile lost only part of its verve as he redrafted his request.

"I meant," he emphasized, "that I'd like to buy one of the dolls you have for sale just like the one in the window."

"I'm sorry, sir, but there are no other dolls like it for sale in the store," she explained. "It's the only one, and it's not for sale."

Jacob tried to sound patient.

"I don't understand. Are you saying you've sold out of the doll? And if so, why can't I buy the one in the display window?"

Apparently, Jed McCallaway had trained his clerks well. She knew exactly what to say.

"Sir, I'm sorry that I can't help you. Would you like to speak to the store's owner? He's in his office in the back. Just follow this aisle until it ends, and then turn to your right and you'll see the sign. It says 'Office.'"

Jacob thanked her and hurried to the back of the store.

"That's right, sir," confirmed Jed McCallaway from behind his desk. "It wasn't one of our dolls. It was for display only, and if you look, you'll see it's no longer there. The person whom it belongs to came last night and took it with her."

Jacob's heart sank.

"Could you suggest where I might go to find another one just like her?"

"You might try the Doll House. It's on the other side of town, but I doubt they'd be able to help you. They may have something similar, but—"

"She can't be something similar," Jacob interrupted. "She has to be the same doll. Could you at least tell me who owns the doll, so I can ask her where she bought her?"

Jacob's voice betrayed his emotion. Jed was sympathetic but refused to tell him the owner's name.

"I'm sorry, but I promised not to say, and I won't betray that confidence."

Discouraged but still hopeful, Jacob called the Doll House from the phone booth outside the store—one of those old-fashioned glass and wrought-iron telephone booths, matching the turn-of-the-century facade of the store. They had dolls with dark brown curls and brown eyes, and dolls with blue eyes and blond or red curls, but no blue-eyed dolls with large dark brown curls, nothing that perfectly matched Jacob's description. The owner even checked his several catalogs but found nothing. Jacob asked for, and he gave him, the names of several other shops in town that might help him. Luckily, he had his phone card, but one by one, none could locate the doll. The third shop owner he talked to gave him the name and number of her most knowledgeable collector.

"There has never been such a doll mass produced," the collector said. "It must be one-of-a-kind, most likely both made and purchased overseas."

Jacob was bitterly disappointed, close to despair. He could feel the anger he had fostered during the past year begin again to boil inside him. He was not an intemperate man—far from it—but it was all he could do to keep his anguish in check, all he could do not to vent his frustration in some physical way. He glanced down at the package he had set on the floor of the phone booth but did not give in to the impulse to crush it with one powerful step. Instead he turned and faced away from the package, away from the lights and the people coming in and out of the store.

"No," he said out loud as the image of Ann in the hospital returned once more to his thoughts. "I will not turn from God again. I will not change the course I have promised to follow. I will not fail again the trial of my faith."

He closed his eyes and uttered again the last verses of his sinner's prayer:

"And yet another year of sin,
of guilt and anger unrestrained,
may leave my unrepentant soul
forever stained.
God grant that when I come to Thee,
the memory of this coming year
may bring a twinkling to my eye
and not a tear."

When he opened his eyes and turned to leave, the first thing he saw was the joy in Molly's eyes. She was standing near the entrance to the store next to the mailbox, some twenty feet away, her excited gaze fixed on the package that was leaning against the inside glass of the phone booth. Jacob instantly understood what he saw in her eyes. She did not look at him, but straightaway turned and ran down the street toward the tunnel. As Jacob watched her disappear into the crowd, he repeated once again his prayer. It would seem that the real test of his faith had just begun.

Jacob was halfway through the tunnel before he realized he had forgotten to buy the lights and the music, so he quickly returned to McCallaway's Store. On his way to the music department, he saw Valerie Lawson partway down one of the aisles in the sporting goods section. She had a baseball glove on her left hand, and he watched her for a few moments as she punched the fist of her other hand repeatedly into the glove's webbing.

"Molly was right," he thought. "She is very pretty."

He tried to imagine her in a dress other than the familiar green one she now wore under her open jacket, but could not. Funny he had never noticed, but it was true: She always wore the same dress. When she turned to try on another glove, he left his shopping cart and approached her slowly from her blind side.

"You're not thinking of leaving us to play in the majors, are you?" he began to ask, but stopped short at Valerie's reaction.

She had flinched and cowered away from him at his first word, her hands springing defensively in front of her face. Jacob noted the sudden flash of terror in her eyes. It was not a normal reaction, and he realized his blunder immediately.

"I'm sorry, Valerie. I didn't mean to startle you. It was very stupid of me. Are you all right?"

Jacob was uncomfortably aware that he had violated her privacy, forcing her to reveal something that she would have preferred to keep secret. He tried to change the awkwardness of the moment by changing the subject.

"You must be doing some last-minute shopping for your son...I'm sorry, I don't remember his name."

"No, *nada*. I'm...I'm the one who's sorry. I...uh...his name is Joseph. Please, Mr. Kikkert, I'm not—"

"Please, Valerie, call me Jacob, or call me stupid. I really am sorry. I should have warned you. Will you forgive me?"

Valerie forced a smile and nodded.

"So..." Jacob continued, taking another glove from the rack and putting it on his own hand, "is that the one you've decided on?"

He did not wait for her answer.

"That one's not bad, but I'm pretty sure he would prefer this one. It's a little more expensive"—he checked the price tag—"well, quite a bit more expensive, but a guy's glove is his best friend. I know. This one will last a lifetime. It'll be a little big for him for a couple of years, but it's definitely the one I'd get him."

He handed her the glove.

"Then this one it will be," she said, returning to her usual confident manner. "And…thank you…Jacob," she ventured and smiled again. "Merry Christmas."

Jacob took this cue to say good-bye and went on his way. He was experiencing feelings he hadn't had for some time, and his first response was to drive them away, censuring himself for having allowed himself the luxury. After all, he had his own lost soul to worry about, but as he picked up the lights and found two new discs in the music section, he continued to contemplate his encounter with Valerie. It seemed to him that buying a son a baseball glove was a father's obligation and prerogative. His curiosity grew as he pondered the other symptoms and clues he had only now recognized as such.

It felt strangely pleasant to be thinking of another's troubles instead of his own, and he wondered what course he might take to help. For some reason, God did not want him to buy Molly the doll she wanted, the doll that was to be the symbol of his change of heart. Perhaps he and Molly—of course, she would jump at the chance—could celebrate Christ at Christmas by helping Valerie.

He stopped by the sporting goods section on his way to the checkout stand. As he suspected, the glove was back on the rack. All the gloves were still on the rack. He put it on his hand again, punched the webbing, smiled, and then dropped it into his cart.

Jacob and Molly spent what was left of their Friday night trimming the tree and fine-tuning their plans for the following day. Molly was elated by the prospect of subbing for Santa.

"You make lists for Joseph and his dad, and I'll make one for Valerie," she suggested.

"I'm not sure that there is a dad," he said pensively, "but I know how to find out."

Jacob hoped that the joy that comes from giving might partially compensate for the disappointment Molly would surely feel when he explained about the doll. He knew it would be better to tell her right away, but he decided to wait until Christmas Eve. On his way home from the store, he had formulated his plan. He would give Molly one other gift in addition to the bike and the surrogate doll, a special gift to be opened Christmas Eve that he hoped would mean more to her than any doll ever could.

His plan also required that he delay—also until Christmas Eve—telling Molly that he had returned to faith and prayer. So that night, Jacob knelt alone in the house so Molly would not yet know that he was praying.

"Father," he pled, "I remember reading that it is a foolish man who asks for a sign, and I am not expecting one. But if it be Thy will, please help me to know that Thou hast forgiven me. I am determined to submit my will to Thine and to follow the example of Thy Son. I am no longer angry with Thee, but it's hard to forgive myself. My hope is that Ann is with Thee and that I can be there with her some day. I miss her terribly. Please, strengthen my feeble faith that I might bear the burden of my guilt, or, if Thou wilt, and when Thou wilt, please take it from me."

Father and daughter woke early the following day. Jacob cut short his morning run. They had much to do. It was still dark when they arrived at the office. In Valerie's file, they found only some of the information they wanted: her address and phone number, of course, but strangely, nowhere had she given any information about her husband, not even his name.

The fifteen-minute drive to Valerie's house was pleasant. It was a cloudy winter morning and felt very much like it might snow. They had yet to explore the several smaller rural communities outside the city. Valerie lived on the outer edge of one of them, in a wonderful, old, white two-story farmhouse. The craftsman in Jacob admired its architectural integrity—especially the large front porch that wrapped around the house on the east, west, and south sides—but also lamented the neglect that had left the home much in need of repair.

Mature trees, mostly ash, and a large lawn surrounded it. It was just the kind of place he and Ann had so often dreamed and talked about. A small barn and three other buildings stood out back, isolated somewhat from the house by a small orchard. A large garden spot on the south side separated the detached garage from the U-shaped pasture that framed what was obviously once, many years ago, a well-kept and prosperous farm. Jacob studied its detail carefully. Molly was more interested in the cows across the road.

They drove past the house several times. Jacob was sure it was the right house—he recognized Valerie's car parked in the gravel drive that led to the garage—but he wanted to be certain that when he returned later that night, he would find no surprises. He could park out of sight some fifty or sixty yards down the road on the other side of the bridge that crossed the irrigation canal. No streetlights and no obstacles were in the way, nothing to hinder what would be a relatively short sprint in the dark, after dropping off the packages and rapping at the door. Best of all, there was no evidence that Valerie had a dog, and he saw no motion-activated lights.

It was plain good luck that the third and final time they drove by the house, Valerie had come out of the front door and was getting into her car. She was dressed in jeans and her familiar dark-green fleece jacket, the first time either Jacob or Molly had seen her in anything other than her green dress.

Only one important piece of information was lacking, information that a phone call from the pay phone at the service station two miles down the road would provide. An adolescent voice answered on the third ring.

"Hello, Lawsons."

"Hello, this is Jack Carlson. Is Mr. Lawson there?"

"He's not. Can I take a message?"

"It's urgent that I get in touch with him. When can I find him home?"

"He doesn't live here anymore. He left a month ago."

The voice paused slightly, then continued. "We're hoping he never comes back."

"Do you know where I can reach him?"

"No, I don't."

"May I speak with Mrs. Lawson?"

"She's not here. She's gone to work and won't be back until late this afternoon."

Part Two
Chapter Seven

Jacob's curiosity was growing. Valerie had left her house going in the direction opposite to the one that would have taken her into town. Once back in the city, he drove past the office to see if Valerie had indeed gone to work, but there was no sign of her.

After breakfast, Jacob and Molly were at the entrance to McCallaway's store when it opened at 9:00. Fortunately, the sales lady in the women's department was exactly Valerie's age and size, so it didn't take Molly long to select two dresses, a skirt, several pairs of stockings, two blouses, and a sweater. In addition to the baseball glove he had already purchased, Jacob picked out two baseballs, a bat, two books (he bought two copies of Dickens's *A Christmas Carol*, one for Joseph and one to read to Molly), a radio-controlled car, and two shirts. Molly wanted to gift-wrap it all at home, but Jacob insisted they have everything wrapped at the store.

"Fingerprints, that's why," he told her. "If we wrap them, our prints will be all over the place."

"Yeah, right," she said sarcastically. "I'm sure she'll check for fingerprints."

"She might; she's very smart, like you. And besides," Jacob added, "Mr. McCallaway tells me his store uses the same wrapping paper that Santa uses. We do want them to think the gifts are from Santa, don't we?"

Molly yielded.

After a stop at the grocery store for a box of oranges, some nuts, Christmas candy, bacon, a loaf of fresh bread, and a Christmas ham, it was off to the sandwich shop for lunch, then home again. It took them several tries to fit everything into the two large mesh bags with the hemp handles they had purchased specifically so that Jacob could carry everything in one trip. They finally took the oranges out of their box and put them into the bag wherever they fit as they packed. While Molly took a nap, Jacob did some rewiring in the house. They had tickets for *A Christmas Carol* at 8:00 P.M. at the community theater. The nap would assure that Molly wouldn't doze off during the play. They would make their delivery after the play ended.

Jacob knew that Valerie would surely suspect them when her son opened the package containing the baseball glove, but he would be ready if she said anything. He and Molly had both practiced during lunch how they would respond if confronted.

"Won't we be lying, Daddy?" Molly asked.

"It's not really lying," he assured her. "It's pretending, and I know for a fact that you are an excellent pretender."

Chapter Eight

Annabelle was glad for a chance to relax and watch the play. It had been a busy two days. Friday's pageant rehearsal went reasonably well. The children were ready. Later that afternoon, as she was baking tarts in the cultural hall kitchen with the Relief Society food committee, Bishop Beckstead called her into his office to show off the books of her poetry that he had picked up that morning from the printers. Saturday's party at the church was well attended. Everyone pitched in to help. Tonight's final performance of *A Christmas Carol* was sold out. Susan played the part of Scrooge's housekeeper, and Mark was one of the town children in several scenes. Like Annabelle, Susan had endured Camille's death through an increase in her service to others and through church and community involvement, sharing her time and talents freely whenever and however she could.

Annabelle had seen the second performance of the play a week ago with Andrew, and she was with him once again tonight. They had seats on the side aisle, six rows from the stage, not the best seats from which to view the play, but the best to see Mark and Susan. Despite the past two days' busy schedule, her thoughts had turned often to Molly and her father. She wondered why she had dreamed her dream and what her role would be as she patiently waited for God to give her His errand. When Jacob and Molly came in just seconds before the play started and sat down in the two vacant seats next to them, Annabelle knew this was no coincidence. She found it hard to concentrate on the play and was eager for intermission. When it at last came, Andrew left immediately to help backstage.

"Hello, Molly, how are you this evening?" she asked.

"You know my name?" was her surprised answer.

"I know the names of all the children who walk by my house on their way to school."

Molly remembered.

"Oh, you're the old lady in the window," she exclaimed, delighted.

"That's right. I'm the old lady in the window. Is this your father?" she asked, looking at Jacob. "Hello, I'm Annabelle McNeely. I live in the house across the street from McCallaway's store."

"I'm very pleased to meet you. I'm Jacob, Jacob Kikkert," he responded, offering his hand. "They tell me we'll be visiting your pumpkin patch next fall."

Annabelle puzzled. She had heard the name before, but where?

"Yes, I hope you will...do you like the play? And you'd better say yes," she warned good-naturedly. "My daughter Susan and my grandson Mark are two of the actors."

"We're enjoying it very much. Aren't we, Molly?" Jacob acknowledged while looking for Susan's and Mark's names in the program. "Let's see here...Susan...Harrison," he read. "Oh yes, Scrooge's housekeeper. She's very good."

"I'm glad you think so. Her best lines come after intermission when she sells dead Scrooge's bedsheets and curtains."

Jacob laughed politely, still looking at the program, then turned pensive. Annabelle noted a slight change in his voice, a trace of nostalgic and wistful sadness.

"I once knew a very special girl named Harrison," he said, still looking at the program. "Her mother's name was Susan...I never really met her, her mother, that is; I never got the chance. She was a pianist—the mother was—back East, where we used to live."

Annabelle desperately tried to keep her countenance from mirroring the light that had suddenly turned on inside her. The meaning concealed between the lines of Camille's last letter, the letter that Annabelle had faithfully read each month for a year, had been revealed to her in a sudden single emphatic stroke: the strange last name, Kikkert; the surprise name of the little girl, Molly.

She remembered, too, Susan and Andrew's story about Camille's encounter with the family they had never met. They had not canceled their scheduled Sunday brunch with the Kikkerts. Jacob and his family had not approached them after the funeral, and Susan and Andrew wondered if perhaps they did not know. But it was also possible that they had indeed attended but because of the crowds—many people had come to the funeral—had decided to wait until their brunch on Sunday to personally express their condolences. Whatever the case, after several failed attempts to reach them by phone, Andrew and Susan were ready to receive them that Sunday afternoon. They had left Annabelle with Mark at the hospital and driven home to prepare a light meal. They thought it odd when their new friends did not come and were even more puzzled that they had not at least called.

They did not pursue it further, nor did they think any less of the Kikkerts. It was an awkward situation, and after all, they had never really met; they would not know them if they were to see them. Their only real contact had been a brief phone conversation. Besides, they had enough to think about with Susan's concert that night and their plans to immediately return home as soon as Mark could travel. Andrew had advised the city of his desire to cut short his sabbatical, a request readily granted—the new director welcomed the chance to begin his tenure with a new hire.

Annabelle reflected now, during her moment of sudden realization, on the circumstances that had combined so that they never did, nor apparently would, learn that Mrs. Kikkert was the driver of the other car. The doctor had told them that the accident was caused by diabetic unconsciousness and that the woman driver, who had died, was not to blame. Andrew had, in fact, asked not to be told the driver's identity, and he and Susan had purposefully not read the obituaries or anything else in the newspaper. Nothing, they reasoned, could be gained by their knowing. Their sudden return home had eliminated any future chance contact with the Kikkerts. Even the unique last name was soon lost in their memory.

Only Annabelle had unknowingly kept alive a tie to the now long-forgotten Kikkerts, and she had no notion that any such tie was even there.

It had seemed fantastically providential when, out of the countless possibilities, the husband and daughter of the driver of the car that had taken Camille's life had come to live in their town. The revelation now that Jacob was also the man whom God had sent to save Camille in her time of need seemed nothing short of miraculous. What may have seemed to most to be an incredible sequence of coincidences was for Annabelle further conclusive evidence of her faith, that a loving Heavenly Father mediates in the lives of his children, and that he had a task for her to do. She recognized the affirmation of the Spirit that swelled inside her.

"Are you all right?" asked Jacob, alarmed by the unexpected pause and change in Annabelle's countenance.

"Yes, Jacob...I'm fine." She searched for something to say to break the tension. "So...where do you live?"

They talked briefly about the history of the old Porter house, the neighborhood, and other neighborly matters. Jacob decided he had better take Molly to the rest room before the second act.

"I need to freshen up myself," said Annabelle. "If you'd like, I can take her with me."

"That's kind of you. Thank you. I'll walk out with you. Now that I think about it, I probably should make a visit to the men's room."

As they waited in line, Molly and Annabelle became much better acquainted. On their way back to their seats, Annabelle could not resist one last question.

"Are you hoping for something special for Christmas?"

Molly's eyes lit up as the lights dimmed slightly to warn the audience to return to their seats for the beginning of the second act.

"Yes, I am." She stopped and pulled Annabelle down within range of her whisper so her father could not hear. "My daddy is giving me Camille's doll, the one that was in the display window of McCallaway's store."

Chapter Nine

Her grandmother's wall clock chimed eleven times—Joseph had fixed it that morning. Valerie sat alone in the dark, staring out the window from her grandfather's favorite chair—the only piece of furniture in the large room other than a small love seat against the bare north wall, a large coffee table in front of the love seat, and a small Christmas tree in the northwest corner by the stairs. It was a moonless, cloudy night, the darkest kind of night. It had started snowing large clumsy flakes, visible to her only in the headlights of an occasional car that sped past on its way back from town. She could not sleep. She thought another good cry might help. She had sent Joseph to bed an hour earlier. He had fallen asleep on the love seat while reading—they had no television. He was growing up so fast, too fast. A twelve-year-old boy should not be so unhappy and withdrawn. She blamed Karl, but she also blamed herself. If she had only been stronger, bolder; if she had stood up to him when it all began, things might be much different now.

Karl was gone. Thank God. She should have thrown him out two years ago, the first time. She had finally gone to the police on Thanksgiving Day. He would never touch her or Joseph again, but he had found another way to hurt them. He had withdrawn what little money they had, all they had saved in what they had agreed was Joseph's "untouchable" college account, and had maxed out the cash line on their credit cards. The police had been looking for him for almost a month. She was sure he was long gone and would never dare return.

"I love this house," she whispered through her tears, then sighed hard. It was her house, her grandparent's house, the house where she had spent her youth, and the house they had left her when they died. They had taken such good care of it. It needed so much work now. Years of neglect had taken their toll. If she was to keep it, the mortgage they had taken out to start the business must somehow be paid. When the business failed, Karl began drinking. Always quick to anger, he became increasingly volatile. She and Joseph endured it as long as they could, longer than they should have. She was sorry now that she had been so foolishly patient. Once a loving and happy child, Joseph was now a bitter and troubled young man.

On the Friday and Saturday after Thanksgiving, she had sold everything she possibly could at the estate sale the bank had helped them plan: furniture, tools, even most of her clothes—everything Karl had not already pawned to support his drinking—so they could keep the house and the farm; even so, the business debt, the second mortgage on the house—now her debt—would take many years—the rest of her life, it seemed—to eliminate.

The bank had been good to refinance a new thirty-year mortgage after she found her new job. It was a wonderful job at a good salary—more than she had hoped for—with good people, an answer to prayer. She was amazed they had hired her. She had competed against several applicants, and she had not worked as a full-time writer for years. She had put all her efforts into teaching and into the business— but because she was bilingual, she supposed—she had spent the first ten years of her life in Central America—the new director had given her the job.

Valerie smiled as she continued to cry. That new director was Jacob Kikkert, a young, handsome widower about her age, with an East-Coast accent when he spoke English and a Castilian accent when he spoke Spanish. He had been so kind and gracious that she had not dared ask for an advance on her first month's salary. Her pride had gotten the better of her. Christmas would simply have to be postponed. They would get by somehow until January. Her small Christmas bonus—she had worked for less than a month—and her Saturday jobs cleaning the Andra and Worthen homes—mansions really—would keep food on the table and gas in the old car she bought after the other had been repossessed. She tried to explain their circumstances to Joseph.

"Whatever," he said indifferently. "I don't really care if you cancel it altogether."

She had no plans to cancel Christmas, just reschedule it.

"January sixth, *el día de los reyes magos*," she promised. "That's the day the wise men brought us gifts in Costa Rica when I was a little girl. And that's the day they'll visit us here this year. It can't be much, Joseph, but you'll have a nice gift or two. I promise." "And a new dress or two for me for work," she promised herself.

She had Joseph's gifts already picked out. For sure, a baseball glove—Joseph loved baseball. His old glove and bat had disappeared early in the spring, as had anything that Karl could hock.

Valerie smiled again through her tears as she thought of her encounter with Jacob in McCallaway's store. She had flinched and cowered instinctively when he had startled her. Surely, he suspected why. He had been so understanding and tender that she soon forgot her embarrassment. In its place was hope that there might be more than kindness behind the extra attention that Jacob had shown her. Karl had never shown her such deference and tenderness, even before he began drinking. Valerie was not much given to fantasy—life had taught her too much—but tonight, alone in the dark, she imagined what life might be like were she to be loved by someone like Jacob.

Thus she mused, gazing out from a dark room into the dark of the night, when a sudden squeak of one of the porch planks startled her from her night's daydream. She leaped to her feet. She had known and feared the sound before. Surely, she thought, Karl would not dare return.

A quick series of hard raps on the door drew her to the window in time to see the figure of a man jump gracefully over the porch railing and vanish into the night. She turned on the switch between the window where she stood and the front door. All but one of the lights in the ceiling over the porch had burned out, but that lone dim light was enough to give her a glimpse of the back of the intruder scampering across the front lawn and into the darkness of the road.

She remained frozen at the window for a long time, straining to feel the slightest movement in the floor or to hear the tiniest sound. If anyone were there, she was sure she would hear him breathing. Nothing—only the lights from a passing car. Valerie wondered momentarily if she should call the police but decided that if it were Karl, he would have assumed that she already had. Besides, the man she saw running was not her husband; the Karl she knew could never have moved that fast.

She turned on the lights in the kitchen just long enough to check the back door. It was locked and secure. Besides the two windows on either side of the front door, three other windows allowed her to see both the east and south wings of the porch. Unless someone stood immediately behind the front door or against the house between two of the windows, there was no chance that anyone was still there. She listened with her ear at the door for a minute or two, just to be sure. Again, nothing.

Convinced finally that there was no danger, she slowly opened the front door and peered out under the security chain. She felt more silly than relieved when she beheld two large mesh bags brimming with wrapped packages. She recognized the wrapping paper from McCallaway's store and instantly knew the identity of her fleet-footed champion. She fell to her knees and started again to cry.

"God bless you, Jacob," she said.

Chapter Ten

"God bless us, everyone!" Jacob read.

Molly's body tensed slightly in his lap, and she adjusted her position somewhat to better look up into her father's face. They had begun reading the story that morning. Molly had enjoyed the play so much the night before that she wanted to read the book right away. Jacob understood the reason for his daughter's reaction. He had read the last lines of Dickens's tale with considerable emotion. His voice had also faltered when he read Scrooge's solemn promise to the Ghost of Christmas Future: "I'm not the man I was before."

Jacob knew he had confused her with his uncharacteristic show of sentiment, but he was glad to see the hope in her eyes mingled with that confusion. It was perfect timing. They had just had an early dinner, and it was still an hour before they had to leave for the Christmas Eve service and pageant at the church—Jacob had not yet told her of his plans to go.

Both he and Molly had been caught up the night before and since then in the excitement of their little project. The play had ended at 10:30 P.M., and it was 11:15 before they arrived at Valerie's house. On their way there, snow began to fall, which combined with the Christmas music from the radio to heighten their general holiday mood and good spirits.

As planned, they parked off the road, a few yards down the lane just on the other side of the bridge that crossed the canal. Here, the willows were so thick that no passing car would see them. Molly would be entirely safe during the few minutes he would be gone. She helped him take the bags from the trunk and adjust and secure the contents inside.

"Be careful not to drop anything. And don't forget to knock," she ordered.

"Okay. Here I go. Give me a kiss for luck," he said.

After Molly was safely inside the car, he ventured onto the road. He could see both ways for several hundred yards and was sure he could reach the porch without being surprised by approaching headlights. He proceeded cautiously over the lawn to the porch. The bags were rather awkward. He was a bit concerned that the falling snow might make the lawn a bit slick for his escape, and he reminded himself to not get too excited and fall on the seat of his jeans.

The house was totally dark, meaning Valerie and Joseph were probably both in bed, so he need not hurry; but after he had left the packages by the door and knocked, his adrenaline kicked in. He was over the rail and off the porch, running with little thought for the slippery lawn. He was fortunate that he had not dallied because a light went on while he was still in the yard. In the light of day, he would certainly have been spotted, but he was sure that even if someone had seen him, he couldn't be identified in the dark.

He and Molly waited for about ten minutes before pulling out onto the road. They drove away from the house for a few hundred yards and then returned, passing it at just over the speed limit—a slow-moving car would be suspect. Their load was still on the porch. Only then did it occur to Jacob that Valerie might be too frightened to open the door. He regretted knocking. It might have been better to let them discover the bags in the morning.

"No," Molly reassured him. "If they don't find it until morning, a cat or dog might eat the ham and the bacon."

Molly was right, as usual, and they both felt much better to discover, after a drive a few miles down the road and then back again, that the packages were safely inside.

"Yes!" Molly shouted triumphantly. "Mission accomplished!"

Their excitement and fatigue had carried over to the next day. Jacob crawled out of bed at 5:00, as was his custom, but this time only long enough to stoke the stove and sneak out to the house to wrap his special gift for Molly, the gift that was the center of his plan. He returned and, before slipping back into bed, placed it quietly under the tree among the packages from Carmen he had put there on Friday.

Molly awoke at 8:30 and was surprised to see her father still in his bed. He should have been back from his run and working on the house by now.

"Daddy, are you sick?" she asked, shaking him gently.

"No, honey. I'm fine. Just tired."

He wanted to tell her that he had decided not to work on Sundays, not even on the house, that Sundays from now on were to be a day of rest and worship, a day for family and close friends, a day for thinking of and serving others, but he didn't. That would have undone his plan.

After a breakfast of hotcakes with maple syrup, they made a snowman on the lawn in front of the house. Back inside where it was warm, they sat to begin Dickens's tale. Jacob put it down only to prepare and eat their late lunch and early supper. Now, they had come to the story's end. Jacob sat in Ann's rocker, with Molly in his lap. Jacob was sure that she had sensed that the emotion in his voice was a preface to something significant.

"Molly," he began, "I have a special present for you, and I want you to open it now. It's under the tree. Why don't you go and find it, and bring it here. I want you to open it sitting here in your mother's rocker."

Molly hugged her father, then jumped off his lap, kneeled down in front of the tree, and pulled out the package.

"It's very heavy," she said. "I can tell you wrapped it."

Jacob smiled at his daughter's quick wit as he stood so that she could take his place in the rocker. She peeled away the paper carefully and recognized her mother's Bible. Her smile vanished. She swallowed hard and turned and looked at her father, questioning him with her hope- and tear-filled eyes.

Jacob knelt down in front of her and took her hand.

"I love you, Molly. Do you know your daddy loves you?" His voice trembled.

"Yes, Daddy," she answered, her face reflecting the emotion of her father's faltering voice.

"And…do you know your mommy loves you?"

There was silence as she hesitated to answer.

"Daddy?"

"Yes, Molly?"

"Did you say 'loves' when you meant to say 'loved'?" Her voice trembled now, and Jacob knew that the light that filled her dark brown eyes was the reflection of the hope in the windows to his own soul.

"No, Molly. I meant to say 'loves.'"

His throat burned as he struggled to continue.

"Your mother loves you. And there's so much more you need to know. She loves you because she lives. She lives and will live forever. She lives with God. Do you know that God loves you? He does, and he loves Mommy and he loves me."

The tears that he had once promised himself that Molly would never see flowed freely now. He did not try to stop them. Molly laid the Bible on the seat of the rocker, threw her arms around her father's neck, and cried too.

"And we will be a family again: you, Molly, your mommy, and I." Jacob was weeping unashamedly now, but he was strangely comfortable with these tears. "Your daddy was wrong…your daddy was so wrong…and your mommy was right. She was right...you must never forget that she was right."

It was hard for him to speak.

"And we must try to live as she taught us. And we will, Molly; I promise you...we will...I promise."

Jacob sensed that Ann was present, too; Jacob, Ann, and Molly, embracing, crying, not wanting to let go, not wanting to break the wonderful spell. Finally, Molly pushed herself from their embrace and looked again into her father's eyes.

"Daddy?" she asked.

"Yes, Molly?"

"Can I pray now?"

Jacob held her little shoulders in his hands and looked deeply into her beautiful brown eyes. He saw reflected there the undeniable evidence of things unseen but true.

"Oh yes, Molly, you can pray. You can pray every morning and every night...and Molly?"

"Yes, Daddy?"

"Will you teach me again how to pray?"

"Yes, Daddy."

Father and daughter knelt together by the rocker.

"Heavenly Father," she began, "thank Thee for all Thy blessings. Thank Thee for Jesus and Christmas, and thank Thee for helping my daddy remember who he is..."

When she finished her prayer, they sat in the rocker, and Jacob opened the Bible to the Gospel of Luke.

"And there were in the same country," he began, "shepherds abiding in the field, keeping watch over their flock by night..."

It started to snow again as, hand in hand, father and daughter walked down the hill, under the tunnel, past McCallaway's store, and on to the church with the white steeple. They arrived twenty minutes early and sat against the left wall halfway down the rows of pews, where they would be out of the way and from where they could watch the congregation and participants fill the chapel.

Molly delighted in every moment of the experience, and Jacob delighted in Molly. She stood and waved each time she spotted a classmate—there were several, dressed as angels, in the choir. When Annabelle McNeely walked in behind them, shepherding the smallest angels to their places, Molly tugged hard at her father's shirtsleeve.

"Look, Daddy," she pointed. "There's Mrs. McNeely."

In the same moment, Annabelle spotted her two lost sheep and left the ninety and nine to welcome them.

"What a surprise! I'm so glad you've come," she said. "Let's find a seat closer to the front, where you can see better."

She ushered them up several rows to the closest available seats on the aisle before returning to finish ordering her little flock of fidgety angels. Just minutes before the beginning of the service, she returned unexpectedly. Jacob sat Molly in his lap to make room on the aisle.

"Jacob, Molly," she began, "please don't say no. I know we've barely met, but I'd like you to come to my house tomorrow for Christmas dinner at twelve noon sharp. I'm cooking a huge turkey with all the trimmings, and my little family and I would love to have you. You'll break an old woman's heart if you don't come."

"Please, Daddy. Can we go?" pleaded Molly.

Molly was much like her mother in that respect, socially minded and at her best around other people. She missed their Sunday-night gatherings at Carmen's, and Jacob missed them, too. He was also eager to expand their circle of friends and welcomed any chance for Molly to spend time with good people.

"There's no reason why we couldn't," he answered, and Molly's curls bounced up and down off her shoulders. "Thank you, Mrs. McNeely. This is very kind of you. Molly will be glad to have someone to talk to besides me for a change, and glad to eat someone else's cooking."

"Wonderful! I'm so pleased," she replied. "And please, Jacob, call me Annabelle. And you can call me Annabelle, too, Molly. All the children do. I'll see you tomorrow then at noon. Enjoy the service."

And they did enjoy it: the music, the sermon, the pageant, and the walk home in the gently falling snow. It was a perfect day before Christmas, at least for Molly, and would have been too for Jacob, if not for the task that still awaited him. He must somehow, some way, tell Molly that there would be no Molly Ann for Christmas. He had determined to tell her on the way home, but he did not. He decided it would be better after evening Scripture and prayer, but it was not. His last chance was as he tucked her into bed, but he again let the chance slip by. Why should he ruin what for Molly had been a glorious day? he reasoned. Why should he spoil her Christmas Eve? Why not delay it until the last possible moment? He would tell her in the morning.

Molly fell asleep to the music Jacob had purchased from McCallaway's store, but Jacob lay awake so that he could bring the gifts down from the house. It took him two trips—the bicycle was a trip by itself—but he left the doll he had bought in the attic. As he filled Molly's stocking, he pondered the events of the day and the words he had just read to Molly from the Bible: "Ask and ye shall receive; knock and it shall be opened unto you."

"Why not ask for a miracle?" he thought, surprised by his boldness yet entirely comfortable with the notion. "Why not ask? Why not knock?"

All right, he would ask. If it was God's will that his petition be granted, it would be so. If not, he would accept God's will, but what harm could come from asking? He would exercise his faith and then submit himself to God's will.

The music had long stopped. Molly slept soundly, contentedly, purring like a kitten. Jacob knelt at the side of his bed and talked with God. He thanked Him for hearing his prayer. He thanked Him for Molly, for the blessing of being her father. He thanked Him one by one for all his blessings, for his change of heart, for the promptings of the Spirit.

"And Father," he at last concluded, "I am yet a child in my faith. I do not understand Thy ways, but if it be Thy will, please take the memory of my guilt from me. Please replace it with another. And—" Yes, he must ask it; something assured him that God wanted him to ask it. His voice broke as the warmth of the Spirit filled his body like the rays of the summer sun—"please bring Molly the doll that was once in McCallaway's store."

Chapter Eleven

As she had done hundreds of times before, Annabelle lovingly moved Molly Ann from the parlor to the bedroom. In the morning, she would bring her back to her place of honor on the piano. This personal physical contact twice each day with Camille's doll had become for Annabelle an almost sacred ritual, her personal liturgy, and her way to cherish the memory of her granddaughter.

Tomorrow Molly Ann would participate in their Christmas tradition. It was she, after all, who would wear the new dress. Annabelle had promised Camille that she would keep her doll with her always. Of all the tangible things she possessed, Molly Ann was her most prized treasure. The prospect of life without her was unimaginable. Surely, God would not ask it of her. Certainly, it was something else He wanted her to do for Molly. She was ready to give of herself in anyway she was directed, but the doll meant so much to her. It could never mean as much to anyone else.

Since her conversation with Molly at the play, Annabelle had done a good job of convincing herself that God would never expect her to part with Molly Ann, but she realized now as she prepared for bed that she was in effect trying to answer her own prayers. It had been God's will that she put Molly Ann in the display window for Molly to see; of this she was certain. She had responded to her dream without hesitation and in total trust, waiting patiently for God to give her His errand. She never imagined until last night at the play that His errand might include giving away Molly Ann.

"No," she had told herself as she watched the rest of the play, "there is something else, certainly something much more meaningful that I must do. It makes perfect sense. God wants Jacob and Molly to have the chance to accept the gospel. Camille began to bring our two families together more than a year ago, and now God has given us a second chance. Perhaps some wound must be healed, something perhaps related to Molly's mother's death that has prepared Jacob to embrace the Savior and his Church. But give up Molly Ann? What could it accomplish? True, it would bring joy to a little girl on Christmas day, but it would also bring loneliness to an old lady for the rest of her life. No, the price is too high, the sacrifice too great."

Her argument was becoming stronger.

"Yes, Molly will be disappointed not to find Molly Ann among her presents, but she won't be the only child disappointed on Christmas day—the world is sometimes a cruel place; thousands of children will feel the same. God sat Jacob and Molly here next to me as a prelude to something much more important. He has arranged for me to meet them. I must now foster the friendship we have begun. Yes," she reasoned, "this I must do. Perhaps Molly's interest in the doll is the excuse I needed to take the next step." Annabelle resolved to have her new friends over for dinner sometime soon after Christmas. Andrew, Susan, and Mark would come too. She would show Molly the doll; she would once again bring the families together.

The opportunity to extend that invitation came much sooner than she had expected. When she spotted Jacob and Molly the following evening in the chapel during her last-minute preparations for the ward's special Christmas Eve service, the idea occurred to her that she should invite them to Christmas dinner. Annabelle was happy to obey such an unmistakable prompting from the Spirit. So, she had boldly asked them to come and was delighted when they accepted. Dinner was planned for 1:00, and she had decided before asking them to tell them to come exactly on the hour, allowing her family time for their traditional opening of Camille's gift and poem before their guests arrived. The Spirit, however, had again intervened, and she had instead asked them to come at noon. It was clear to Annabelle that God wanted them to be part of the tradition. After she returned to her seat in the choir, she started to formulate her plan. Molly's disappointment would not last for long. She would invite her to come and see Molly Ann as often as she liked. She would even allow her to help change her dress on occasion.

"Yes," she told herself. "Molly Ann is to stay with me so that Molly will come often to see me. Yes, this must be what God wants me to do."

During the service, Annabelle observed her new friends often and carefully from her place in the choir. She had never seen anyone so attentive. Molly's eyes were wide with wonder. Jacob's were full of faith. There was an unmistakable aura in their countenance that told her that God was with them.

After the service, at their family Christmas Eve party and devotional, Annabelle sat Susan, Andrew, and Mark down to listen to what she promised would be a remarkable story. She told them everything, beginning with her encounter with little Molly Kikkert in the hospital and concluding with the news that Jacob and Molly Kikkert were joining them for Christmas dinner. They listened intently; Susan cried. Annabelle was thorough; they had very few questions.

"So, what do you think?" she asked.

"I don't know what to say," said a tearful Susan. "One thing's certain: Our Heavenly Father loves us very much. I'm looking forward to meeting them."

"I'm glad you invited them," said Andrew, his voice cracking with emotion. "It's going to be a wonderful Christmas."

Mark looked particularly pensive. He had responded to Camille's death in a far different manner than his parents had. They had relied on each other and on their faith. Mark had at first turned his sorrow inward and his anger heavenward. His emotional scars had not healed as quickly as had his bodily ones. It had taken him longer to mourn, much longer to find the inner peace that sustained his parents. But he had at last found it and was better for it. Annabelle was proud of her grandson.

"And what do you think, Mark?" she asked.

"I think," he said, "that Camille would want you to give her the doll."

Chapter Twelve

Jacob often had dreams—common dreams that, once awake, were quickly and easily forgotten—but none like the dream he had that Christmas Eve. He would remember this dream every day for the rest of his life. He was in a dark and damp prison, a cramped cell, hewn out of solid stone, locked behind a rusted iron gate, welded to its frame. He had been there a long time, cold and alone, hungry and weak. His only solace was that through the bars he could see a warm and pleasant meadow surrounded by a forest of tall trees and filled with brightly colored flowers and children dressed in equally brightly colored clothes, hundreds of happy children singing, laughing, and playing on the grass. Molly was among them. She turned and waved to him, and Jacob longed to be with her. He threw himself against the gate until he was bruised and broken, and pulled until his strength was gone.

Then he began to weep and to pray, and as he prayed he looked through the bars of his cell and saw a woman in a beautiful white dress coming out of the trees. Many of the children ran toward her and greeted her enthusiastically. Molly was the first to reach her and was swept up in a loving embrace. From her arms Molly pointed toward Jacob's cell. Only then did he recognize the woman, and in an instant Ann stood outside the gate of his prison. Her face was serene yet radiant, full of joy and love. She opened the gate effortlessly and, taking Jacob's hand, led him out of his prison into the light and warmth of the meadow

Together, they stood on the grass among the flowers, Ann watching Molly play with the other children, and Jacob watching Ann. Her deep blue eyes shown with a brilliance he had never imagined possible in human eyes.

Some of the children again ran toward the forest, where another woman also dressed in white had come out of the trees. Again, Molly was the first to reach her and was again swept up in a loving embrace. Molly pointed once more toward Jacob, and he recognized Camille; her long red hair glistened in the sunlight. She was holding a box wrapped in the paper from McCallaway's store. She left the children and in an instant was standing with Jacob and Ann.

"Hello, Jacob. We're all glad you're finally here," she said, as she handed the box to Ann.

Ann unwrapped it quickly, effortlessly. Inside was the doll, the doll from the window of McCallaway's store.

"Here, Jacob," Ann said, handing him the doll. "You have passed the trial of your faith and remembered who you are. Here is your sign, Camille's doll, Molly Ann. She wants you to give it to our Molly. You see, Jacob, God does know us better than we know ourselves. Your adversity has shown you the way, the direction He wants you to go… and, Jacob," she added, "Valerie is very pretty."

Ann touched his cheek, then his lips with her finger, kissed him softly, and smiled, a smile that spoke volumes, then turned and with Camille walked back into the trees. It was that smile, that image of Ann, that remained with Jacob when he awoke from his dream to what sounded like a knock at the door.

It was first light, Christmas day. It took Jacob several moments to orient himself. It had all seemed so real. Unlike all his other dreams, images that were quickly confused with those of a thousand other dreams, this dream would not leave him. It was as clear in his memory as anything he had ever experienced while awake. He knew it was a dream sent from God.

Molly had not stirred. Although there was some light outside, it was still dark in the garage. Jacob quickly pulled on his jeans, donned his shirt, straightened his hair with his hands, and made his way in the dark to the door. Who could it be? Who would be up at this hour on Christmas morning?

He opened the door. No one. But on the doorstep were two packages, both wrapped in the paper from McCallaway's store.

Jacob wasn't sure what to think. Who? he wondered. Perhaps Valerie. An attempt to reciprocate? But how? They had made their delivery Saturday night, long after McCallaway's store had closed, and it was never open on Sunday. Perhaps someone else from the office, perhaps his boss, Mr. Poulsen. Perhaps Mrs. McNeely. Yes, Annabelle

McNeely. She had been so kind to invite them to Christmas dinner, and she did live across the street from the store. But if they were coming for dinner, why would she not wait until then?

Jacob turned on the Tiffany lamp above the table to examine the packages more carefully. They were wrapped immaculately; no tape showed anywhere. Each package was trimmed in gold and silver ribbon. Both were quite large but not heavy, and both had small white cards tucked in under the ribbon with Molly's name perfectly inked on them by a skilled hand. The card on the larger of the two added the footnote: "open first."

It was too early to wake Molly, so after he had placed the two gifts under the tree, Jacob stoked the fire and lay back on his bed. His dream had not left him. He recalled it in all its precise detail. He closed his eyes and could see Ann's face exactly as it had been in his dream. He tried to recall the images that had been with him so long, the images from the hospital, but could not. They had been taken from his memory and replaced with those of his dream. That part of his prayer had been answered, and he was filled with wonder and gratitude as he now pondered God's goodness. He also wondered if the second part of his petition might be granted. "Here is your sign," Ann had said, and as the light from this Christmas dawn filled the room, he stared at the packages under the tree and began to cry. He knew what was inside one of them. How could he doubt it? But how was it possible? How had it happened?

Part Two
Chapter Twelve

He could wait no longer. The room was cozy and warm. He plugged in the lights on the tree and turned on the disc player, selecting "God Rest Ye Merry Gentlemen."

"Molly, honey, it's Christmas morning," Jacob whispered in her ear, "and Santa has been here."

Molly smiled with her eyes still closed and then opened them slowly as she stretched and yawned.

"I had the coolest dream," she exclaimed, then stood up on the bed and jumped into her father's arms.

"It wasn't as cool as mine," he challenged.

When she saw the bike next to the tree, she jumped out of his arms and rode it twice around the table. Her stocking was next, and she emptied its contents onto the table item by item.

"Let's open some gifts," suggested Jacob, trying not to sound impatient.

"This one says, 'Open me first,'" said Molly as she sorted through the presents under the tree.

"Then you'd better open it first," Jacob replied.

Molly tried to act stunned when she pulled the doll from the box. Jacob eyes welled with tears. It was Camille's doll, but her eyes and smile had changed. They now reminded Jacob of his dream.

"What's the matter, Daddy?" she asked.

"I'm just very happy, Molly. Merry Christmas."

"Merry Christmas, Daddy," she said, running into his arms for a big hug, and then turned her attention immediately back to the doll.

"Look, Daddy. I told you it was Camille's doll. I told you it was Molly Ann."

She showed him the embroidered name on the dress hem. It was written in the same style as Molly's name on the card.

Just how Camille's doll had found its way into Molly's arms was a mystery Jacob was anxious to solve. He knew it was God's hand that had put her there, but he ached to understand just how. The second package brought more tears of joy to both daughter and father. Inside were twelve other dresses, each with "Molly Ann" embroidered on the hem in gold and silver thread.

Chapter Thirteen

Everyone was in the kitchen busily preparing Christmas dinner. Besides the usual sausage and celery stuffing, mashed potatoes and gravy, and the other holiday turkey trimmings, Annabelle was making everyone's individual favorites: stuffed mushrooms for Mark, sauerkraut for Andrew—no one else would touch it—and candied yams for Susan. In all cases, she had doubled the recipe just in case their guests' tastes required it. The house was decked in holiday finery. Every room evidenced Annabelle's acclaimed knack for beauty. Holly graced the parlor mantel, and fir boughs accentuated every shelf, doorway, and window. Candles and nutcrackers, figurines and carvings adorned even the smallest nooks and crannies. In the parlor the fir tree guarded its spoils, open gifts segregated in piles by recipient, each easily identified by the name on its attendant Christmas stocking.

As they labored, Andrew sang along with the carols broadcast from the stereo in the adjacent dining room. If he didn't know the words, he made up his own, and Susan and Annabelle snickered at both the liberties taken and the sour notes that accompanied them.

All were excited to at last meet the Kikkerts. Susan was a little nervous, worried about protocol: Who would answer the door, who would sit where, what she would say.

"Just be yourself," Andrew counseled. "Just let it happen."

They had all been up since an hour before dawn. Annabelle had awakened them with her 6:00 A.M. phone call.

"I'm sorry to wake you so early," she had explained, "but I need Andrew to make a delivery for me right away."

Annabelle gave no other details. She knew that they understood immediately what she meant. Andrew, always the teacher, brought Mark along to share in the adventure, and it was Mark who placed the two packages on the doorstep, knocked several times, then slid through his footprints down the snow-covered driveway to where Andrew and Annabelle waited in the getaway car.

Later that morning, when all were gathered in the parlor to open their gifts, Annabelle explained her decision. She was not one to liberally share her personal spiritual experiences but felt that she owed her family an honest explanation.

"Mark's words shamed me," she began. "I'd thought only of what I wanted, what I believed was best for me. Molly Ann is Camille's doll, not mine, and thanks to you, Mark, I began to think of what Camille would tell me. I decided to act on faith, and I wrapped Molly Ann and her dresses, then I prayed. In my prayer, I promised God that if Camille wanted me to give little Molly the packages, they were wrapped and ready to go. I lay awake for quite a while waiting, listening for some answer, but none came. I was as confused as ever."

Annabelle had started to cry. Susan moved from her place on the love seat next to Andrew and sat down by her mother on the couch and took her hand.

"Then a wonderful thing happened," Annabelle continued through her tears. "For the second time in my life, I dreamed. In the dream, Camille walked through a large meadow surrounded by trees and filled with flowers and happy children. Many of them greeted her. She seemed to know them all. Some of them sat on the grass with their parents; others played in small groups of five or six, but none was alone. Camille was dressed in a beautiful but simple white gown. When she saw me, she smiled and hurried toward me. We embraced. She thanked me for taking such good care of Molly Ann, then turned and took the packages from the piano in the parlor. 'Good-bye,' she said. 'I'll see you again soon.' Then she returned to the meadow to where a couple and their little dark-haired daughter sat on the grass. It was Jacob Kikkert, and the little dark-haired girl was his daughter, Molly. Molly's mother, a beautiful blond-haired, blue-eyed woman also dressed in white, rose to greet Camille. Camille gave the packages to her, then she gave them to Jacob, and he in turn gave them to Molly, who opened them. Molly cried with joy and then turned and waved to me. Camille and Molly's mother walked together into the trees at the edge of the meadow. That was my dream. I awoke. It was almost six in the morning. I called you right away."

Chapter Fourteen

Jacob and Molly had decided to walk to Annabelle's. Jacob could not recall ever being happier. Except for the main road that turned west at McCallaway's store, the streets had not yet been cleared of the two or three inches of powdery snow that had fallen during the night, giving them a view of the cityscape before them as they emerged from the tunnel a aura of unspotted cleanliness and freshness that mirrored his own mood and sentiment.

They arrived at the door exactly as the bell in the city's clock tower chimed noon in the cold clear air. Jacob was carrying a small wrapped package, and Molly carefully held Molly Ann. Andrew met them at the door.

"Hello, Jacob. Hello, Molly. I'm Andrew, and I'm very pleased to meet you," he said, offering his hand to Jacob and then crouching down to offer it to Molly, too. "We've heard a lot about you. Come right in. Annabelle and the rest of the family are in the parlor."

Molly pulled Jacob down and whispered into her father's ear, "He's very tall!"

After only a few steps down the entry hall, they turned through an arched opening into the parlor where Susan, Mark, and Annabelle waited to greet them. Instantly, Molly let go of her father's hand and ran to the large portrait hanging on the wall behind the sofa.

"Look, Daddy!" she said excitedly. "It's Camille! It's a picture of Camille!"

Jacob's mind quickly connected the pieces of the puzzle: Annabelle, Susan, and Andrew Harrison, the doll named Molly Ann. The color left his face in an instant. Every muscle in his body tensed and then joined together in one colossal shudder he could only partially restrain. He felt weak and helpless and out of breath. His knees buckled slightly. He took a half step backward to regain his balance, and the package he was holding in his left hand fell to the floor.

Susan stepped forward, taking his trembling hands in hers; her exquisite fingers wrapped around his in a motherly caress.

"Yes, dear Jacob, we are Camille's family, and we're so pleased and happy to finally meet you."

Jacob tried to speak.

"I...I don't...I don't know what to say," he stuttered.

Tears had filled his eyes; he took a quick, deep breath, bowed his head, and began to cry.

Susan reached behind his shoulder with her right hand and pulled him into her embrace. Together they wept, Jacob's face buried between her neck and shoulder.

Annabelle cried, too, holding Molly close to her side. Andrew put his arm around Mark's shoulder, and they joined in.

"It's all right, Jacob. We understand, we understand," Susan repeated.

After several moments, Susan broke their embrace and led Jacob by the arm to the sofa and sat him down beside her. By then, Andrew had tissues for everyone. Mark sat down next to his mother, and Annabelle and Molly claimed the facing love seat while Andrew sat in the chair he had pulled from the parlor desk.

"Jacob, dear Molly," began Annabelle, "God has brought us together. He wants us to be good friends. And we will be, if you'll let us."

Jacob bit his lower lip to help stay the tears that continued to well in his eyes and fall. His throat burned.

"I'm so sorry," he said. "I'm so sorry about Camille—"

"Jacob," Andrew gently but firmly interrupted, "you need to know we feel only gratitude for what you did for our daughter. You saved her. We blame no one for her death, and I mean that genuinely. We have accepted God's will. We feel His love with us, and I believe you feel it, too. We've no doubt that we'll be with Camille again, and no doubt that you and little Molly will be with Ann also. I'm equally sure that what we're beginning here now today, this wonderful Christmas day, is an association that will last for the eternities."

Jacob nodded his agreement.

"I believe so, too," he said. "And thank you, all of you. God bless you for what you've done for Molly...and for me."

"God bless us, everyone," interrupted Molly, remembering her Dickens.

"Yes, Molly," said Annabelle, smiling, "God bless us, everyone...I love happy endings, or should I say happy beginnings? Now if it's all right with you, Jacob and Molly, we'd like you to be part of our family Christmas tradition."

Annabelle took the package from the piano.

"Molly," she asked with a slight tremble in her voice, "would it be all right if we put Molly Ann on the piano while we open Camille's gift?"

Molly smiled and nodded, then jumped out of her seat and set the doll tenderly on the doll stand on the piano. Annabelle handed the package to Mark, then sat down again next to Molly. Mark stared thoughtfully at the package in his lap for a few moments in uncomfortable silence, then winked at his grandmother and handed it to Molly.

"I suggest we change our tradition slightly and have Molly open it," he said.

Molly recognized the lettering on the card and began again to cry. She turned and put her arms around Annabelle's neck.

"I love you, Annabelle," she whispered.

"I love you, too, Molly. The envelope inside is for Susan to open," she added.

Molly carefully opened the package, thumbed the embroidered lettering on the hem, and then held up the dress for all to see. She next handed the envelope to Susan.

"I think I'd like to change our tradition slightly also," she said, looking at her mother for approval.

Annabelle nodded her agreement.

Susan rose from the couch, took Jacob by the hand, and led him to the chair where Andrew was sitting.

"You two need to change places," she said, handing the envelope to Jacob. She sat on the couch next to Andrew, snuggling into his open arms.

Jacob's eyes pleaded for some explanation.

"It's Mother's Christmas poem," Susan answered. "Every year, she writes one in Camille's memory."

"Are you sure you want me to read it?" he asked.

"I'm very sure," Annabelle nodded.

Jacob carefully broke the envelope's seal, pulled out the gray parchment pages, and read.

Running the Trail
(for Camille)

Why does life contain heartache and sorrows?
Why does God permit suffering and pain?
What is there from uncertain tomorrows
that mankind stands to gain?
I'll not quote you a lesson from Scripture;
a theologian, indeed, I am not.
Sometimes lessons from life help us picture
what hard doctrine cannot.

Years ago, I discovered that running
on a track, twice a week in the morn,
caused a change in my life. It was stunning,
  much like being reborn.
Though it took me a while to get used to,
to reach optimum distance and time,
once I'd realized my goal, I can tell you,
  I was feeling just fine.
The track was inside a large building,
a grand complex of concrete and steel.
Its surface was even and yielding:
  the conditions ideal,
the temperature; comfort, perfection.
It was safe, not a chance I would fall.
Those who ran faced the self-same direction:
  no distractions at all.
And yet, once I had reached my objective,
when my quota for fitness was full,
what before had been novel and festive,
  now became rather dull.
As time passed, given any good reason,
I would skip a day's workout or two.
And if not for a change in the season,
  my conditioning was through.
With the spring and a break in the weather,
on the side of the road, oft I'd see
people running, alone or together;
  it just might work for me.
But the road held one obvious danger.
The solution, good luck would avail:

in the canyon I spotted a stranger
running safe on a trail.
Though its course ran the self-same direction
as the road, it was nearer the stream.
Trees concealed it from sight and attention;
it could hardly be seen.
I discovered its origin and distance
and determined to give it a try.
It refurbished my fitness persistence.
I'll explain to you why.
From the trail, I can see God's creations,
from the cliffs to the rocks in the creek.
Sights and smells, sounds, and other sensations
are diverse and unique.
Each new day brings a different adventure,
something new for my soul to be taught;
and there's no one around who can censor
any feeling or thought.
And few details escape my reflection;
God has blessed us with so much to see.
Every object from nature's collection
holds a lesson for me:
the new colors that autumn delivers,
the first butterfly hatch in the spring,
the soft snowfall and ice on the river
that the wintertime brings.
Running trails brings joy if one chooses,
but the privilege exacts its own price.
There are blisters, sore muscles, and bruises,
and you fall once or twice.

The trail's surface is bumpy and jagged,
often treacherous in rain or in snow,
and its course runs uneven and ragged;
often progress is slow.
But I've never once missed the convenience
I've forsaken by leaving the track,
and in spite of its promise of lenience,
I could never go back.
For by doing what's hard, I grow stronger;
and in light of the chance I might fail,
I run slower, but farther and longer,
when I run on the trail.
And I sense a rapport, a strange kinship,
with the runners I meet on my way;
and a curious unspoken friendship
tempers each running day.
In the struggle in heaven, two brothers
waged a war to determine life's course.
Our two-thirds chose a trail, while the others
found a track to endorse.
Why does life contain heartache and sorrows?
Why does God permit suffering and pain?
What is there from uncertain tomorrows
that we all stand to gain?
It's from doing what's hard that we're stronger;
and in light of the chance we might fail,
we run slower, but much farther and much, much longer
when we run on the trail.

Chapter Fifteen

It was 3:00 A.M. Saturday morning. Jacob leaned back in his chair, stretched his arms forward and yawned as hard as it was humanly possible to yawn. His interlocked fingers, scarred and rough, the fingers of a carpenter, popped at the knuckles. The poem was finished, and just in time. Today was *el día de los reyes magos*, his excuse for giving the poem as a gift to Annabelle. He had worked on it for an hour or so every night since Christmas, but in order to make his holiday deadline, he hadn't left his post under the light of the Tiffany lamp for six consecutive hours, except twice to put another log in the stove.

He was exhausted and was thankful that it was Saturday. He would sleep until 9:00 A.M. At 10:00 he, Andrew, and Mark were going out to Valerie's to finish fixing her roof. The January thaw had come early that year, and they hoped to finish what they had started last Saturday, before the weather turned cold and it snowed again. What they had done already would see Valerie through until spring, but they would finish the job now more for Joseph's than for the house's sake. He and Mark had gotten along well, and Joseph could use a friend like Mark.

"He needs good adult role models too, like you and Andrew," Valerie had said.

Molly, Susan, and Annabelle would do more than tag along again, too. During their last visit, they had painted the living room, and today they planned to surprise Valerie again by painting the kitchen while she was at work. Later that night, everyone planned to gather at the Harrisons' where Jacob and Valerie would introduce Annabelle and her family to their "day of the magi" traditions. Valerie would cook a Costa Rican dinner, and Jacob would bring everyone a small gift—also a surprise. Of all the gifts he would be giving, his gift to Annabelle was the most important.

Susan had given him three books of Annabelle's poetry, the books Bishop Beckstead had compiled for the ward members. There was much he admired in her poems. The one he had read in the parlor on Christmas day had moved him deeply; it had been written especially to him, he was sure. That night, he had begun the poem he hoped would communicate to Annabelle his gratitude for her sacrifice.

Molly, too, had understood in part that sacrifice. She was sleeping soundly now; a vigilant Molly Ann sat above her on the dresser that served as headboard for the bed. Molly had visited Annabelle often during the past two weeks, almost every day after school, and always accompanied by "our Molly Ann," as she always called her in Annabelle's presence. She could easily have stopped to visit on her way home but came home first so she could wave with the rest of the children from in front of McCallaway's store and to tell Jacob where she was going. Those were reasons enough, but the real reason she came home first was so she could take Molly Ann back with her—Jacob had made her a wooden box with a carrying handle for safe transport—and place her tenderly on the stand which never left the parlor piano. On New Year's Eve she had insisted that Molly Ann "sleep over." Annabelle had been delighted and deeply touched by the powers of perception in her little new best friend.

Jacob also had a new best friend. Valerie had called late Christmas night to thank him. Molly had chatted for a few minutes, then handed the phone to her father.

"*Hola*, Valerie. I hope you've had a merry Christmas."

"We have, Jacob, thanks to someone very kind and generous, someone who knows a lot about boys and baseball."

She didn't give him time to respond.

"Listen, Jacob…" she began awkwardly, "if your offer still stands, I…I really could use a good listener sometime…maybe you and Molly would like to come over some evening for dinner."

"Is tomorrow night too soon?" he suggested, surprised by his boldness.

"Tomorrow night would be just fine, Jacob."

Jacob knew by the timber and tone of her voice that she was smiling.

"I've got a small turkey we never cooked. Should I bring it along?" he asked.

"No, save it for another time. I think we'll have leftover ham and oranges."

Annabelle and her family met Valerie and Joseph the following Saturday. They had invited Jacob and Molly to their weekly waffle breakfast, and when they learned that later that afternoon they were going out to a nearby village to mend a friend's roof, they asked if they could come along and help. Technically, Valerie was still married. It was nice to have others involved in their friendship. Valerie and Susan had become especially close.

Jacob copied his poem for Annabelle onto several sheets of white paper. His penmanship was clean and legible, but nothing like Annabelle's. He read it aloud once more before he enclosed it in the envelope.

The Doll in McCalloway's Store

It was cold, but the stove held no fire.
Molly's schoolbooks were not by the door.
Once again she had stopped to admire
the doll in McCallaway's store.
The doll had been nothing but trouble
ever since she had spotted it there.
And its presence served only to double
the guilt I seemed destined to bear.
"Look, Daddy, her hair's dark and curly
like mine, and her eyes are deep blue
just as Mommy's were. Daddy you surely
remember her eyes, 'cause I do."

They were blue, and I'll always remember
and miss them most this time of year;
but for children, the month of December
should be joyous. I held back the tear
from my own eye, that first tear I never
would allow little Molly to see.
I was sure I had lost Ann forever;
tears could never return her to me.
The glimmer of faith she had kindled,
through her love, in my hard, doubting heart
was growing, but rapidly dwindled
and vanished once we were apart.
And I asked how a Heavenly Father
could allow a young mother to die.
Or was He too busy to bother
to respond to a little girl's cry
when she pled, "Please make Mommy better;
please God, do not take her away"?
"There's no Santa to read a child's letter,
and there's no God who hears when we pray.
"If there were, He'd have given her warning
of the illness she harbored inside.
After all, she had prayed night and morning;
the gospel she trusted had lied."
These were my thoughts as she languished,
as I helplessly watched my Ann die,
without faith, without hope, and I anguished
for a six-year-old girl who asked why.
For me there was no God nor Savior
I could blame; the blame was all mine.

It was my dreams, my selfish behavior
that had kept us from knowing in time.
I believed that my style had no rival.
Full-time work left me no time to write.
Ann would work for our family's survival.
We'd be thrifty while money was tight.
And since doctor's exams were expensive,
her fatigue and slight pain went ignored.
She saw no cause to be apprehensive;
she insisted we trust in the Lord.
"I'm young, and I've always been healthy,"
Ann argued, "I'll do it next spring.
By then you'll be published and wealthy.
I feel God will help us and bring
a blessing. I'm sure that he knows us
much better than we ourselves know.
Oftentimes our adversity shows us
the direction He wants us to go."
But Ann died. I abandoned my writing;
the well that inspired me ran dry.
All in life that was good and exciting
was now burdened by guilt, so why try?
It was only my love for our daughter
that gave me my reason to live,
and the love that her mother had taught her
gave me strength to go on. I would give
all I could, all I had in my power
to assure my dear Molly would be
safe and happy, I'd spend every hour
of my worthless life working so she

would no more feel heartache nor sadness,
   so she'd have no more reason to cry.
I would fake my contentment, my gladness;
   for my Molly's sake, I'd live a lie.
Ann's devotion and faith had proved fruitless.
   I resolved to spare Molly such fraud.
I'd determined that prayer had been useless,
   so we'd live out our lives without God.
We moved west, and I found good employment
   far from memories I hoped to ignore,
a good school and a cozy apartment
   up the street from McCallaway's store.
Molly walked by the store every morning
   and again on her way home from school.
On December nineteenth, without warning,
   it appeared sitting there on a stool
in the window between the toy trolley
   and the red and green stitched patchwork quilt,
the doll that reminded my Molly
   of her mother, and me of my guilt.
Each morning she ran to revere it
   and stayed till she heard the first bell.
All the day through, she longed to be near it.
   After school it delayed her as well.
She said, "Daddy, I named her for mother
   and for me too. Her name's Molly Ann.
I asked Santa to bring me another,
   but I'd rather have her, if I can."
I scolded her gently, insisting
   that she walk home from school with a friend;

The Doll in McCallaway's Store

but I saw in her eyes that resisting
was futile, and besides, it would end;
for I'd that day determined to buy it
and present it to her Christmas day.
I would give her the box; she'd untie it.
I was eager to hear what she'd say.
Next day, on the job, I was pleasant.
My coworkers were stunned by my glee.
I was anxious to buy Molly's present,
to wrap it and put up the tree.
For the first time in months I had reason
to find some fulfillment in life.
Together we'd weather the season
alone without mother and wife.
After supper, while she cleared the table
and swept up the crumbs from the floor,
making up some excuse, I was able
to run down to McCallaway's store.
And I pondered in anticipation
of my purchase, perhaps I'd been wrong
to foster such guilt and frustration;
perhaps Ann had been right all along.
Molly Ann would become my salvation.
Perhaps through my daughter's pure heart,
I'd rekindle forgotten sensation,
and religion would find a fresh start.
But my window of faith quickly shattered,
replaced by alarm and despair.
It was gone, and nothing else mattered;
my salvation was no longer there

in the window between the toy trolley,
and the red and green stitched patchwork quilt;
it was gone, the doll for my Molly,
and the hope I might conquer my guilt.
In the store, I asked for assistance
in finding who'd purchased the doll;
and McCallaway's rigid insistence
there was no way that he could recall
soon softened, but only to say it
had never been offered for sale.
Its owner had asked he display it,
and her name he had sworn not to tell.
And she'd taken it back only hours
before I had entered the store.
There was nothing in anyone's power
to do. He could say nothing more.
I searched every store in the city,
but the doll was one of a kind.
Did I turn back to faithless self-pity?
Not so; I was desperate to find
someone to atone for my suffering,
some savior my pain to relieve,
some power to save me by offering
some sign that could help me believe.
By the light of my Christmas-Eve candle,
I knelt at the side of my bed.
"Please, Father, alone I can't handle
much longer the anguish," I said.
"I was so wrong to doubt Your compassion,
so foolish to question Your grace.

The Doll in McCallaway's Store

Forgive me my sin; let the passion
of Christ give me strength to erase
the damage my pride has inflicted
on Your daughters You gave me to love.
The doubt that my soul has afflicted,
please, replace with Your light from above."
Whether a dream or night's vision,
I can't say. As I prayed on the floor,
I saw my own soul locked in prison.
My Ann came and opened the door.
Unmistakably happy and radiant,
she moved from her arms into mine
Molly's doll, which was likewise resplendent,
and whispered, "Here, here is your sign.
It's His answer; you see, He does know you
much better than you yourself know.
Your adversity this time has shown you
the direction He wants you to go."
It was Christmas, I'd slept until morning.
I awoke to a knock at the door
and discovered, my doorstep adorning,
the doll from McCallaway's store
and a box filled with doll clothes all ordered,
and on each dress or garment, some hand
had lovingly stitched or embroidered
the name of the doll: Molly Ann.

Once faithless, and hopelessly stranded,
the love and compassion you gave
is forever indelibly branded

on the soul that you helped God to save.

Jacob said his prayers and climbed quietly into bed. He reflected for several minutes on his good fortune, "his blessings," he corrected himself. Molly continued to sleep peacefully in her bed. How he loved her! Perhaps he would finish his novel now, for her, or perhaps he would write another. The light from the full moon shining through the window illuminated Molly Ann's piercing yet gentle eyes, eyes as blue as the clear winter sky, eyes that reminded him of Ann, the happy radiant Ann of his dream, the Ann that he and Molly would always have and always love, the love that would always be reflected for them in the eyes of the doll from McCallaway's store.

Acknowledgments

First of all, I thank my family for humoring me as I pursued what to them seemed an impossible dream. Secondly, of all the lessons gleaned from this, my first attempt at fiction, the absolute necessity of a talented editor was perhaps for me the most surprising. It was my good fortune to have two very capable editors. Don Eamon's initial recommendations helped me identify several bad habits and taught me to give greater attention to detail. When he was unable to complete the task for personal reasons, Allan Macpherson grabbed the oars midstream and skillfully guided me through the troubled waters of "point of view." His observations were especially valuable in helping me to better see my work through my reader's eyes, and for that, and for doing all in his power to make up for lost time, I am extremely grateful. Finally, for creating a cover design that personifies so beautifully the story inside, I express my sincere appreciation to Jana Rade and Karl Andrews.

About The Author

Kevin Krogh grew up milking cows, hauling hay, and wandering the forests and mountain valleys of northern Utah. He has spent most of his professional life teaching Spanish language, culture, and literature; and designing and constructing residential gardens and other exterior spaces. In the fall of 2000, he decided that reading, analyzing, and teaching what others had written was no longer enough, and landscape design no longer fully satisfied his need to see the tangible results of his creative nature. He had always wanted to write creatively, so when circumstances and an increased desire and confidence finally combined to allow him to seriously venture an attempt, he quickly discovered his penchant for writing poetry. In *The Doll in McCallaway's Store*, the poet has turned novelist, and he now divides his writing time between the two genres. As compelling as Kevin's passion for poetry and fiction is, it takes a backseat to his devotion to family and faith. His wife, Nancy, son, Mark, and daughters Valerie, Sandy, Ruth, Susan, and Katie are his greatest treasures. They make their home in one of northern Utah's beautiful mountain valleys, and his life with them and his grateful service to church and community are his highest priorities.

To learn more about the author and his novels and poetry, visit www.kevinkrogh.com.